STAR TREK®
THE NEXT GENERATION

STAR TREK:
THE NEXT GENERATION NOVELS

STAR TREK:
THE NEXT GENERATION GIANT NOVELS

STAR TREK®
THE NEXT GENERATION

GUISES OF THE MIND

REBECCA NEASON

TITAN BOOKS
LONDON

STAR TREK **THE NEXT GENERATION 27:**
GUISES OF THE MIND
ISBN 1 85286 464 8

Published by
Titan Books Ltd
42-44 Dolben Street
London SE1 0UP

First Titan Edition September 1993
10 9 8 7 6 5 4 3

British Library Cataloguing-in-Publication Data. A catalogue
record for this book is available from the British Library.

Printed and bound in Great Britain by Cox and Wyman Ltd, Reading,
Berkshire.

Therefore the wise man . . .
. . . does not collect precious things.
He learns not to hold on to ideas.
He brings men back to what they have lost. . . .

. . . Having and not having rise together.
Difficult and easy complement each other.
High and low rest upon each other. . . .

Lao Tze, Tao Te Ching

Lord, make me an instrument of thy peace.
Where there is hatred, let me sow love.
    Where there is injury, pardon,
    Where there is doubt, faith,
    Where there is despair, hope,
Where there is darkness, light. . . .

Saint Francis of Assisi

It is logical that one should desire peace. Before a peace can be obtained, one must learn to rule one's passions. To gain mastery over the emotions, one must first embrace the many Guises of the Mind. . . .

Surak of Vulcan

Chapter One

THE YOUNG LIEUTENANT on the transporter platform looked at Troi with haunted, frightened eyes.

"You'll be all right, Geoff," the counselor said, giving her voice more confidence than she felt. Standing behind her at the controls, the new transporter chief, Samantha Tuttle, cleared her throat.

"The starbase is signaling, Counselor," she told Troi.

"Thank you, Chief," she acknowledged without taking her eyes off her departing patient. "Doctor Fletcher will be waiting for you, Geoff," she continued. "Everything is arranged. The *Skylark* will be here in thirty-six hours to take you back home to Beta Arcturus. Doctor Fletcher will be traveling with you. He has a copy of all your records and the doctors at the clinic are waiting. It's almost over."

The terror in the young man's eyes did not abate.

1

He ran a dry tongue over his lips and tried to make his voice work.

"Thank you," he finally managed to say. "I'm sorry I . . . I wasn't a good patient."

Troi smiled her best professional smile. "You were a fine patient. Just remember, there are no magic cures. Everything takes time."

The lieutenant nodded. Troi stepped back next to Chief Tuttle, who was still waiting to work the transporter controls.

"Just a few more days, Geoff, and you'll be home. Are you ready?"

Again the lieutenant nodded. Troi touched Tuttle's arm and the transporter chief's hands moved across the board before him. There was a hum, a shower of light, and the lieutenant's body began to fade.

"Good-bye, Geoff," Troi said softly as he disappeared. "Good luck."

"The starbase is signaling that Lieutenant Salah has arrived," Tuttle told her.

Troi looked up at her and gave a weary smile, then she turned away. It was over; there was nothing more Troi could do now except go back to her quarters and make the final entry on Lieutenant Salah in her log.

Troi left the transporter room. Crew members greeted her as she walked down the corridor toward the turbolift and she nodded to them, but she did not truly see them. Her actions were automatic and professional, and unrelated to her thoughts, which were still of Geoff Salah. In her mind she still saw the look of scarcely controlled panic that had become etched upon his face in these last weeks.

Troi had always known, and accepted, that Starfleet psych-profiles were not infallible. But even in its latent stage, this phobia should have been diagnosed, she thought for the hundredth time as she stepped into the turbolift and gave her destination to the computer. Geoff Salah should never have been on a starship. Yet he had been here. And she should have been able to help him. She had failed, and it hurt.

Troi reached her quarters and stepped inside. Behind her, the door slid silently closed. Only then did she let her facade of professional calm slip away. Her shoulders drooped as she leaned back against the wall and closed her eyes. For a few, brief moments, the slender frame of Deanna Troi bore a resemblance to Atlas, bowed beneath the weight of the world.

Then she took a deep breath and straightened her shoulders. She had work to do.

She walked over to her desk and sat down. As she did, she touched a button on the computer terminal, switching it to silent recording mode; at this moment, even the pleasant artificial voice of the computer was more than she wanted to hear.

"Personal log: Counselor Deanna Troi," she began. "Stardate 45741.9. We have just concluded a six-hour layover at Starbase 212, where we picked up the passengers who will be traveling with us to Capulon IV and . . ." Troi stopped and drew another breath, searching for a way to express the finality she felt. "Where I lost a patient. On my recommendation, Lieutenant Geoff Salah has been granted extended medical leave to his home planet. It is unlikely he will ever be able to return to duty aboard a starship."

Troi sat back and closed her eyes again. A deep weariness washed through her. She was exhausted from all these weeks of trying to help Lieutenant Salah combat the sudden explosion of fear that had ripped apart his life and left his sanity tottering on the brink of extinction. His increasing paranoia had pounded in her brain each time they were together. As the manifestations of his phobia grew, Troi had found herself

3

having to battle through the attacks of anxiety and sleeplessness, the lack of concentration and the burgeoning sensation of impending doom that were Salah's symptoms—not her own.

Nor had she been able to tell Salah that his fears were groundless. It was a reality that the *Enterprise,* that any starship, traveled through a vacuum. The dangers of such travel—systems failures, hull breaches by asteroid bombardment or enemy fire, unknown and sometimes hostile life-forms, ion storms, novas and supernovas, and a thousand other things, were too varied to name. They were the conditions one accepted when one chose a life in Starfleet. They were part of the adventure.

And they were the very things Lieutenant Geoff Salah could no longer endure.

Once more the specter of his pained and troubled expression rose up to haunt Troi, bringing with it another wave of weariness. Depression sent its first wispy tendrils through her brain, whispering to her of futility and failure.

Troi ended the entry. Later, after she had brought her own feelings into focus, she would record more. She took a deep breath, let it out slowly, and called up the schedule for her afternoon appointments.

The first one, only a few minutes from now, was with Bio-tech Theodore Aske and Chief Roberta Plummer of geo-sciences. Standard voluntary prenuptial counseling. Troi gave a small, wan smile, glad that these were the next people she had to face. There had been nothing in her past three sessions with Aske and Plummer to indicate anything ahead for them but a long, happy marriage.

Reading the next name on her schedule, Troi's dark eyes grew troubled. Ensign Johann Marshall. More pain to deal with—grief and guilt and anger. In the month since Marshall had received word of his father's death and began coming to Troi for counseling, these emotions had been the essence of their time together. Denying that he felt anything but loss and sorrow, Marshall would often sit in her office saying little. Then his dark, brooding emotions would fill the room and reverberate through Troi's mind.

She would endure them, though she knew she could raise her mental shields and place a firm, protective wall around her empathic talent. Yet, then she might miss some vital clue as to why the ensign's self-accusations were greater than his grief. Until that was brought into the open, Ensign Marshall would not heal. Troi did not want to fail with Marshall as she had with Salah. She knew she would keep her shields lowered.

"And who counsels the counselor?" she wondered aloud as she stood and composed her body into the posture of a confident professional—shoulders back, chin lifted—and mentally prepared herself to go to her office and face the rest of the day's appointments.

The comm button on her uniform chirped. She tapped it lightly. "Troi here," she said.

"Counselor." The rich timbre of Captain Picard's voice came over the comm channel. "Tomorrow evening at nineteen hundred hours, I will be hosting a dinner party to welcome our guests on board. If you have no other plans, I would be pleased if you would attend."

Always on call, the words flashed through Troi's mind. Even at a social event like a dinner party, she knew that the captain would expect her to be sensing the emotions of the people in the room. He did not understand; no one on board the *Enterprise* fully understood how exhausting such constant sensitivity could be.

Troi tried not to let these thoughts sound in her voice when she answered the captain. "Thank you, sir," she said. "I'll be there."

Picard signed off. Troi stepped toward her door, and as it slid silently open she knew that tonight she was going to treat herself to her favorite form of personal therapy. As soon as she was off duty, she was going straight to Ten-Forward and have Guinan make her this galaxy's biggest, gooiest, chocolatiest . . .

Up on the bridge, Captain Jean-Luc Picard was feeling very pleased with life as he settled himself comfortably into his command chair. Their passengers, the Little Mothers, were remarkable individuals —members of an organization that had lasted through the centuries. Picard knew that many of his contemporaries, while admiring the work of the Little Mothers, felt that religious organizations such as theirs were anachronistic. Picard did not agree. As a student of history, he was keenly aware of the part religion had played in the spread of civilization.

Picard was too honest a researcher to ignore or deny the many atrocities that had been committed in the name of religion. Earth's past was as studded with them as many other worlds' histories, and much more than some. Yet it was the organizations of religion that had kept the light of law and learning, the essence of civilization, alive during eras of darkness that might otherwise have seen those lights extinguished.

The Little Mothers—now theirs was a history that exemplified what Religious Orders could be. Picard had first learned of them as a schoolboy and had admired them since. Over the years he had watched for any mention of them, both in history books and current Federation news communiqués. The Little Mothers' work with the unwanted children of the galaxy, regardless of physical or mental condition, of species or planet, was legendary and inspirational. Picard was pleased to be able to introduce them to his crew—and to introduce his crew, of whom he was justly proud, to them.

Picard turned and found his First Officer watching him. "Your expression reminds me of an old saying about a cat and a canary," Riker said, a smile tugging at the corners of his mouth.

"Yes, Number One, I am pleased. By our passengers, and by our mission."

"That's something I don't quite understand, Captain," Riker continued. "We're going to Capulon IV for the signing of the final treaty between that planet and the Federation—"

"Yes."

"Why are we taking two nuns with us?"

Picard studied Riker for a moment, then gave a small, enigmatic smile.

> "'One man with a dream, at pleasure,
> Shall go forth and conquer a crown;
> And three with a new song's measure
> Can trample an empire down.'"

"Captain?"

"A poem, by a nineteenth-century Irish poet named O'Shaughnessy. It means that a small number of individuals with vision and dedication can make or change history. From what I have read of the young King on Capulon IV, I think he is such an individual. It is my guess, Number One, that the King intends, with the help of these nuns, not to 'trample an empire,' but to build one."

Chapter Two

JOAKAL I'LIUM, the King of Capulon IV, walked down the corridor toward his apartments on the third floor of the palace. He walked with an easy, long-legged gait, the walk of someone accustomed to few obstacles. He was clothed in the colors of the House I'lium. A long crimson tunic with full sleeves, gold buttons and sash gave breadth to his slender shoulders, and the loose pants, also of crimson, that gathered at the ankles inside his boots added height to his medium frame. His dark hair was worn long in back, in the fashion of young men. Wisps of it curled around the high neck of his tunic and touched the cropped beard and mustache that hid the fine lines around his mouth and made him look younger than his twenty-nine years.

By his side walked Aklier, member of the Council of Elders. He was dressed in a similar style to Joakal, but in the orange and brown of his own House, and wore the knee-length sleeveless vest of adulthood.

Aklier was shorter than Joakal and more stout. At the age of sixty-seven, the proud carriage of early manhood that was so much a part of his companion's walk, had long departed from Aklier. His shoulders were stooped and his feet no longer left the floor as sprightly as once they had. His hair and beard were the dark silver gray of black hair aged. Although his beard hid many of the lines that had embedded themselves on Aklier's face, he knew those lines existed and were growing deeper with each passing year.

As the two men walked side by side down the palace corridors, their boots clicked dully on the stone floor, punctuating the silence of the late hour. Joakal hardly noticed the sound, nor did he give much thought to his companion. His mind was filled with details of his upcoming coronation and with the dreams and plans he had nurtured for so long.

For nine years, ever since his father had died and Joakal came to the throne, he had ruled through the Council of Elders, as was the custom of his people. Now his Coming to Age was only a short time away. In twenty-seven days he would be thirty years old, and three days after that he would be crowned *Absolute*.

For the last nine years Joakal had dreamed of the changes he would make for his people. He had spent those years, and many years before them, studying the laws and the histories, and making plans. They were secret plans, for the changes he would make involved the reinterpretation and reordering of many of the old ways. This he could only do after he was *Absolute*. Soon his dreams would come true. He would be known as Joakal the Just, Joakal the Lawgiver.

And there was Elana, his beautiful, beloved Elana. She had been gone this past month, spending time in her childhood home while she decided whether to marry him or enter Service at the temple, but she promised to return on the day of his coronation with her answer.

She *will* marry me, Joakal thought. She *must*. Joakal loved her too deeply to consider any other answer. It was with her alone that Joakal had shared all of his many plans and dreams. She was the only one on this world who knew what action he had already taken to make the first of those dreams come true. She would stand by his side when he made the proclamation. She would rule by his side, and together they would guide this world into a new and golden age.

The young King turned to his companion. "Have you heard anything from the Federation ship?" he asked. "Are you certain they'll arrive on time?"

"We have received no word from the ship," Aklier answered. "You would have been told, but I am certain they will arrive on schedule."

"Think of it, Aklier," Joakal said, his eyes shining with his unspoken dreams. "Think of what it will mean for our people. The stars will be open to us and all the people on all the worlds of the Federation will be our brothers. We will learn of their ways, and we will teach them ours."

The Federation ship and the treaty; all of Capulon knew of these. It was who the ship carried and what they represented that was the secret Joakal hugged to himself. To cast off the superstitions of the past, and embrace the scientific wonders of a hundred worlds— that was the tomorrow he planned to build for Capulon IV.

He was so entranced by his vision of the future, he did not notice the furtive glances his companion was casting at the doorways they were walking past, nor notice the sudden sweat that beaded on Aklier's forehead.

Joakal kept walking. Behind him, a door swung open on silent, well-oiled hinges. A figure slipped through.

Suddenly hands gripped Joakal's shoulders and spun him around. Joakal gave a startled cry. He saw the fist coming toward him. Just before it connected, just before the world exploded into pain and darkness, Joakal saw his attacker's face.

And it was his own.

Chapter Three

TROI BENT CLOSER to the mirror as she secured the last pin into her hair. Then she clipped her earrings into place and stood back to survey the total effect.

Not bad, she assured herself, turning slightly from side to side. For the dinner party this evening, Troi had chosen a new dress from the ship's catalogue and she decided she liked both the style and the color. The high back and gently heart-shaped neckline gave her throat a long, graceful look, and the deep garnet color of the dress complemented her skin. Not bad at all, she told herself again as she ran a hand down the fitted bodice to the folds of the full skirt, smoothing away a small fold in the fabric.

Troi glanced at the chronometer display: 18:45—ten minutes before Will Riker would arrive to escort her to the dinner. Troi walked over to the food replicator dispenser.

"Hot chocolate," she ordered. But when her drink arrived and she took a sip, she grimaced. It was not what she wanted. The rich, sweet liquid did no more to lift her mood than had the chocolate sundae last night, or the double workout she had done in the gym this morning. She was still worried about Lieutenant Salah, still depressed over her inability to help him—and still very, very tired.

"So, what do I want?" Troi asked herself as she started to pace about the room. She, of all people, should be aware of her feelings, able to define and examine them.

Okay, she thought, applying a technique she had used often with her patients, I'll make a list. Number one: Work, her profession—Did she still believe in what she was doing? Yes. Troi knew that her choice to become a psychologist and to join Starfleet had been the correct one. She harbored no doubts or regrets.

So, number two: Her assignment—Would she rather be stationed somewhere else, on a starbase or planet, maybe even at Starfleet Command or the Academy? No. She loved the *Enterprise* and the people on board.

Number three: Her personal life? No—*emphatically* no. She was not ready for marriage and children. She would be less than honest if she said she never thought of them, but it was not an *active* consideration. They were for some later time in her life. For now she had friends, dear and cherished friends like Will Riker and Beverly Crusher, like Captain Picard, like Geordi and Worf and Data—like so many others. They kept her from being lonely.

Lonely. The word made Troi stop pacing. She was never lonely—that was the problem. She was never *alone.* Even here in her quarters, she could feel the presence of the fifteen hundred people around her. The loves and hates, griefs and sorrows, joys and triumphs not only of the crew members, but of their spouses and children, were like a constant white noise inside her brain.

As ship's counselor it was Troi's duty to be *aware,* not only of the mental and emotional condition of the crew, but to guard against the unseen threats that could attack the minds of the people on board. For this Captain Picard relied upon her—and through him, so did everyone else.

What I need, Troi thought, is a vacation. I need a time when no one is relying on me. I need to put things back in perspective.

The door chime sounded. "Come in," she called and the door obediently slid open. Commander Will Riker stood framed in the doorway, looking handsome and virile in his dress uniform. His eyes caressed her, sliding slowly up and down her form, and he let out a slow, appreciative whistle.

"Deanna," he said. "You look magnificent."

"Thank you, Will."

Riker held out his arm and Troi walked over and took it. As they headed down the corridor toward the turbolift, Troi let herself bask in the familiar touch of Riker's mind. His approval and affection were a balm to her weary soul.

This is a dinner party, she thought to herself as they walked. It's a social event. No threats, no dangers— no warring dignitaries or tricky negotiations that hang in the balance. We're traveling through well-known space on our way to a peaceful mission. Other ships get by without a Betazoid counselor, maybe for a while I can block everyone out of my mind and just enjoy myself. A mini-vacation.

Troi turned her head and smiled up at Will Riker.

She was pleased by the warmth in his eyes as he smiled back.

The other guests had arrived when Troi and Riker walked into the dining room on Deck 8. Troi saw that the male officers had opted to wear their dress uniforms while, like herself, Beverly Crusher had chosen civilian dress. Standing next to the captain, the doctor looked exotic in an oriental pants-dress of pale green Chinese silk.

Troi did not need her Betazoid senses to read the emotions in the room. Captain Picard, as he stood next to Doctor Crusher, was smiling one of his rare broad smiles. He radiated pride and pleasure as obviously as Beverly did serenity. To the captain's left, Geordi was busy being sociable and, as usual, he was on the verge of laughter. Troi wondered what story he was telling as he waved his arms through the air. Worf stood near him, but a little apart. The Klingon's eyes shifted around the room continually, his body tense and ready to spring into action. Data, meanwhile, watched everyone with an expression of fascinated curiosity.

At the center of this group stood two nuns. Both wore identical ankle-length dresses of a heavy brown material, girded about the waist by a braided rope. On their heads each wore short white veils, and their feet were encased in sandals. One nun also had a wooden pectoral cross on a leather thong around her neck. She stood with her head bent and her eyes downcast as if she was deep in private meditation.

Troi breathed a silent sigh of relief—all here was as it should be. For a while she could, and would, rest. She raised the mental shields around her mind, smiled, and stepped further into the room. The captain glanced up and saw her.

"Good—Counselor, Number One," he said. "I'm glad you've arrived. Come and meet the Little Mothers."

Still arm in arm, Troi and Riker advanced to the captain's side and waited while he made the introductions. The nun with the cross was Mother Veronica, the Head of the Order. The other nun was Sister Julian. They were going to Capulon IV to make the initial contact with the government; others of their Order would be following in a few weeks.

The dinner proceeded with polished smoothness. Troi could not help but admire the way the captain played host. With well-timed questions and comments, he kept the conversation moving and interesting, all the while keeping his eye on the plates and goblets of his guests, unobtrusively making certain their wineglasses were refilled, food dishes were passed around, and delicacies placed within easy reach.

Troi was seated across the table from Mother Veronica. The nun had stayed quiet throughout the meal. Troi noticed she had not eaten much more than a mouthful. To the counselor's practiced eye, the nun looked troubled and exhausted.

Seated to Troi's left, Sister Julian was as animated as Mother Veronica was reticent. "It was 1873, not 4, when our Order was founded, Captain," she was saying. "In October. The fourth of October—the feast day of Saint Francis of Assisi, whose Rule we follow."

Then Sister Julian stopped and laughed. "You'll have to forgive me, Captain," she said. "I find history a fascinating subject, and I tend to become rather passionate when I'm discussing it."

Picard smiled. "I am a bit of a history enthusiast myself," he said. "In fact, aside from the wonderful work you do—which I hold in the highest esteem— part of what interests me about your Order is the fact that you have survived the centuries. Even now, when religions no longer play such a pervasive part in society, your Order seems to be thriving."

"It was not always easy for us," Sister Julian said solemnly. "Many times our Order nearly died out. Each time a span of religious apathy would occur, the numbers in our Order would dwindle. Yet a few of us always remained to carry on the work."

She cocked her head slightly to one side and studied the captain. "As for religion no longer playing a part in society," she said. "Which society? The Vulcans, whose discipline of pure logic, the Kolinar, exists side by side with their mystical teachings of the Katra? The Bajorans who unanimously claim that it is their spiritual beliefs that have held them together as a society throughout the long years of Cardassian domination? I could name dozens more."

"Perhaps I should have said that religion is no longer as important on Earth as it once was," Picard replied.

"Oh, come now, Captain," Sister Julian said. "You don't mean that. Just because we no longer fight wars over our beliefs, you don't think that they are gone, do you? Religious beliefs, their myths and practices have been with humankind since its beginnings. By the time the first god figure was painted on a cave wall, the myths of that god had already been told around the campfire, told and believed. I think it is, rather, that we have learned to let religion be a matter of the heart, personal and not political. We have at last learned tolerance."

Picard smiled at her. "You are a fine debater, Sister Julian."

Troi watched Sister Julian nod a pleased acknowledgment of the captain's compliment, then cast a quick glance across the table to Mother Veronica, as if trying to pull the other nun into the conversation. Mother Veronica did not notice or look up from her attitude of contemplative withdrawal.

"Back to our original subject," Sister Julian said after an infinitesimal pause. "Our Order was founded —in 1873," she shot Picard a small smile, "in Spain, on Earth. The country was torn by one of the many civil wars of that era. The need for us and for our work was very great. There were so many children whose families had been killed and whose villages had been destroyed. The first of our Sisters took these children into their convents, then built dormitories and infirmaries to house and care for them. They endeavored to raise the children in an atmosphere of love despite the wars that raged all around them. Our Order was given the name Mothers of the Hopeless.

"If you are a student of history, Captain," she continued, "you know that the next two centuries were filled with outbreaks of war, and not only in Spain. Some of these wars were termed small wars or internal power struggles, others were global confrontations. They all left homeless, helpless children in their wake."

"Then your work is mostly with homeless and war-traumatized children?" Riker asked.

"Oh no, Commander," Sister Julian answered. "That was only how our Order was established. Our work, our *mission* to use the Church term, is to provide a loving home for all children. *Any* child, regardless of need or condition, is taken in and cherished. And throughout the centuries there is little we have not seen—the homeless, the abused, the sick—sometimes terminally—the openly rebellious who are really looking for security, the autistic who

18

are locked behind the curtain of their own minds, the mentally deficient, the physically challenged—all of them find a home within our walls."

"But Earth, in fact most of the Federation worlds, have solved these problems," Doctor Crusher said. "Our planet is no longer torn apart by wars. Medical science can detect, and cure, most physical defects—often before birth—and our psychological sciences have learned how to overcome the mental conditions, like autism, that were so debilitating and such a frightening part of our past."

Sister Julian smiled a little sadly. "You are an idealist, Doctor," she said. "That is a good trait in a healer. No wars—not on Earth, but what about the war with the Cardassians? Cardassian children can be homeless and frightened and in need, too. And many of the other worlds within our galaxy do not feel the same way about their children as we humans do. That is why when we began encountering other worlds, other peoples and cultures, our Order took our mission from Earth to the stars. You would be surprised how many worlds ask for us to come and set up one of our homes on their planets."

"So you no longer have any houses on Earth?" the captain asked. "I thought I read—"

"Oh yes we do, Captain." Sister Julian interrupted. "Our main Mother House is on Earth—that will never change. But we have many Mother Houses now. Our home was on Perrias VII."

Captain Picard's brow wrinkled slightly. "Perrias VII," he said slowly. "That's not a member of the Federation."

"No, Captain," Sister Julian replied. "It is not. But then, we are not ambassadors or members of Starfleet —nor do we have any political affiliations. If we hear of a need, we go."

"How do such reports get to you?" Commander Riker asked.

Again Sister Julian smiled. "Oh, they get to us. Sometimes, such as the case with Capulon IV, the government of a planet asks us to come. But that is more rare than I like to think. Usually it is word of mouth—rumors, news reports, even anonymous communiqués. Word gets to us."

While Sister Julian continued to talk, Troi became aware of a vague feeling of disquiet. It was like an itch slowly growing between her shoulder blades, or a steady, monotonous beat too quiet to be truly heard, but too loud to be ignored. The relaxed glow of the evening fled and Troi was on duty once more. Slowly, she lowered her mental shields. Immediately her mind was under siege, bombarded by desperate confusion. It was like stepping into the middle of an exploding star.

Too many . . . too many . . . The words crashed through Troi's mind. *Go away . . .* they echoed. *Too many. . . .*

Across the table, Mother Veronica sat with her head bowed. Her body was tense and stiff, and her cheeks were as pale as chalk.

She's a telepath, Troi realized.

The voice inside her head grew stronger. Mother Veronica has no shields, Troi thought, feeling the desperation mounting in the other woman's mind. A telepath can't survive without shields.

Troi focused her gaze, and her mind, on the nun. Although not a true telepath herself, Troi could communicate with others so gifted, especially when the telepathy was as strong as she was receiving from Mother Veronica.

It's all right, Troi sent. *I can help you.*

Mother Veronica's head snapped up. Her eyes

locked with Troi's and the counselor felt the sudden flood of terror that filled the nun's mind.

It's all right, Troi tried again. *Don't be afraid.*

Mother Veronica sprang to her feet, her chair scraping loudly across the floor. She raised her hands to her temples in a quick, staccato motion.

"I'm sorry. I . . . I have to go," she stammered. "Headache. You all stay. Please." She moved away from the table and toward the door with the speed of a deer in flight.

"I'll go see if I can help," Doctor Crusher said, starting to push herself away from the table. Before she could rise, Troi was already out of her chair.

"No, Beverly," she said. "I'll go." The doctor gave her a curious glance, but she nodded. Like the rest of the crew, the doctor trusted Troi's abilities. Troi was relieved; it would have taken too long to explain.

Troi turned and left the dining room. As she stepped into the corridor, she saw Mother Veronica waiting for the turbolift. Troi hurried toward the nun. Mother Veronica saw her and shrank back against the wall.

Troi slowed her pace. She began speaking softly, trying to use her voice to calm, to soothe.

"It's all right," she said, repeating the message she had told the nun a few moments before. "Don't be frightened. I understand. I know how exhausting it can be to have other people's thoughts always in your mind. I can teach you how to block them out. Let me help you."

Troi was in front of Mother Veronica now, and being this near Troi could look into the nun's eyes. Mother Veronica reminded her of an animal in a trap—hopeless and terrified.

"Let me help you," Troi said again. "I understand."

Mother Veronica slowly shook her head. "No," she

whispered. The turbolift arrived and Mother Veronica stepped inside. "Leave me alone," she said as the doors slid shut.

Troi stood there looking at the closed doors. Mother Veronica needed help—soon, before her sanity snapped. Troi took a deep breath and let it out slowly as she turned away from the turbolift. She must return to the dinner party. The others would be waiting for her; the captain, in particular, would want to know Mother Veronica's condition.

What could she tell him? Troi wondered. What did she have the *right* to tell him? Mother Veronica was not a member of the crew. She was no threat to anyone but herself. Until she asked for help, she was entitled to the privacy of her own life, her own mind. Meanwhile, until she was willing to accept help, there was nothing that Troi, trained psychologist, counselor on Starfleet's flagship, Betazoid and empath, could do.

Once again there was someone who needed her and once again, she had failed.

Chapter Four

THE NEXT MORNING, at ten-thirty, Captain Picard stepped off the turbolift on Deck 16. He had promised the Little Mothers a tour of the ship and had decided to guide them himself, but he was surprised to find only Sister Julian waiting for him in the hall.

"Good morning, Captain," Sister Julian said as he approached.

"Good morning, Sister," he replied. "Isn't Mother Veronica joining us?"

"No, I'm afraid not. This traveling has been so hard on her," Sister Julian said with a sigh. "I have traveled before, but not Mother Veronica. She came to the convent when she was only four years old, abandoned one night on the convent steps, and this is the first time she has left it."

"Why now?" Picard asked as he and his companion began walking back down the corridor toward the turbolift.

Sister Julian shrugged. "Mother Veronica has a talent for order and organization that will make her an excellent leader for our new Community. I think this is why traveling, with its constantly changing routine, is so upsetting for her."

"But surely, if leaving her home planet causes her so much distress, she would better serve your Order where she was."

Sister Julian stopped walking and turned to the captain. She stood for a moment studying his face. "If you were ordered to give up the *Enterprise,* would you do so?" she asked.

"Of course. It would be my duty as a Starfleet officer."

Sister Julian resumed walking. "We have duties also, Captain," she said. "And we are vowed to obedience. Do not let her current indisposition cause you to underestimate Mother Veronica. She has an extraordinary gift for working with children, especially troubled children. She will be needed where we are going."

They reached the turbolift and while they waited for the doors to open, Captain Picard changed the subject. "Are your accommodations satisfactory?" he asked.

"Our accommodations are more than satisfactory, Captain," Sister Julian replied. "They are quite luxurious. A stateroom converted for our use, and a chapel—it is most generous and kind of you. It is a delight to pray in that beautiful chapel. We have been on three transports and two starbases, and they have not contained anything so lovely."

"Thank you," the captain said. "It is a copy of the parish church in my home village on Earth, in France. I had it replicated for your use."

The turbolift arrived. "Where would you like to

start your tour of the ship?" he asked as he and Sister Julian stepped inside.

"Is it true, Captain, that you have whole families, even children, on board?"

"Indeed."

"Then that is where I would like to start—with the children."

The captain and his guest spent the morning visiting the classrooms and playrooms. At each of the stops, Sister Julian sat among the children, patiently answering their many questions. Picard was fascinated by the instant rapport between the children and the nun.

As he watched, Picard realized how his own attitude toward children had changed over the years he had captained the *Enterprise*. When he accepted command, he had thought the inclusion of entire families on a deep-space vessel, especially children, to be one of Starfleet's less intelligent decisions. Now he knew that they had been right and he wrong. Having spouses and children on board made his crew happier. That aided in their performance of their duties and gave his ship a greater sense of community. Picard was now pleased to count the children of the *Enterprise* as part of his command.

After leaving the classrooms, Picard took Sister Julian to one of the holodecks and showed her several of the programs that were commonly used for family outings and "outdoor" play. Now they were on their way for a tour of the medical facilities.

As Picard and his companion neared sickbay, a young ensign stepped out into the corridor. When he caught sight of the captain and the nun coming toward him, the color drained from his face. He looked for a moment as if he would faint. Then he shook himself and hurried in the opposite direction, but he kept shooting quick, frightened glances back over his shoulder.

Picard had rarely seen anyone move so fast without actually running. He almost called out to the ensign; he would have, had he been alone. Instead, Picard could only wonder whether it was himself or the nun that had so terrified the young man. I will have to mention this to the counselor, Picard thought.

Deanna Troi sat in her office waiting for Ensign Marshall. She glanced again at the chronometer display on the wall: fifteen minutes late. This was not like Marshall. He might come to her office and say little or nothing during their entire session, but he always showed up—and on time.

"Computer," she said aloud. "Location of Ensign Johann Marshall."

"Ensign Marshall is in Ten-Forward."

Something's definitely wrong, Troi thought as she headed for the door.

She found him sitting in one of the far corners of the lounge, staring at the cup in front of him. Even from across the room Troi could feel the turmoil raging inside him. She glanced at the bar and caught Guinan's eyes.

"He's been here for a half an hour," Guinan said quietly. "He ordered a cup of coffee, but he hasn't touched it. He just stares at it."

Troi nodded. Steeling herself to endure the young ensign's emotions, she walked over to his table. He did not look up when she approached; his eyes never strayed from the dark liquid in the cup.

"Johann," she spoke his name softly. The ensign flinched at the sound of her voice, but he blinked once and looked up.

"Johann," she said again. "We had an appointment. When you didn't show up, I was concerned."

"I'm . . . I'm sorry," he stammered. "But I can't talk to you now. I can't—"

Something's happened, Troi thought. Go softly, Deanna. This could be the breakthrough he needs. Softly now. Gently.

Troi sat down. "We won't have our appointment today," she said. "We'll just sit here and have a cup of coffee together. There's no need to talk if you don't want to. All right, Johann?"

The ensign nodded. Troi looked up, prepared to signal Guinan, and saw the Ten-Forward hostess already coming toward her, cup in hand. Troi smiled; somehow Guinan always knew.

Aklier, Head of the House Ti'Kara, member of the Council of Elders, was not at the palace. Although he lived, worked, and spent most of his time at the royal residence, he also owned a small holding outside the city confines. Most of the Elders who served on the Council had second homes somewhere in or near the city where they could get away from the pressures of court and still be near enough to return quickly if the need for them should arise. Yet, to Aklier, this small house and the five acres on which it stood was more than a refuge. It was the home of his happiest and most bittersweet memories. This was the place that held his heart.

The house and land had been a gift to Aklier and his wife when they were newly married and their early years together had been spent here. When Aklier's father had died, Aklier became Head of the House Ti'Kara. He had inherited all of the lands and titles, but it was never the family seat in which he felt at home. It was here, where he and his wife had known

27

so much happiness. Here their daughter, their only child, had been born, and it was here that Aklier's ife had died and was buried, among the gardens she loved so well.

Aklier walked down the long path toward those gardens. He strolled slowly beneath the fruit trees they had planted together. How strange it was now to remember that these trees that shaded him from the sun's glare with their fruit-laden branches had once been little more than twigs he and his wife had labored to put in the ground.

She could make anything grow, Aklier thought as he neared the gardens. She had been dead for almost fifteen years, but he almost expected to see her amid the flowers and shrubs, wiping the dirt from her fingers as she stood up and smiled at him. He could see her, with his mind and his heart.

The sun was hotter here, out from under the trees, and the scent of the flowers and the soil rose like a cloud of perfume around Aklier as he passed. He breathed it in deeply; it was her smell.

Aklier walked to the heart of the gardens where his wife was buried. The grave was marked only by the stones that encircled it. They were barely visible now, almost overgrown with the abundant vegetation. Aklier knew that was how she would have wanted it. With his own hands, he had planted the small purple and white flowers that had been her favorites on her burial mound.

He sat on one of the stones and began idly pulling out the weeds that had sprung up among the flowers. He often came here, to sit in her company and tell her of his hopes and frustrations, just as he had through-out the years of their marriage. And today, today particularly, he wanted to talk to her.

"I've done it, Ilayne," he said out loud. "Just as I promised I would. Not another child will have to die the way our daughter did. That law will be abolished soon. At last I've found the way to give her death, and yours, some meaning."

Tears welled in Aklier's eyes; he missed her so much. "Oh, Ilayne," he whispered. "Are you with our daughter now? Have you ceased to grieve at last? I pray the God will forgive me for what I have done. I've betrayed my King, Ilayne. I had no choice. I did it because I love you and because I hate the law that caused you to grieve yourself to death. It's almost over now, Ilayne. It's almost over."

Aklier did not bother to wipe away the tears that wet his face. The sun would dry them.

While Aklier sat in the warmth and sunlight of his garden, Joakal I'lium sat on the floor of a small, bare cell. The luminous green veins in the stone of the walls cast an eerie light through the room. Joakal knew where he was. This stone had been used in only two buildings—the palace and the temple; Joakal was not in the temple. This cell, and several others like it, were in the subbasement of the palace. They had not been used for generations.

When Joakal had first regained consciousness, he had tried calling for help. He had screamed until his throat was raw and his voice gone. No one had answered. No one would come looking for him in this silent, lonely place.

He sat now as he had sat for hours—in the far corner of the cell, his back pressed against the wall and his head cradled on his knees. The cold from the stone felt as though it had entered his body and penetrated through to his soul. Time was measured in breaths and heartbeats.

It was the sound of a key turning the lock of the cell door that finally brought Joakal out of the stupor that had taken hold of him. He tried to jump to his feet, but the cold had entered his muscles and made them stiff and unresponsive. Using the wall for support, Joakal had barely gained his feet when the door swung inward. His captor stepped through.

Joakal gasped. Even in the dim light of the cell, it was like looking in a mirror. The same face, the same hair, the same body—only the eyes were different. The eyes that met his own burned with a hatred Joakal had never before encountered.

"Who are you?" he whispered, his voice still hoarse and painful.

His captor's eyes narrowed. "I," he said, "am your brother."

Joakal slowly shook his head. "I have no brother."

The man's lips twisted into the parody of a smile. "You do," he said. "And not just a brother—a twin. I had the misfortune to share a womb with you—and to be born a few minutes late. That made me an *abnormality,*" he spat out the word. "My life became forfeit."

"You're lying," Joakal whispered.

"Our *dear* mother," the man continued as he came further into the cell and began to pace back and forth before the still open door, "was required by law to leave me at the temple to die. But she wanted someone else to do her dirty work for her, so she gave me to a guard. He had more compassion for me than my own mother. He took me home to his wife and they raised me, but it was a life of secrecy and fear. As I grew older, we moved farther and farther into the country, always afraid that someone might see my face and think of you. My—parents—never let me forget who I was. Who I *am.* When they died I swore I would come to the palace and take back my own. I am Beahoram. Beahoram I'lium."

As Joakal listened, a part of his mind screamed that

30

this could not be real. He had planned to abolish this law as one of his first acts when he became *Absolute*. The Little Mothers who were on their way here—they would help him take care of those children already abandoned. That was why he had sent for them. It was inconceivable that this law was the reason he was locked in a cell and facing—what?

"Beahoram," Joakal said. "I would be glad of a brother. Come with me to the Council of Elders. I'll make them accept you."

Beahoram laughed. Joakal's mind raced, quickly searching for something to say to break through the arrogance he felt emanating from the other man and the anger he saw clearly on Beahoram's face.

"Listen to me," Joakal said. "I said I would be glad of a brother, and I meant it. You could help me. I've made plans for so many changes for our people. You could be part of making those changes come true."

Beahoram's eyes narrowed. "What changes?" he asked in a guarded voice.

There are so many, was Joakal's instant response. Which ones would mean anything to his brother? he wondered.

"The old law condemning abnormal children," Joakal began, "the law you were victim to—that will be the first to go. I've already begun arranging for that to change. And the law of isolation that has kept us locked on this world. There are people on their way here now, people from an organization called the United Federation of Planets. Our world is going to join them."

Joakal felt himself growing excited, in spite of the situation. "There are many other laws, too," he said. "The ban on scientific studies and technical advancements beyond our current level—in my studies I've learned that we once honored the sciences and used

31

them. I want that to happen again. Our law says too much technology is an offense to the God. I don't believe it. I believe we are meant to *use* our minds. Once I'm elevated *Absolute,* I'll be the Voice of the God and I can change the old ways. I want our people to be part of the future."

"I almost believe you," Beahoram said. "But it doesn't matter. For thirty years, you've had everything and I've had nothing. I watched my father work himself into his grave, accepting any job he could find to put food on the table. I watched my mother wither into an old woman, always afraid that someone would drag her 'son' away. And all the while, wherever we went, I heard your name. Joakal—what a good prince he is, how studious, how pious; what a good King Joakal will make. I grew to hate the very sound of your name. Well now, Brother, now it's my turn."

"Beahoram—listen to me," Joakal pleaded. "I'm *willing* to share it all with you. You don't have to kill me to get what you want."

Beahoram laughed, a low grating sound. "I'm not going to kill you, Brother."

"Then what—?"

"Have you ever wondered about the old legends, Brother?" he asked. "They're true, you know. All my life I've felt the truth of them within myself. I have your face. I live in your place in the palace and I answer to your name. Everyone who sees me thinks I am you. Soon I will wear your crown and then you will learn how true the legends are. When I am crowned in your place, when I am elevated and the power of *Absolute* comes to me, I will strip your memories from you one by one and make them my own. I will not take your life, my brother—I will take your mind."

Joakal could not keep the horror from his face, or the icy chill from his heart.

Chapter Five

TROI AWOKE at seven o'clock the next morning. It was later than she had planned to arise, but she felt no rush. She had checked her appointment schedule the night before and although her duty shift began at eight, her first patient was not scheduled until ten o'clock. Since she was not needed on the bridge, her morning plans included a workout in the gym, a half-hour of T'ai Chi, then a bath and a leisurely breakfast. She spent so many hours sitting in her office listening to her patients, that this morning routine had become increasingly important to her. The exercise kept her body toned and flexible and allowed her a safety valve of sorts, a way to vent the pressures and frustrations, especially the subliminal ones, that went with her profession. The fluid movements of T'ai Chi helped her focus her mind for the day ahead. The long soak and a lingering breakfast that she planned for today, were luxuries she added only when time allowed—not very often.

Troi ordered a cup of ginger tea from the food dispenser. She sipped on it as she began brushing the night tangles out of her hair. The hot liquid and delicate bite of the ginger were invigorating. By the time Troi had finished brushing her hair and gathered it into the clasp that would keep it out of her way while she worked out, she had finished the cup. She ordered another as she went to her closet and pulled out her favorite turquoise and pink exercise suit.

After she had dressed, she glanced at the wall chronometer. It read 07:38. Still plenty of time, she thought as she headed for the door. Just then the captain's voice came over inner-ship communications.

"Counselor Troi," he began. "Will you come to the briefing room at oh-eight-hundred hours? Now that we are underway, I think it time to review our mission to Capulon IV."

"Certainly, Captain," Troi said evenly, stifling a mental groan.

"Thank you, Counselor. Picard out."

Troi turned back around, sighed once, and pulled the clasp from her hair.

Twenty minutes later, attired now in the deep crimson jumpsuit she, as ship's counselor, wore instead of a standard uniform, Troi stepped off the turbolift and onto the bridge. She crossed to the briefing room where she found Data, Worf, and Will Riker already waiting. A moment later, Beverly Crusher and Geordi arrived. They had all just taken their seats when the door opened a final time and Captain Picard stepped through.

"Good morning," he greeted them as he took his place at the head of the long table. "As I told each of you," he began, "I think this an opportune time to review our mission. Mr. Data—if you please."

"Certainly, Captain," the android said. His fingers played across some buttons set into the table before him and the holographic image of a planetary system appeared in the air.

"Capulon IV," he began, "is a class M planet in the Sigma Delphini system, near the Blanchard asteroid belt that is currently being mined by the Starfleet Corps of Engineers.

"In terms of its technology, Capulon IV is on a level approximating that of mid-to-late twentieth-century Earth. However, when the Federation sent cultural analysis specialists there to observe, they reported that more advanced technology does exist, but is not used."

"A retrograde society?" Geordi asked.

"No," Data replied. "Not in the true sense of the word. It is not that they have lost the knowledge. It appears to be a willing abandonment of certain areas of advancement. However, the cultural specialists felt that the society, and especially the King, was ready for first contact. The contact was made five years ago and a preliminary treaty was signed."

"Why a preliminary treaty?" Riker wanted to know.

Data looked at the captain, who nodded slightly, indicating that the android should continue.

"The government of Capulon IV is a monarchy," Data explained, "but it is not until the King reaches the age of thirty that he is allowed to rule. Until then, all governmental decisions are passed through the Council of Elders, a committee made up of representatives of each of the twenty-nine provinces, with the King presiding as Head of the Council. At the age of thirty, however, the King is said to 'Come to Age' and be wise enough to rule alone. He then goes through a new coronation, after which the King is said to become the God-embodied and bears the title of *Absolute*. Although the council may still act in an advisory capacity, the King's decisions become an order of divine mandate."

Data's fingers moved again and the planets disappeared. "The present King," he continued, "is Joakal I'lium. He will turn thirty two days before we arrive at Capulon IV. His crowning as *Absolute* is set to occur the day following our arrival. The final treaty between Capulon IV and the Federation is due to be ratified following the coronation. King Joakal is reported to be very forward thinking and it was because of him that contact was made. According to all reports, the King is quite eager for his world to join the Federation."

"Thank you, Mr. Data," Picard said. He leaned forward and clasped his hands before him on the table. "Our mission here is twofold. First, as the Starfleet Flagship, we are here as representatives of the Federation to witness the coronation and the signing of the treaty. We are also here, at the King's request, to escort the Little Mothers to Capulon IV. The King's reason for this request has not been announced. It is my intention to lead this Away Team."

"You, Captain?" Commander Riker spoke up.

"Yes, Number One. Those are my orders. I understand their reason and I agree with them."

"But, Captain—"

"Will," the captain said, "Joakal I'lium is about to

be crowned *Absolute,* and absolute monarchs do not deal with seconds-in-command."

Picard held up his hand to silence his first officer before he could object further. "Mr. Data," the captain said as he turned again to the android, ignoring the scowl on Will Riker's face. "What is our ETA to Capulon IV?"

"At our present speed of Warp Two—twenty-three days, nine hours, eleven minutes, forty-three—"

The captain made a quick gesture which stopped the android mid-word. "Very good," Picard said. "Now if no one has anything to add, this briefing is adjourned."

Everyone except the captain stood. But as Troi turned to leave, Picard asked her to remain.

"Counselor," he said after the room had emptied. "During our tour of the ship yesterday, Sister Julian expressed an interest in spending some time with the children, perhaps helping in one or more of the classrooms. I know that you have occasion to work with the teachers and are more closely aware of their needs than I am. Do you think this might be possible? I've seen Sister Julian interact with the children and she does have an amazing rapport with them."

"I'm certain a number of the teachers would welcome her input," Troi replied. "And there is also the recreation areas for the non-school-age children. There is always room for more help there."

"Very good, Counselor. Would you please see to the necessary arrangements?"

"Yes, Captain."

"Thank you, Counselor," Picard said as he stood. Together they walked out of the briefing room.

Troi went directly to the turbolift, all thoughts of a leisurely morning before her first appointments vanished. Maybe this evening she would have time for her workout.

It had been another long day. Counselor Troi entered her quarters, slipped off her shoes, and thought how good a long, hot bath would feel. Maybe later she would truly indulge herself—lots of steamy water, scented candles, Mozart playing softly in the background. Peace. Quiet.

Troi stretched, trying to work the tension out of her shoulders, then walked toward her favorite chair. As she passed her desk, she noticed the message light blinking on the computer. With a sigh, she sat down and pressed Display. Instantly a communiqué from her mother filled the screen.

Little One, it began. *It has been so long since I have heard from you, I was beginning to become concerned. Then I realized that if anything was wrong, dear Jean-Luc would let me know. Still, a mother does worry.*

I am on Celestra visiting our old friends Targ and Melli. You remember them, don't you, Little One? You were so crazy about their son Sear when you were younger—before you met Commander Riker. Well, Sear is married and has three children now—two boys and a little girl. The girl is such a dear little thing. She reminds me so much of you. I look at the children and think. . . .

Troi groaned. She was definitely *not* in the mood right now to read about her mother's desire for grandchildren. The door chimed and Troi gratefully reached out and pressed the Hold button on her message.

"Come in," she called, prepared to greet *any* visitor with a smile. But when the door opened, Troi's smile vanished.

Mother Veronica stood in the doorway. Even from where she sat, Troi could see how the nun's body trembled. Her face was ashen and there were dark circles under her eyes.

"Help me," she said, her voice a tortured whisper.

Troi jumped to her feet and rushed to the nun's side, trying to ignore the turbulence of Mother Veronica's emotions. They stormed through Troi's mind as if driven by hurricane winds and she was forced to raise her shields before she could help the nun into the room.

Troi led Mother Veronica to a chair and the nun sank wearily into it. Troi sat down across from her and waited until the nun's trembling subsided. Slowly, Mother Veronica's breathing became more steady.

"Talk to me," Troi urged gently.

Mother Veronica raised her troubled eyes to Troi's face. "Please," she whispered. "You said you could help me shut out the voices. I can't stand any more."

Troi nodded. "I can help you—and I will," she said. "But you have to give me someplace to start. Talk to me."

Mother Veronica reached up and began fingering the wooden cross that hung about her neck. That seemed to comfort her.

"At the convent," she began slowly, "at home, it was so peaceful. I had lived with the thoughts of the other sisters all my life. They were thoughts of God and of our work—calm, ordered thoughts. Then we received word of this new mission. A bishop came, sent from our Mother House on Earth, to speak with our Mother Provincial. His presence upset everything. He stayed for weeks, talking with Mother Felicitas, making arrangements for the sisters and priest who are to follow us, helping Mother Felicitas decide who was to stay and who was to go. Finally the

Community was called together and told the decisions. I didn't want to go, much less be named Mother for the new Community. Oh, my dearest God, I didn't want to leave my home."

"Why didn't you tell your Mother Provincial and the bishop?"

"I . . . I couldn't."

"But if they knew how much distress—"

"No!" Mother Veronica jumped to her feet. "No—no one knows."

Troi, who had grown up as a member of a telepathic race, was puzzled by Mother Veronica's outburst. What trauma is behind her fear? Troi wondered. She needed to keep the nun talking.

"It's all right," she coaxed. "Tell me what happened then."

Mother Veronica sat back down. "We left Perrias and began traveling. Three other ships, two starbases —all filled with people thinking different thoughts— all gathering, repeating inside my head, never leaving me alone. They just keep getting louder and louder. I can't sleep—I can't eat. I can't even pray anymore."

Mother Veronica's hands were on her temples now, rubbing and pushing as though she could somehow force the sounds from her mind. Troi reached out and gently lowered the nun's hands, then sat there holding them and waiting. She knew there was more to come.

Mother Veronica took a ragged breath. "One of your crew members came to me. He wanted comfort and reassurance. His parents were religious people and he had been raised in the Church. His father had wanted him to become a priest but he had run away and joined Starfleet instead. Now his father is dead."

Ensign Marshall, Troi thought quickly. Many missing pieces clicked into place.

"But I couldn't comfort him," Mother Veronica

continued, the anguish in her voice mounting. "I couldn't be in the same room with him. All his grief, all his pain—I ran. I left him sitting there and I ran away. Oh God, what kind of nun can I be if all I can do is run from someone who needs me?"

"Mother Veronica," Troi said, keeping her voice quiet but firm and even, "your reactions are normal. The name for your talent is *telepathy*. There are many telepathic races throughout the galaxy, and each of them has developed disciplines or techniques for putting a barrier between themselves and the influx of other people's thoughts. A telepath *must* have ways of shutting out the voices or they'll lose *themselves*. If you'll let me, I can teach you my people's disciplines for mental control. Will you let me help you?"

Mother Veronica disengaged her hands from Troi's and stood. She began pacing about the room. Troi slowly lowered the shields she had raised when the nun arrived and immediately felt Mother Veronica's turmoil. Indecision, followed by waves of panic that crested and crashed through her, pushed by the nun's powerful but undisciplined talent. The force of the storm was too much for Troi and she again put a barrier around her mind.

Finally Mother Veronica stopped pacing. She turned and faced Troi. "All right," she said. "Please."

Troi slowly let out the breath she found she was holding. "I'll rearrange my schedule," she said. "We'll begin tomorrow morning."

Mother Veronica nodded. "Thank you," she said, and turned away. When she reached the door, she glanced back over her shoulder. Her eyes locked briefly with Troi's. Again the counselor was reminded of a wild, trapped animal, and again she wondered about the source of the nun's terror.

The door slid shut. Troi immediately touched the

comm button on her uniform. "Troi to Captain Picard," she said.

"Yes, Counselor?" his voice came almost at once.

"Captain, I need to talk to you. It's important."

"Very well, Counselor. I'm in my quarters. Please come join me."

"Thank you, sir. I'm on my way," she said as she reached out and turned off the display panel of her computer. Her mother's letter would have to wait.

"A telepath," the captain said, his voice sharp with surprise.

"Yes, Captain—a very gifted one. But she's had no training at all. In fact, she fears her gift."

"Any idea why?"

"Not yet."

The captain sat back in his chair and took a sip from the cup of tea he was holding. Troi did the same; the hot liquid was soothing and the smell of the bergamot, distinctive to Earl Grey, was like a restorative—as was the captain's company.

Sitting here in the captain's quarters, Troi was surrounded by the personality of the man. An individual of eclectic tastes and interests, he was an intellectual: a philosopher and adventurer, a student of the arts and of history, and a dreamer who yearned after the strange, new worlds of their charter. Yet, above all, he was *The Captain*—strong, disciplined, a leader of indomitable will who had infused the ship with his personality and yet never lost the ability to be compassionate. Troi liked him and liked serving with him.

"What is it you want to do?" he asked, bringing Troi's thoughts back to the problem of Mother Veronica.

"I want to help her, to teach her the Betazoid method for shielding the mind. You have to understand, Captain, a telepath without shields cannot survive. Her sanity, and her life, are in danger."

"Her life, Counselor?"

"Yes, Captain. When I studied at the hospital on Betazed, there were cases of telepaths who had been unable, for one reason or another, to develop their mental shields. Some of them were Betazoid, some were from other races brought to us for help. But we were not always able to reach them. Believe me, Captain, the anguish of an unshielded mind, of a mind imprisoned by the constant cacophony of other people's thoughts, other people's emotions, is a terrible thing. You remember Tam Elbrun, don't you? He was one of the lucky ones. It is a brutal existence that most choose not to continue. I don't want that to happen to Mother Veronica."

"I agree, but are you certain you can help her?"

Troi nodded. "The fact that she has survived this long with her sanity intact means that her mind and her will are very, very strong. I know I can help her develop at least rudimentary shields, but it will take time. I'd like your permission to be excused from bridge duty. I'll also rearrange my appointment schedule to free as many hours as possible to work with Mother Veronica."

"Very well, Counselor. I'll inform the bridge officers. We're due to reach Capulon IV in just over three weeks. Do you think you can do what needs to be done in that time?"

"I hope so, Captain."

Picard's forehead creased into a frown. "One thing, Deanna," he said. The use of her first name warned Troi that whatever the captain was about to say was of deep, personal concern to him. She listened very carefully, hearing the nuances as well as the words.

"You are an excellent ship's counselor," he said,

"and I don't presume to tell you your job—nor do I claim to understand, except in passing, the nature of telepathy. But I do know something of the faith that allows the Little Mothers to do the work they do. Are you certain that in helping Mother Veronica to develop these shields, which you say she needs—and I believe you—you won't be interfering with that faith, or taking from her the essence of who she is as a nun?"

Troi looked down and studied the tea in her cup, then looked back up and met the captain's concerned, questioning eyes.

"Only Mother Veronica can answer that, Captain," she said. "My work is with her mind, not her soul."

Troi finished her tea and left the captain's quarters, prepared to go back to her rooms, call up tomorrow's schedule on the computer, and begin juggling the appointment times. But as she stepped off the turbolift, she saw Ensign Marshall waiting outside her door.

He looked up as she approached. Troi saw that his eyes were red and swollen, as if he had been crying. His catharsis has begun, she thought. He's ready to talk.

With more confidence that she had felt in many days, Troi smiled at him. "Come in, Johann," she said.

Chapter Six

ON THE PLANET Capulon IV, Elana, First Daughter of the House E'shala, strolled aimlessly through the rooms of her childhood home. She had been home for over a month now. During that time she had visited all the favorite haunts of her childhood. She had climbed trees as if she were still a young girl, and gone on picnics, wandering through the fields where she used to play. At night she had spent many long hours watching the stars through her bedroom windows. Yet she was not trying to recapture those lost days, but to discover her future.

Still she could not choose between the two paths that lay before her. The first path that led to life at the temple was the one she had always thought to follow. Since she was eight years old, Elana had dreamed of becoming a Servant and of dedicating her life to the God—perhaps, even becoming an instrument of the God's Voice.

Nine years ago, when her father had been appointed to the Council of Elders that would advise the new King, Elana and her mother had accompanied him to the royal city. Elana had been ecstatic, for in the royal city stood the most ancient temple on all of Capulon IV. To Elana, it was the most holy place on their world and it was there she dreamed of making her Oblation of Service.

Her father, as Head of the House E'shala and member of the Council, had stayed at court. Through him, Elana had met Joakal. Elana often remembered that day: Joakal sitting on the throne in the Great Chamber, looking ill at ease as he received the oaths of his newly appointed Council of Elders; the way their eyes had met; the smile that had tugged at the corner of his mouth when he looked at her. Somehow over the last nine years, that shy attraction they had both felt had changed into friendship. Somehow, some *when,* that had deepened into love.

She loved him; Elana admitted her feelings, but her questions remained: Did she love him enough to give up her dream of Service to the God? Did she love the God enough to face the future without Joakal? More and more, the answer to the second question was no. She had only been gone from him a month, yet she found herself listening for the sound of his footsteps, his laughter, his voice calling her name.

Elana E'shala was finding the world to be a very empty and silent place without these sounds.

Troi waited for Mother Veronica in the observation lounge on the port side of Deck 35. It was a small room and the view here was not as panoramic as from many of the other observation ports. That was an advantage, for they were less likely to be disturbed and Mother Veronica would need this quiet to concentrate. There was so much for her to learn and so very little time.

Troi had arrived early so she could be here to greet the nun. While she waited, she thought about last night's visit from Ensign Marshall. It had been a good session, one of the best they had had. The ensign had finally been ready to talk. He had sat in her quarters for nearly two hours, sipping tea while he told her about his childhood and the home in which he had grown up, his family and the plans they had harbored for his future, plans he had disrupted by joining Starfleet, and the rift that had caused between himself and his father. Marshall had not been home in two years. He had never mended that rift, and now his father was dead.

Parents too often seem immortal to their children, Troi thought a little sadly. As if there will always be time later to say what needs to be said. Then death comes, and so much is left unresolved. Maybe now that Marshall accepted his pain and brought it out into the open, he can begin the long process of forgiving—his father, and himself.

Troi heard the door open. She looked up and smiled as Mother Veronica stepped into the room. The nun's fear filled the small area like the reverberating echo of discordant music. Troi had to force herself not to raise her shields against it. Now, more than ever, she needed all her empathic abilities. She kept her voice soft and her expression welcoming as she greeted the nun.

"You're right on time," she said. "Why don't you come and sit down. We'll just relax for a few minutes before we begin."

Mother Veronica sat next to Troi, but she did not

relax. She held herself rigid, like a rabbit ready to spring at the slightest sound.

Troi swallowed a sigh. "I thought you might enjoy meeting here instead of my office," she said, still keeping her voice pleasant and light. "It's quiet here, and the view is one I like."

Mother Veronica looked up and let her eyes scan the windows. "'The heavens declare the glory of the Lord,'" she whispered. "'And the firmament showeth his handiwork. . . .'"

"Is that from a poem?"

Mother Veronica nodded. "In a way," she said. "It's from the Psalms, which are a series of prayer-poems."

"Do you know all of the Psalms?"

Again the nun nodded. "I began learning them as a child, shortly after I came to the convent. They comforted me—and have gone on comforting me throughout the years."

"Tell me how you came to the convent," Troi said.

"I was a small child—I don't remember much about it."

Troi could feel that the nun was lying. She does remember, Troi thought, and it frightens her. Why?

The counselor turned and faced Mother Veronica. "I think we should get started," she said. "I know this is very difficult for you, so I want to begin by explaining a bit about telepathy and its uses. As I said last evening, there are many telepathic races throughout the galaxy, and we encounter more all the time. It is a normal condition, a talent, and as with any talent it can be trained and used."

Troi could feel the nun's disbelief. "If it is so normal," Mother Veronica said, "why am I the only one of my sisters cursed with it?"

"Although there are many races—many humanoid

48

races—with telepathic abilities, there are just as many, or more, without them. Among the humans of Earth, for example, telepathic communication is rare. But it is also *not* nonexistent. When it does show up, that person is valued as having a very precious gift—as you do."

Troi shifted a little in her seat, trying to find the words to reach through Mother Veronica's prejudice. "Telepathic communication," she continued, "can be a source of great good. It can open the way for understanding between peoples. It can break down the walls of mistrust and fear or reveal sentience where none was thought to exist. It has been known to reach across distances and to bring hope in a time of despair or rescue when none seemed possible."

Still Troi could feel the nun's disbelief. But the counselor had the conviction of truth on her side and she pressed on, trying to find one example that might light a spark of interest in Mother Veronica. A single spark was all Troi wanted—from that she could build a beautiful, warming flame.

"Medicine has its uses for telepathic communications as well," Troi continued. "Tricorders and diagnostic beds, all of the wonders of medical science, cannot reach a trapped mind. But I can—and so can you."

Was that it? Troi wondered. Was that the flicker I've been waiting for?

"Sister Julian told the captain that you have an extraordinary talent for reaching troubled children—"

"You don't understand," Mother Veronica interrupted. "Their thoughts scream in my head until I have to help them. Yes, I want to—but for *my* sake as well as theirs."

"I do understand," Troi assured her. "I know how difficult and how painful life has been for you. That is why we are here. But," Troi paused and looked into the nun's eyes. "Our lessons will require deep mental communication. Will you trust me?"

Mother Veronica looked away. Her eyes strayed to the viewports and she sat silent for several minutes regarding the stars. Troi felt her inner struggle and said nothing more. Mother Veronica's agreement to be here today had been an act of desperation; from this point on, if they were to succeed in the short amount of time allotted to them, each act must be one of decision.

The nun turned back around. "One question," she said. "There are things within my heart and soul, private things between myself and God. Will they remain private?"

"I will not force myself into any part of your mind you do not willingly share with me."

"All right," Mother Veronica said. "What must I do?"

Troi reached out and gently took Mother Veronica's hands into her own. "Physical contact often strengthens the bond," she explained, "particularly between student and teacher. Now, close your eyes. Think of nothing. My mind will reach out and touch yours, establishing a link between us. Once that is done, I will guide your thoughts back into my mind and show you how mental shields work. I will do this several times, and each time the link between us will be severed and have to be reestablished. Then I will give you some exercises for concentration. That is all we will do today."

Mother Veronica nodded.

"Then let's begin."

Troi watched the nun close her eyes, and did the same. Softly, trying not to cause her student's already overburdened mind too much distress, Troi endeavored to establish the link between them. Each time she touched Mother Veronica's thoughts, chaos erupted, spewing forth pain and fear, and the nun's mind retreated out of reach. After the eighth such try, Troi opened her eyes. She found she was sweating with exertion.

"Mother Veronica," she said. "There is something in your mind that is keeping us from reaching the level of communication that we need. I believe it is something from your past, and that we must deal with it before we go on."

Troi paused. She knew what must be done, but would Mother Veronica agree? She chose her next words carefully.

"I asked you how you came to the convent and you said you don't remember. I know you do. I believe much of your fear stems from that time and I think we need to examine it."

Mother Veronica started. She tried to pull her hands from Troi's, ready to run away, but the counselor did not let go. She knew she had to get through to the nun.

"I am not here to judge you," Troi said, "but to help you. You are not a little child anymore, but somewhere deep inside your mind, the little girl you were is crying to be healed. She cannot be healed while she is hidden and buried. Let's heal her together."

Mother Veronica was no longer trying to pull away. She was sitting quietly; her expression was haunted as her eyes slowly filled with tears.

"Close your eyes again," Troi said. "And this time I want you to think about when you came to the convent. Think only about that time. Remember every detail—every voice, every action. It cannot hurt you anymore. It is in the past."

Troi spoke softly, letting her voice lull and guide the nun. Again the counselor reached out to touch Mother Veronica's mind with her own. At first it was the chaos of before, then slowly, the memories emerged . . .

"Kill her . . . she's evil . . . a demon-child. . . ."

Voices split the silence of the night, loud even through the walls of their home. Light from the torches flickered through the window. Pounding—they were pounding on the door, trying to get in.

In the back of the house, the little girl's mother picked her up and lifted her toward the bedroom window. The little girl could feel her mother's hands were shaking. "Their thoughts hurt, Mama," she said. "Why do they hate me?"

"I don't know, baby. Now shh, you must be very quiet. You go on. I'll be right behind you."

The little girl scrambled out the window. Her mother followed and once they were on the ground, again picked the little girl up. From inside the house came the sound of breaking glass. The smell of smoke grew stronger.

The woods, the little girl heard her mother think. *I have to get into the woods, get my baby away.*

The mother began to run, desperate to reach the trees on the other side of their small garden, praying that the darkness of the night would be enough to hide them. The twenty yards seemed like a chasm of miles. Her breath was loud in the little girl's ear, her fear pounded in the child's mind.

"Mama?" she said, uncertain what was happening. "Shh, baby. Quiet."

They ran until they were under the cool, dark

boughs—and they kept on running. *I've got to get my baby somewhere safe. Where can I go? . . . The convent,* the mother thought, changing directions as she ran. *The Little Mothers will protect her. . . .*

Through the trees the little girl could see the blaze that had been their home. Her world faded into a haze of dark confusion: the feel of her mother's arms clutching her, holding her so tightly she could feel the pounding of her mother's heart, hear each panting breath in her ear; her mother's feet colliding with the ground as she ran, each step jarring the child in her arms; above all, the echo of her mother's fear filled the little girl's mind.

Up ahead, through the trees, a soft light shone. Relief swept through the mother and she ran faster. They reached the convent steps; the little girl felt herself being lowered.

"Listen to me, baby," her mother said as she knelt down in front of the child and looked into her large, frightened eyes. "Listen very carefully. You have to stay here for a while—I'll be back for you when I can, when it's safe again. The Little Mothers will be good to you. Will you stay here for Mama?"

The little girl nodded, her eyes filling with tears. The mother reached up and pulled the bell-rope. From inside the convent a single gong sounded.

The mother pulled the little girl into her arms. "Promise me, baby—promise me you'll never again tell anyone you can hear their thoughts."

"I . . . I promise."

"That's my good girl. Remember Mama loves you, baby." Footsteps sounded, coming closer; the mother's arms tightened. "I'll always love you."

The mother let go. She kissed the child once on the cheek, then stood, and fled into the night, leaving the little girl alone on the convent steps. Behind her, a door opened and a woman dressed in a long brown robe stepped through. She put her hands on the little girl's shoulders.

"Come inside, child," she said. "There's a home for you here."

"She never came back," the woman who was now Mother Veronica sobbed. "Oh, Mama, I kept my promise—I never told. It was so hard without you."

Troi opened her eyes and saw the tears that ran unchecked down the nun's cheeks, tears that the frightened child had never shed. Troi reached out and put her arms around her companion's shoulders, silently holding her, silently letting the wounds start to heal.

After a while, Mother Veronica's tears ceased. "I didn't talk for weeks," she said aloud, finishing the story her mind had shared. "I wouldn't even tell them my name. But the Little Mothers were patient with me. They loved me, and I grew to love them. I never left the convent—until now."

She sat up straight and wiped her cheeks with the back of her hand. "Now you know," she said.

"Now I know," Troi repeated softly. "But you're not that child anymore. It's time to let the memory go, like a nightmare banished by the daylight. It's time to come into the light and stay there."

Chapter Seven

THROUGHOUT her afternoon appointments, most of Troi's thoughts remained with Mother Veronica. Even after the nun had shared those tortured memories from her past, establishing the teaching link with her had not been easy. The child within Mother Veronica still dwelt in a world of self-recrimination and fear. She blamed herself that her mother did not return, fearing that she had been killed for what her child's mind contained. This fear had festered over the years. Now it was like an improperly cleaned wound that reopened and must drain away the infection of self-hatred.

The last appointment finally concluded, Troi went to the bridge to talk with the captain. They withdrew to his ready room where she could explain Mother Veronica's condition to him in private.

"So you see, Captain," Troi concluded, "this is going to be a more difficult task than I had anticipated. It is important that Mother Veronica learn to shield her mind. But equally important, perhaps more important, is for her to realize, and *accept,* that the loss of her home, and perhaps her mother's life, were not her fault. A part of her knows it, but another deeper part does not. And this pain goes very, very deep."

"Is there any way of finding out what happened to her mother?"

Troi shook her head. "I've already checked," she said. "Perrias VII is not a member of the Federation and the records from them are sketchy at best. Most of what we know comes from the Little Mothers themselves."

"And an incident like this one is not likely to show up on an official report," the captain said with a nod. "Have you learned anything about the planet and its people?"

Troi sat a little forward, her mind sorting through the reports of the Little Mothers that she had read, narrowing the information down to a few succinct statements.

"Most areas of Perrias VII are still very primitive. The inhabitants believe in a number of deities and demons that guide, or interfere in the case of the demons, in every aspect of an individual's life. That which is thought demonic is *cleansed* from their society. This cleansing is immediate and often brutal. The Little Mothers lost several nuns to such cleansings when they first arrived, until they convinced the population that they were there only to help. Now they seem to have integrated themselves into the society. Their presence may even be having a beneficial and stabilizing effect."

"Given this information, its not likely that Mother Veronica's mother survived the night, is it?"

Troi shook her head. "No, Captain, it is not. It makes Mother Veronica's attitude toward her telepathy more understandable, but it does not alleviate her need for training."

"I agree," the captain said with a nod. "Thank you for your report. I realize this is creating a great deal of extra work for you and I want you to know I appreciate it. Mother Veronica could not be in better hands."

Troi felt a flush of gratitude. A slow smile spread across her face as she and the captain went to rejoin the others on the bridge.

When she stepped through the doors of the ready room, Lieutenant Commander Data looked up from his station at Ops. He turned to her. "Counselor," he said. "May I ask you a question?"

"Certainly, Data."

"It is my understanding that one of the Little Mothers is an untrained telepath whom you have taken on as a student. Is this correct?"

"Yes."

"Then you have been in contact with her mind—how is it different from other minds?"

"I'm not certain I understand your question, Data. Do you mean as a telepath?"

"No, Counselor. Telepathic communication and other occurrences of psychic abilities have been well documented by many cultures. The writings of the Vulcans are perhaps the most illuminating on the subject. They are certainly the most concise. However, I was referring to Mother Veronica's mind as a nun. What has made her choose such a life?"

Leave it to Data, Troi thought. She walked over and sat in her customary seat to the captain's left, trying to think of a way to answer the android's question.

"The question you have asked," she said after a moment, "could refer to anyone, Data, and to any profession. Why are we"—she waved her hand to indicate the bridge personnel—"in Starfleet? We are here because of the belief that this is the life and work we are meant to do—because of a *calling.*"

"I concede that point, Counselor," Data replied. "Yet outside the parameters of our Starfleet duties, each of us is free to pursue what is frequently termed a normal life. My research indicates that this is not true for nuns."

"But then we come to the question of what is *normal,*" Troi returned. "My mother would not say that my life is normal, because it would not be normal for her—yet, for me it is."

"If I may," Captain Picard interrupted.

"Certainly, sir," Troi said, relieved to have someone else take over.

"While I agree with what Counselor Troi has said," Picard continued, "I believe the answer to your question, Mr. Data, is much more complex."

Troi watched Picard switch into what she considered his teaching mode: legs crossed, elbows on the armrests of his command chair, one hand raised as if to punctuate the points he would soon be making. She thought them a well-matched pair, this android second officer who was constantly seeking to learn and the captain/philosopher who, though he might not admit it, loved to teach.

"Consider this," Picard was saying. "In all the myriad cultures we have encountered, every one of them has included a philosophy, a religion, that deals with the questions surrounding the meaning of existence. Are we more than a cosmic accident, and if so, why are we here? Where did we come from? Is there a God? Is death a finality or a transition? Where do we go? These are the questions asked by every sentient civilization—and in every one of them there have been those individuals whose lives are dedicated to striving for the answers."

"So what are the answers, Captain?" Data asked with the frank, trusting innocence of a child.

Picard's expression was one Troi was glad she had not missed. His eyes grew wide and he blinked twice; his cheeks paled slightly and his Adam's apple bobbed several times as he swallowed back his astonishment. Next to him, Commander Riker was vigorously rubbing his hand down his mustache and beard, struggling to contain his laughter.

"Data," the captain finally managed to say, "I don't claim to know any Ultimate Truths. I know only what I believe, personally, and each person must come to such beliefs for him- or herself."

"Yes, Captain. How?"

Picard drew a deep breath. "By study—by careful thought and consideration, some would say by prayer and meditation—by talking to others—by cultural background—"

"But Captain," Data said, "I possess no cultural background to draw upon."

"Then I would suggest you begin by reading history. Many of the greatest minds and greatest philosophical writings have come out of monastic settings and disciplines. But do not limit yourself, Mr. Data. You are in a unique position. Not many of us come to these questions so free of preconceived opinions and prejudices."

"Do you have any suggestions as to where I should start, Captain?"

Again Picard drew a deep breath. He shifted in his seat, recrossing his legs as if his command chair had suddenly become uncomfortable. He considered Data's question very carefully; there were so many writings that he valued: the Discourses of Plato and the great Dialogues of Epictetus; the philosophy of the Tao Te Ching; the Summa Theologica by Thomas Aquinas and the mystical vision of The Cloud of Unknowing—and those only named a very, very few. Away from Earth, there were the Teachings of the Katra from Vulcan and the Xhari'a of the Felicus; the Orisha of the Yoruba, whose complexity had taken him so long to understand, but who expressed the ideals of union so eloquently, and the Ik-Onkar whose religion was expressed not in words but in symbolic notations.

"No, Mr. Data," Picard said at last. "I do not—I don't want to influence your search. I will only recommend that you investigate as many cultures as possible before forming any opinions."

"Thank you, Captain," Data said as he turned back to his duty station. "I shall do so."

Joakal I'lium sat in his cell, surrounded by the silence of his captivity. He was not ill-treated; he had food and water, blankets with which to cover himself against the cold, but he was alone, more alone than he had ever been before.

And yet, he was not alone. In a way he would not have thought possible, Joakal could *feel* the nearness of his brother. He could almost hear Beahoram's thoughts echoing in his head. And more than the thoughts, it was the other's emotions—the hot flashes of anger, the triumph that was without elation, the dark and bitter need for revenge—these surged through Joakal and left him trembling.

Upstairs in the main council chambers, Beahoram sat in his brother's place at the head of the long table, eyeing the old men gathered around it. There were twenty-nine of them, the Council of Elders, and together with him they made the number thirty—the number that was supposed to denote wisdom and divine inspiration—the age the King would be crowned and elevated to *Absolute*.

I am here, Beahoram thought with grim satisfaction. It has taken me a long time, but I am here. And you, you old fools, you don't know the difference.

Tygar, the Elder seated to Beahoram's right, cleared his throat and took some papers out of the folder on the table before him. Beahoram turned toward him.

"Sire," Tygar said, "we have received the final set of petitions from those families eligible to participate in your coronation. With your permission, we would like to review them this morning. Time is growing short and we need to reach our decisions."

Beahoram inclined his head in assent. He glanced down the table at Aklier and noticed that the Elder's hands were shaking slightly as he, too, took out the papers before him.

He's more nervous than I am, Beahoram thought. The old fool will give us away if he's not careful.

Tygar cleared his throat again and began to read. "From the Southron, the House Masalai petitions that the Head of their House be allowed to walk in the procession, to receive and carry the Robe of Youth that will be lifted from you during the ceremony. As precedent, they cite their similar function in the coronation of seven past Kings, including your grandfather, Nygaar the Third."

"And in my father's coronation?"

"No. At that time, the Head of the House Masalai was still a youth himself and, therefore, not allowed to take part in the coronation. The honor passed to the House L'Snium, and they, also, have petitioned."

"What precedents do they cite?"

61

"Their claim is based on distant relationship to Your Majesty—they are seventh cousins on your mother's side—and on a personal friendship with your father."

Beahoram felt his stomach tighten; friends of his father, of the man who would condone his son's death, relations to the woman who would give her son away—these were none he wanted near him.

"The honor will return to the Masalai," he said aloud.

"Next, Sire," Tygar said, "there are a number of petitions for the honor of attending Your Majesty during the vigil of your Coming to Age. All of the petitioners are worthy, and I beg Your Majesty to consider most carefully."

This was the one tricky petition. Beahoram wanted no one but Aklier to attend him until after the coronation. He glanced down the table. Aklier was staring fixedly at the papers in his hands, beads of perspiration lining his forehead.

Beahoram turned his eyes away. He gathered a royal hauteur about him like a cloak and lifted his chin. "I have already decided," he said. "Aklier shall attend my vigil."

The murmurs around the table erupted at once. "But . . . but Sire," Tygar stammered, "this is most irregular. The petitions must be—"

"It is *my* Coming to Age," Beahoram snapped. "It is a *private* vigil. Aklier has been my trusted adviser and friend and I wish to reward his faithful service." Beahoram turned toward the head of the Council and let his long-nurtured anger flare briefly in his eyes. "Am I not the King?" he demanded.

Tygar subsided. "Yes . . . Your Majesty," he said.

Beahoram looked around the table, staring at each

62

one of the councilors in turn. One by one, they dropped their eyes.

So easy, Beahoram thought. They are such fools. "Next petition," he said aloud.

Tygar shuffled the papers before him, laying several aside unread. While he waited, Beahoram's thoughts strayed to the man who was his brother, sitting alone in the cell in the palace subbasement. Like Joakal, Beahoram could feel the other's presence, but unlike his brother, it bothered Beahoram not at all. It filled him with satisfaction, even dark glee.

Again, unlike Joakal, Beahoram had spent his life knowing of the other's existence. He believed the legends of the priest-kings of old, whose minds were so powerful they could rip the thoughts from their enemies' brains and bend them to their will. He believed; he had felt that latent power within himself all his life—believed, built upon it, strained to make it happen.

And now, more strongly than ever before, he could feel another's thoughts. So near, he needed only the coronation—and the ceremonies that accompanied it—to make his power complete. His mind would become fully awakened then, and he would take his brother's thoughts, his memories, the essence of who he was. He would strip them away and consume them.

He would be the *Absolute,* the God-embodied. Nothing would stop him. He would only have to do this—

Beahoram gathered his thoughts. He pictured his mind like a lance of light and hurled it toward the man downstairs, focusing his will on capturing his brother's mind and sucking it out of him.

But it was like diving headfirst into a wall. Pain lanced through Beahoram's brain; fire exploded be-

63

hind his eyes. His hand flew to his head and he doubled over. The contents of his stomach gushed from his mouth onto the floor. He fell from his chair.

He barely heard the scraping chairs or the voices calling for the healers. He barely felt the hands that turned and lifted him. All he knew was the searing pain behind his eyes. White hot. Blinding.

Far below, Joakal, too, writhed in agony on his cell floor.

Chapter Eight

MOTHER VERONICA stood outside the door of the observation lounge on Deck 35. She knew Counselor Troi was inside waiting to begin today's lesson, and Mother Veronica knew she needed the counselor's help. The invasion of Mother Veronica's mind had not lessened; the battle for her own peace, for her sanity, still raged on. Yet, as she stood alone in the corridor, Mother Veronica was still afraid. What other memories might have to be dredged up and relived, what further pain would she have to endure?

"'Yea, though I walk through the valley of the shadow of death . . .,'" she whispered aloud. Holding the canticle of the Shepherd's care like a shield about her soul, Mother Veronica stepped to the door. It slid open and she walked through.

As she had known, Troi was awaiting her. The nun tried to return the counselor's smile and failed. She took the seat Troi indicated and sat staring at her hands, folded neatly if not serenely, on her lap. She heard the counselor sigh.

"Mother Veronica," Troi said. "I can feel how upset you are. Can you tell me what I need to do to set your fears at rest?"

Mother Veronica shook her head. What could she say—make the strange ability in my mind go away? Make my thoughts like other people's? Take away the years I have suffered this, hated this? She shook her head a second time.

"Then let's try to begin," Troi said. Mother Veronica turned to face her.

"As we did yesterday," the counselor continued, "I will need to establish the teaching link between us. Today we will begin the first lesson toward your development of mental shields. In the ancient language of Betazed, this exercise is called the *D'warshra,* which means The Place of Peace and Identity."

"Peace and identity," Mother Veronica whispered. It was what she had sought all her life. She felt some tiny measure of her fear drain away. Looking up, she met Troi's eyes, and again the counselor smiled at her.

"Ready?" she asked. Mother Veronica nodded and Troi held out her hands. The nun placed hers in them.

"Close your eyes," the counselor repeated her opening instructions of yesterday. "Think of nothing. You will feel my mind touch yours. Do not be afraid. It's all right. Now."

Immediately, Mother Veronica felt the touch of Troi's mind. She was surprised; this was not the tenuous thread they had struggled so hard to achieve yesterday. This time the bond was strong, the flow of communication was unhindered and she found that the mental sharing between them was different from anything she had ever known. There was none of the rushing torrent she was used to receiving. There was no fearsome bombardment, no confusion and pain. This touch between their minds ran cool and fresh and clear. Mother Veronica's fear again lessened, just a little.

It is time to begin, Troi's thoughts told her. *The mind of every sentient being, every creature of thought and self-awareness and will, is unique. It has its own form and feel, and in order to learn to shield it, you must first learn to recognize the mind that is our own. Follow me now as we find the awareness that is uniquely yours.*

Up on the bridge, Data was talking to Lieutenant Worf. The Klingon was trying to master his outrage and remember that his fellow officer meant no offense.

"A Klingon does *not* discuss the gods he follows," Worf finally managed to say. "Especially with a member of another species."

"Actually, Lieutenant," Data replied evenly, "it could be argued that I am not a member of any species and therefore such a statement is rendered meaningless."

Worf clenched his jaw and tried again. Tact was a human skill he was trying to develop, but it was one the Klingon found both difficult and irritating.

"I do not believe your—programming—makes you capable of understanding our warrior gods," he said.

"An interesting point," Data replied. "However, in accordance with the captain's suggestion, I have begun my research into the religious and philosophical questions of the purpose of existence by reading history. Since both the captain and my creator, Doctor Soong, are human, I have begun by reading human history. I spent last night reading the history of the planet Earth, particularly in regard to the development of myth and religion. Although there are many esoteric writings I have yet to cover, I believe I now have a basic working knowledge of the subject. Many cultures worshiped warrior gods and valued warrior abilities. Among the most notable were the Aztecs from an area once known as Central America, the followers of Ba'al in the Middle East, the Celtic members of the Cult of the Head, the followers of the Norse gods Odin and Thor, the Samurai culture of ancient Japan—"

"Enough!" roared the Klingon.

"But, Lieutenant, that is a most incomplete list. In fact, I found that nearly every culture throughout Earth history has at one time or another followed the Way of the Warrior. Even those religions that claimed to teach peace espoused the concept of holy war at some time in their development. I found it quite confusing—perhaps you could explain it to me."

Again the Klingon struggled with his temper. "Is that why you have come to me?" he asked.

"No, Lieutenant. The captain also suggested that I talk with people before forming any religious opinions. The logical place to start is with my crewmates. The ship's library contains very little on Klingon culture and history, and almost nothing on Klingon religion."

"I am not a *G'luuc'taha,* a teacher of the gods," Worf said sternly, ready to tell Data to continue his inquiries elsewhere. Then Worf remembered the times he and the android had fought side by side. They had faced death together; in his culture they were brothers of war. He relented.

"If you will come to my quarters this evening," he said, "I will instruct you in the gods of my house. But it is a *private* instruction. You will not mention this to others."

"Thank you, Lieutenant," Data replied as he turned away. "I think I will now go talk to Geordi."

Data walked toward the turbolift; behind him, Worf emitted a low growl.

"Run that one by me again, Data," Geordi said a few minutes later. He was down in engineering making some notes on a pet project of his when his android friend found him. His thoughts were so filled with sensor-array equations he was not certain he had heard Data's question correctly.

"I asked—do you believe there is a God?"

Geordi put down the computer pad and stylus he had been holding, thoughts of energy-flow curves evaporating like a widespread particle beam. He considered himself used to Data's idiosyncratic inquiries, but this one caught him off guard.

"Why are you asking, Data?"

"My creator, Doctor Soong, did not imprint my programming with his own religious beliefs. Perhaps he did not have any, or perhaps he wished to leave me free to draw my own conclusions. I do not know. It is an aspect of human development I have never before considered."

Geordi did not have to ask why Data was considering it now; the presence of nuns on board ship had many people questioning what they believed.

"Why are you asking me?" Geordi wanted to know.

"The captain suggested I talk to people. You are my best friend. Should I not talk to you?"

"Well, sure, Data, you can talk to me about anything. It's just that your question is a difficult one to answer."

"Then you do not believe in a God?"

"Whoa. I didn't say that. The word *God* means different things to different people. I don't believe in a man with a big white beard, sitting on a throne somewhere. But we've been to too many places and seen too many incredible things for me to believe that it doesn't mean anything, or that we're all just a cosmic accident. *I* don't *feel* like an accident."

"Then you are religious?" Data asked.

Geordi blew out a breath in a silent whistle. "It's not as easy as that," he said. "I'm not religious in the same way the Little Mothers are, but I believe in—something—that gives shape and reason to the universe. And that something is inside of us, too—making us strive to be better than we are, helping us recognize that all life-forms are a part of one another."

"That is not very precise, Geordi."

"I know, Data." The engineer shrugged his shoulders. "But it's the best I can do."

Chapter Nine

"THIS ISN'T GOING TO WORK," Aklier said as he paced back and forth in the King's private apartments. "It's been six days since your collapse in the Council chambers and the other Elders are beginning to wonder if you're fit to rule."

"It will work, Aklier," Beahoram said. He rose from the massive, brocade-covered chair in which he had been sprawling, walked over to the carved sideboard in the corner, and poured himself a goblet of wine.

He held the goblet up until the light shone through it. It was made from a single Flame Crystal and the stone was cut so that its deep red heart was embedded in the stem. It seemed to dance with life as the light hit it, shooting flame-colored rays through the golden liquid that filled the cup. Beahoram closed his fingers around it possessively.

Beahoram lifted the cup to his lips and drank, downing half the contents in a single swallow. Then he set the goblet down and began to walk slowly around the room letting his fingers hungrily caress each thing he neared. His touch lingered on the back of the chair in which he had been sitting. It and its mate were carved from single pieces of dark-grained wood and covered with heavy brocade worked in crimson and gold. A low table stood between them, made of the same dark wood carved in the identical pattern as the arms and legs of the chairs. The center of the table was inlaid with luminous green-veined stone.

Beahoram continued to walk, to claim by touch the contents of the room. He ran one finger along the gilded edge of the frames on the paintings that lined the wall. He stopped to gaze at the window that ran from the ceiling to floor, bracketed on either side by drapes of the crimson-and-gold brocade and crowned by panes of colored glass. He took a few more steps, watching how his feet buried themselves noiselessly in the thick pile of the deep red carpet while he crossed the room to the fireplace. It was empty now, but the green-veined stone from which it was made, the Living Stone it was called in ancient times, was filled with light. It looked as if the fire had one time entered it and become trapped there.

Beahoram's fingers tightened on the mantle. It was his now, all of it, as it should always have been.

He turned and found Aklier watching him. "It will work," he said again.

The Elder swallowed audibly. "These headaches," he said. "You've had too many of them—the first one in the Council chambers and now four more in as many days. The others are beginning to talk. They're wondering if the headaches might be the God's way of telling us you should not be raised to *Absolute.* If it happens again, the Council will begin to look elsewhere for its divine ruler."

"It won't happen again. I was trying to force something my mind was not yet ready to do. I'm content now to wait until after the coronation. The power will come to me then."

"I've risked everything, Beahoram. If we're caught, my life will be forfeit, too. Don't forget that."

Beahoram's eyes narrowed. "I forget *nothing*," he said.

There was a knock on the door. Aklier jerked around nervously, but Beahoram strolled languidly back to his chair and seated himself, a small, self-satisfied smile on his lips.

"Come," he called, and the door was opened by a young boy in royal livery.

"Sire," he said with a bow. "The Lady Elana E'shala is here. She asks for an audience with Your Majesty."

Beahoram glanced at Aklier. The Elder was sweating, his body taut and nearly trembling with fear. Beahoram dismissed the reaction; Aklier was easily frightened.

"The Elder and I are still in conference," Beahoram told the waiting servant. "We will ring when we are finished."

"Yes, Your Majesty," the boy said as he bowed out of the room.

"You must not see her," Aklier said as soon as the door closed. "She could ruin everything."

"Why? Who is she?"

"The woman your brother hoped to marry."

"Then I must see her. Tell me everything you know."

"But, Beahoram—"

"Don't call me that," Beahoram said through clenched teeth. "Never again. Now, tell me."

Aklier swallowed audibly. "Elana E'shala is a

Gentleborn of the Westron Province. She and your brother have known each other for the past nine years and have been with each other almost daily. Joakal loves her very deeply. He has asked her to marry him after he is Elevated and free to wed. I believe Elana also loves Joakal, but she is very devout. A month ago she returned to her childhood home in the Westron to meditate on her decision whether to marry your brother or enter Service at the temple. She was not due to return until the day of the coronation."

Aklier stopped; Beahoram waited impatiently. "What else?" he demanded.

"Else?"

"Yes. What personal things can you tell me? You were in my brother's confidence—I need to know everything."

"I know nothing more. There were some things your brother did not confide even to me."

"No matter," Beahoram said with a shrug. "No one doubts I am my brother. Neither will this Elana. Ring the bell, Aklier."

The Elder pulled the bell cord. A few seconds later the same servant entered.

"You may admit the Lady now," Beahoram said.

The servant again bowed and left. While they waited, Beahoram watched Aklier. The Elder's nervousness irritated Beahoram.

When this is over, Beahoram thought, I'll replace him with someone who has more courage. I'm certain I can arrange for some—accident—to rid me of Aklier.

The door opened and Beahoram turned his attention from the Elder to the woman who entered. His eyes widened slightly at the sight of her.

She was small and delicate, dressed in flowing pants

74

and sashed tunic similar to the ones worn by both Beahoram and Aklier, but in the blue and silver of her House. Her hair rippled in golden curls nearly to her waist. Her eyes were the same blue as her tunic, the color of a cloudless sky in early evening, and even from a distance they seemed to sparkle and dance. When she smiled at Beahoram, a little dimple appeared by the corner of her mouth. Beahoram's opinion of his brother elevated a little; it seemed they shared the same taste in feminine beauty.

"Elana," he said, testing the feel of her name in his mouth. She rushed across the room to him. He stood and enfolded her into his arm.

"I couldn't wait until after the coronation," she whispered, her mouth close to his ear. "I missed you too much."

"And I missed you," Beahoram lied.

Elana stepped back and searched his face, a little frown tracing a line between her brows.

"Have you, Joakal?" she asked. There was a slight waver to her voice.

Beahoram smiled at her. He took her hand and held it, feeling the softness of her skin.

"Of course I have," he said. "Tell me about your trip home—what did you do, who did you see? Tell me everything."

Again Elana studied his face. She glanced from him to Aklier standing unobtrusively by the far wall, and back to Beahoram.

"Don't you . . . don't you want to know my decision?" she asked uncertainly.

"Only if it's good news," Beahoram said, trying to sound pensive.

Elana smiled at him. "It is good news," she said. "The best news. Yes, Joakal—I will marry you."

Beahoram pulled her again into his arms, savoring the feel of her body against his. His lips found hers and closed upon them greedily.

This, too, shall be mine, he thought. But even as the words were in his mind, he felt Elana stiffen. She pulled back from him with a low cry. Her eyes again searched his face, then she turned and ran from the room.

Daylight was beginning to dim and the late afternoon breeze had picked up force as Elana E'shala stood at the base of the temple steps. She pulled her dark blue cape closer to her sides and held her head high, refusing to give in to the tears that waited so near the surface of her thoughts.

Was it only three hours ago? she wondered, feeling as if these last hours had brought her to some remote and ancient era of her life. Only three hours since she had told Joakal she would marry him and had rushed so willingly into his arms? Three hours since his lips had fastened on hers in a kiss devoid of love, filled only with avid, predatory hunger. With that kiss, Elana's world had grown dark and still. Her heart felt as chilled as the breeze that blew across her cheeks and stung her already red and weary eyes.

She would not marry now; that one kiss had changed everything. She would enter the temple and Serve the God, as it seemed she was meant to do.

She put her foot on the first step and began to climb, though her feet felt as heavy as stone. The tears she promised she would no longer shed sprang again to her eyes. She blinked them away, but it was no use; the pain was still too fresh. Oh Joakal, her thoughts cried, what happened? What changed you?

Elana reached the top step. Recessed behind four towering pillars that filled the temple porch, the great doors stood open. For the first time in Elana's life, the temple did not welcome her. Its interior did not look cool and inviting. Today the doors of the temple seemed like a huge gaping maw, waiting to devour her, greedy for her life, her happiness, her soul.

Elana shook her head, trying to clear away the unwelcome image. This was to be her home now and the love she would have given, had given to Joakal, she would turn to the God. Defiant of the pain in her heart, she lifted her chin and walked into the temple.

Silence was the first thing to greet her—a deafening roar of silence. The air was heavy with it; the stone walls and vaulted ceiling dripped with it. It was woven into the light from the lamps that shone in their sconces along the walls. It darkened the shadowed corners and swallowed the sound of Elana's footsteps as she walked down the wide center aisle, past the myriad seats where worshipers could sit or kneel.

She stopped before the altar and knelt at the base of the wide steps. Her heart did not fill with prayers and supplications. "I am here," was all she could find to say.

She continued to kneel, staring at the altar towering six steps above her. It, like the pillars outside, glowed with the pale green light of the Living Stone, and on the altar stood the large golden bowl that symbolized the receptive mind.

My mind is not receptive, Elana thought. Nor is my heart. They are filled with Joakal. Still. I must find out what's wrong. Even if his love for me is dead, I have to find out what has changed him.

Elana raised herself off the cold stone floor. She bowed stiffly to the altar then turned toward the small door on her left that led to the cloistered buildings behind the temple. She would make her Oblation of Service here, at this temple as she had always dreamed, but she would do so to remain where she could watch her beloved.

Elana found the Chief Servant, Faellon, in his office sitting behind a desk covered with the equipment necessary to monitor the daily needs of the temple. The Chief Servant's halo of white hair, his slight stoop-shouldered body dressed in the dark green robe of Service, his sleepy eyes and patient expression looked out of place next to the computer terminals and communication screen that took up most of the surface area of the massive wooden desk.

Elana sat in the chair across the desk from him and told the Chief Servant everything. She started with her childhood hopes and ended with the reason she was here. She left out none of her dreams, her doubts, or her pain.

She was not oblivious to the emotions that played across Faellon's face as she talked. Elena saw the patient resignation in the set of his shoulders and the lines around his mouth that shifted to an ill-concealed expression of boredom long before Elana finished speaking. Although he tried to hide it behind sagacious nods, Elana could tell that Faellon had ceased to listen to her, to hear, or care, what she was saying.

"I think, Daughter," he said when Elana had finished speaking, "you have been hasty in your judgment. Our young King's mind is on his coronation, as it should be. He is preparing himself for the Wisdom which the God will soon impart to him. If he seemed distant or preoccupied, that is only natural. The burden of becoming the *Absolute* is a heavy one."

"He wasn't exactly—distant," Elana tried again to explain. "He was gracious, pleasant. He welcomed me back. Yet when he looked at me, it was with a stranger's eyes, and the lips that kissed me were not Joakal's."

"How could they be anyone else's?" Faellon said, dismissing her words. "Daughter, you are over-wrought. Calm yourself. You've been away—perhaps you have not heard of the headaches that plagued His Majesty for a time. Thank the God they seem to have passed now, but when they would come upon him, he would fall to the floor in agony and have to be carried, only partially conscious, to his bed. Perhaps these account for the change you sensed in him—who knows what the God might have been imparting to his mind during those times."

Elana listened to the Chief Servant's assurances, weighing them against her intuition. She knew this explanation was not enough. Something more lurked behind the change in her beloved. She could not tell how she knew, but her certainty was unequivocal. She also knew that further discussion with the Chief Servant would be futile.

Faellon cleared his throat and changed the subject. "Now, daughter," he said. "You spoke of entering Service. I do not believe you are ready for such a step. The Service of the God must be entered with a calm and quiet heart. Why don't you stay with us for a time of meditation. Perhaps here, in the tranquillity of the temple, the God will direct you."

Elana hesitated only a moment. Where else could she go? To the palace where she usually stayed? No, what she had seen in Joakal's eyes made that impossible. Back to her home in the Westron Province? No, not yet, not until she knew.

"Thank you," she said aloud. "I will stay."

"Good," Faellon replied with a smile as he pressed a button on the top of his desk. After a moment, another green-robed Servant, a woman, entered.

"Show the Lady Elana to the women's quarters," Faellon directed, "and issue her a Servant's robe. She will be staying with us for a time."

The Servant silently stepped back and held the door open for Elana. As she stood to go, Faellon stood also.

"Remember, daughter," he said, "Faith is the first step toward the Wisdom of the God." But his words had the hollowness of rote and his eyes were filled with weariness.

After Elana had gone, Faellon seated himself and dropped his head into his hands. It was almost time for the evening hour of worship to begin. Any moment the other Servants would file into the temple to be joined by those inhabitants of the city who wished to spend time before the God.

Faellon knew he must now go into the temple, also. He must stand at the altar and elevate the great Golden Bowl that was the symbol of his faith and Service, and lead the evening rite, as he had done for the twenty-two years he had been Chief Servant. Each night he stared into the heart of the great bowl, trying to understand the mysteries it represented and achieve that state of holy emptiness that would make him a true receptacle for the Voice of the God.

But he was old now, and tired, and lately his prayers had been changing. How long, O God? the words formed again in his mind. How long will you require this Service from me? Every day they come to me, bringing their questions and problems and pains. I give them the answers of our faith. But the words have become just words that I have said a thousand times before. Let this burden pass from me, O God. Let me rest.

But, as Faellon rose slowly from his desk and started out of his office, there was no answering echo to his prayer. No gentle assurances swept through his mind or caressed his soul. There was no lessening of the weariness in his heart and he knew that for whatever purpose, the God was not finished with him yet.

Faellon stopped at the door and bowed his head until his chin pressed into his chest. He raised his arms out to the sides in an attitude of utter submission. If you will not let me go, he prayed, grant me the strength to endure.

Beahoram stood outside his brother's cell. He knew he should be preparing himself to go to the temple, keeping up the facade of piety for which Joakal was known, but he could not resist coming here, looking through the small grating in the cell door and watching Joakal pace back and forth in his captivity like a caged animal longing for its return to the wild.

But to watch silently from outside the door was not enough. Beahoram wanted to see his brother's face when he told Joakal that Elana had come to *him*, had told *him* how eager she was to marry. The need to prove his mastery over his brother was like a gnawing hunger in the pit of Beahoram's stomach. His heart began to race as he took the key from his pocket and unlocked the cell door.

Beahoram pushed the door open and stepped into the cell. He noted with pleasure the dark smudges that circled Joakal's eyes; the lank and dirty hair, his unkept beard—and he, Beahoram, was clean and groomed, dressed in Joakal's own impeccable clothing.

Beahoram closed the door behind him and walked about the small room, reveling in the way his brother's eyes followed his movements.

Are you comfortable, Brother?" Beahoram asked in a silky, sardonic voice. "Is your new kingdom to your liking?"

Still Joakal said nothing. His only movement was a slight narrowing of his lips. That was enough to make Beahoram's heart jump with triumph. He took a step nearer to Joakal.

"I had a visitor," he said, a smile twisting across his lips. "A very beautiful visitor. Do you know who it was? Can you guess? Elana—beautiful Elana. She came to tell you that she had chosen marriage. Are you pleased? I am. Such long, silken hair, like strands of gold. I can hardly wait to bury my face in it while I run my hands over the skin of her soft neck, down her shoulders, her back. After our wedding night, she too will forget you."

Joakal lunged. His hands grabbed for his brother's throat, murder in his fingertips. Beahoram was ready for him. His fist caught his brother in the solar plexus and the air gushed from Joakal's lungs. He fell to the floor, his eyes wide as he struggled to breathe.

Beahoram lifted his foot and swung. It hit Joakal in the back, sending him into a spasm of agony. Beahoram kicked again; it felt so good.

"When I kill you," he said, "no one will know—or care. You are *nothing.*"

Beahoram stepped back, panting. He forced his lifelong rage back under control. Not yet, he told himself, but soon. He looked down at his brother, still writhing on the floor. No spark of pity moved him.

He turned on his heel and left the cell.

Chapter Ten

CAPTAIN JEAN-LUC PICARD stepped onto the turbolift near his quarters on Deck 6 and headed for the main bridge to start the day's duties. Yet, even as he gave the order and the lift began to move, he changed his mind.

"Computer, hold," he said, and immediately the movement ceased. For a few seconds he looked down at his shoes, weighing his decision. Then he raised his head and gave a new order.

"Deck Sixteen," he said, and the turbolift changed directions.

A few seconds later the doors opened and Picard stepped out into the corridor. At this time of the morning he knew that Mother Veronica would be with the counselor, and Sister Julian would be occupied with the children or with the studies that had filled her time for the weeks the Little Mothers had been on board. Although the quiet presence of the nuns was felt throughout the ship, evidenced by the reactions of many of the crew—especially Lieutenant Commander Data—they were, in reality, rarely seen.

Picard himself was acutely aware of the Little Mothers, as he was aware of the room that was his destination. He tugged at his uniform top in an automatic gesture and began to walk down the corridor in even, measured strides.

He reached the door directly across from the stateroom that housed the Little Mothers. Here was the chapel he had ordered replicated and arranged for their use. He hesitated only a moment, then moved close enough for the computer to sense his presence and open the door.

He entered the chapel and it was like stepping back in time and place, back to the years of his childhood and the home of his youth. Silence enveloped him as he stood just inside the door and waited while his eyes adjusted to the dim light. It was not an empty silence. Picard smiled as he listened to it. In a brief, uncommon flight of fancy, it seemed to him as if the silence smiled back, like an old friend welcoming his return.

It had been more years than Picard liked to count since he first stepped through the doors of the little parish church after which this chapel was fashioned. He had been eight years old. It was a hot summer day and his older brother, Robert, had been tormenting him, as usual—about what, Picard could not remember now. But it had mattered then, very much, and the eight-year-old Jean-Luc had run from his bullying brother, looking for a place to hide.

The little church stood in the heart of the town. Picard had run in no particular direction that day, but as he had neared the church he heard Robert's voice too close behind him. The church had offered a refuge; Jean-Luc had opened one door and slipped quietly inside.

Picard remembered how on that day, too, it had been the silence that first greeted him. The church had been cool after the heat of the summer sunshine and the interior of the building held the faint aroma of incense that after the centuries had permeated the wood of the altar, pews and kneelers. It had awakened the young Jean-Luc's curiosity and drawn him farther inside.

The older Picard now walked into the chapel, moving not with the hesitation of an eight-year-old boy, but with the confident tread of a starship captain. He took a seat in the third pew and looked at the altar. Tall candlesticks and flowers adorned it. The immaculate covering of linen seemed to glow in the reflected light of the candle flames.

It had been the same all those years ago and he could almost see himself as that small boy, staring at the altar for the first time, going up to touch the linen, the candles, turning and running his hands along the communion rail, looking for long, fascinated minutes at the stained glass in the windows, the statues with their rows of votive lights, and the names on the engraved plaques along the walls. The beauty of the place touched him now as it had touched him then, and countless times thereafter.

Picard never told anyone about his new hiding place, though he went to the little church often. At first it had only been a place where he could go and dream his dreams of the stars in peace. Soon, however, the building began to intrigue him. There was something almost mystical about the silence of the place. Picard wanted to know when it had been built, how and by whom. He began to study, looking for those answers, and that study had sparked a love of history and archeology that had grown over the years.

The younger Picard had found the facts about the

parish church in the town library. But it was this older Picard who understood the people behind the facts. *Captain* Picard knew about duty and devotion, and if the ideals that moved him were different from the men and women who, stretching back through the centuries, had built the church, served at its altar and worshipped in its pews, it did not matter. The essence was the same.

It was a good heritage and Picard was proud of it. He stood and again tugged at his uniform, straightening and settling it firmly about his shoulders. When he reached the door, he noticed the little brass cherub that formed the holy water font. He reached out and ran a finger caressingly over its outstretched wings. Then he turned back around and let his eyes embrace the chapel a final time. He was glad he had come; in just over a week the Little Mothers would be leaving the ship and this room would revert to its original form.

Perhaps I'll enter a holodeck program of this chapel, Picard thought when he stepped once more into the corridor and the door slid shut behind him. Yet as he walked toward the turbolift, he knew he would not. He would hold the image in his heart, a dear and cherished memory, but his path lay with the future, not the past—even his own.

Troi was encouraged by her student's progress. The nun had learned the rudiments of *D'warsha;* she could now separate her own mind, her own thoughts, from the myriad that daily assailed her, and she had learned to produce the most elementary of shields. These shields were not strong, nor could Mother Veronica bring them to mind without a great deal of concentration yet, but she was learning.

Today, Troi and her student had begun the discipline of *Kitue,* which would strengthen the nun's shields and aid her in the technique of voluntary raising and lowering. As with the initial steps of all mental training among Troi's people, this lesson combined telepathic communication and guidance with mental imaging. Mother Veronica had chosen the picture of a lake as her personal representation.

See the sunlight upon the water of the lake, Troi's mind guided her student once more through the lesson. *Strengthen the light; make it grow brighter in your mind. Brighter still, until you cannot see the water. Remember the lake is the expression of your mind. The light is like a wall that protects your mind and covers it. The light is a shield. It is yours to possess and yours to control. Now, slowly, let the light fade and see again the peaceful lake beneath it.*

Mother Veronica's attention faltered; the images disappeared. Troi sighed, disengaged her mind from the nun's, and opened her eyes.

"It has been a long morning," she said, "but you've made real progress."

Mother Veronica did not answer Troi or give any indication that she had heard the counselor's words. She stared off at nothing while her right hand reached up to finger the wooden cross that rested on her chest. After a silent, strained moment, she turned toward the counselor.

"How long?" she asked. "How much longer before I can lock my mind away and no one need know that I am . . . a telepath?"

Mother Veronica lowered her voice on these last words and again looked away. Troi sighed. She had hoped Mother Veronica was coming to understand her gift and accept it.

Troi searched for a way to answer her. Even as a trained psychologist, the right words were not always easy to find. Especially with Mother Veronica. There were so many layers of fear to be overcome, layers that had been built over a lifetime. But if they were not revealed and vanquished, how much longer would it be before the nun collapsed under the burden of her own self-hatred?

Troi knew she had to say something.

"What is it that you're still afraid of?" she asked. "Are you still afraid that if you learn to use your gift, you'll be betraying the promise you made to your mother?"

Mother Veronica's head jerked up. She stood and walked over to the viewport, leaning her head against the clear partition.

"When your mother demanded that promise from you, she knew of no other way for you to be safe. It was an act of love," Troi continued, "but it was also an act of hopelessness. The reason for it is long past. It's time to let it go. Your mother did not understand what she was asking. It is impossible for anyone who is *not* a telepath to understand the pressures of such a gift."

"You don't understand," Mother Veronica whispered.

"But I do," Troi countered. "I understand the years of ignorance and the superstition that have kept you from realizing the truth."

"But I don't want truth!" Mother Veronica cried out. "I just want some peace."

She turned and fled from the room.

Troi turned and watched the door slide closed behind Mother Veronica's fleeing form. She felt as if something inside of her had wilted. She lifted her eyes and sat looking at the beautiful, impersonal stars that shone in dopplered streaks outside the viewports. She wanted to help the nun; she wanted it as much as she had ever wanted anything. Even more than learning to shield her mind, Troi wanted to help Mother Veronica learn to rejoice in her own uniqueness.

Troi knew that acceptance, personal acceptance, could be difficult. There had been a time when she, like Mother Veronica, had rejected her gift as worthless. It was her mother who had taught her differently.

Troi had been twelve years old, the age when the psychic gifts of most Betazoid children begin to manifest themselves, when she realized she would never be a full telepath. With this realization had come feelings of isolation and inadequacy. While the other children played the ancient thought games with one another, games that would hone and focus their talents, Troi was excluded—from their thoughts but not their emotions. Her newly budding empathy made her aware of all the pity and ridicule from her peers.

Her mother had known how she felt—her mother had *always* known, then. One night, when Troi was lying on her bed crying, her mother had come into her room and gathered Troi into her arms as if she had still been a child of five.

"Do you want to tell me what's wrong?" her mother had asked.

Troi shook her head.

"Then I'll tell you. You're crying because you think you're different and that makes you feel alone and unloved. Am I right?"

"I just want to be like everyone else," Troi had cried the plaintive litany of adolescence.

"Like all your friends, you mean," her mother said. "Think for a minute, Little One, and answer me a question. Why do you want to be like everyone else? Think about the people you love, and tell me if they're just imitations of the people around them."

Deanna did think about it, and she started with her

father. There was no one else in the universe like her father—at least to her. He was big and strong and gentle. He had a brilliant mind and yet a sense of humor that let him laugh at what he called the follies of existence. He did not find it uncomfortable or intimidating to live among a race of telepaths when his own mind was silent.

And there was her mother, Troi thought as she glanced up at the woman beside her. Forthright and formidable, she had a way of dominating everyone, except her husband, and infusing each situation with her own *joie de vivre*.

Troi loved both her parents. Yet just now, with the rejection of her peers still fresh in her mind, Deanna Troi did not find it comforting to be descended from two such *unique* individuals.

"I don't want to be different," she protested aloud.

Her mother chuckled and tightened her arms around her daughter. "Oh, Deanna," she said. "Everyone is different. That is one of the most precious gifts from the Gods of the universe. Be grateful, Little One, for that difference."

"Will I ever be a telepath?" Troi asked, wiping her eyes with the back of her hand.

"Some telepathic abilities will probably surface later—after all, you are my daughter—but they will never be your greatest talent. However, your teachers tell me that your empathy rating is very high. Your challenge is to learn to use it—and members of our family *never* back down from challenges. *We* meet them, head-on. Now, let's go downstairs. We'll make a cup of hot chocolate and talk about where you should start your training. Empaths need to develop their minds just as telepaths do."

Her mother had been right. Such telepathic abilities as Troi possessed had developed slowly over the next few years, but they were not impressive for a Betazoid. She could share her mind with other telepaths, especially members of her family, and persons with whom she shared an emotional bond. It was enough.

Troi's empathic talents had also continued to grow. Her mother had arranged for Deanna to study with some of the finest teachers on Betazed, and she surprised them all. Even among her race, a race known for its empathic as well as telepathic abilities, Troi's rating was one of the highest seen in over two centuries. When she had chosen psychology as her profession, she had found that special place to use her gifts and in a way that, for the most part, filled her with purpose and joy.

Most of all, Troi thought as she leaned back in her chair on board the *Enterprise,* I learned what my mother started to teach me years before she put it into words. I learned to value myself. This is the lesson Mother Veronica needs, and I don't know how to reach her with it.

Troi's communicator chirped, pulling her from her reverie. "Troi here," she answered it.

"Counselor," came the captain's voice. "We are about to make subspace contact with Capulon IV. I would like you to be present for our initial communication."

"Yes, sir," Troi said. "I'm on my way."

"Is Mother Veronica still with you?"

"No, sir. Our lesson ended a few moments ago."

"Since the King of Capulon IV sent for the Little Mothers, I think Mother Veronica should be here as well. Will you bring her with you?"

"Yes, sir," Troi said again, signing off. She stood and turned toward the door with a sinking feeling in the pit of her stomach. She was the last person Mother Veronica would want to see right now.

Chapter Eleven

MOTHER VERONICA hesitantly agreed to come to the bridge with Troi, but they walked through the ship's corridors in a tense and heavy silence, the nun refusing any of Troi's attempts at conversation. When they reached the main bridge, Mother Veronica stayed by the turbolift door while Troi walked down the ramp and took her seat on the captain's left. Picard motioned to Lieutenant Worf, and the Klingon hailed the planet.

"They are responding," he announced.

"On screen," the captain ordered. Immediately the view of the stars was replaced by the larger-than-life-size face of a young man in his prime. His dark, curly hair was longer in back than in front and wisps of it curled around the collar of his high-necked shirt. The mustache and beard that darkened his upper lip and curled along the straight line of his jaw accented his full mouth and finely chiseled features.

Captain Picard stood and walked toward the viewscreen. "I am Captain Jean-Luc Picard of the Starship *Enterprise*, representing the United Federation of Planets," he announced.

"Our greetings, Captain. I am—Joakal I'lium."

Troi wondered if anyone but herself heard the slight hesitation before he said his name, or noticed the calculating look in the young King's heavy-lidded eyes.

"Greetings, Your Majesty," the captain was saying. "I am honored that you have answered our hail yourself. The *Enterprise* will arrive on schedule for your coronation."

The King's eyes shifted. "I'm not sure that is necessary, Captain," he said. "As my coronation approaches, I have begun to have doubts about the agreements I made in my youth. I am no longer certain that joining your Federation would be the best thing for my people. Our culture is an ancient one. We have known many generations of peace following our laws and our God. Joining your Federation could change that."

These words took Picard by surprise. Troi could feel the emotion crest through the captain and she could read it in the way he pulled his already straight back a little straighter. An infinitesimal movement, but Troi knew its meaning.

Yet, the captain's expression never wavered as he spoke to the King.

"It is the highest law of our Federation," Picard said in his best diplomatic voice, "not to interfere with the culture of our members. The Federation welcomes differences and honors them."

"So you claim, Captain."

Troi shifted uncomfortably in her seat. The King

was radiating deceit in waves that were almost visible to the empath.

"I think perhaps, Your Majesty, we should meet and discuss your concerns," Picard continued.

"Of course, Captain," the King answered. "You and your people are welcome to come to Capulon, but I cannot guarantee I will sign your treaty."

"Understood, Your Majesty. It is my hope that together we will find a solution that will unite our people."

Once the transmission ended, Troi sprang to her feet. "He's hiding something, Captain," she said as Picard turned around to face her. "And he's lying."

"About what? Any ideas, impressions?"

"Nothing specific—only what I've told you."

Troi heard the gasp behind her. She turned to look at Mother Veronica still stationed by the turbolift doors. The nun was white with shock and terror, struggling to force air down into her lungs. Troi rushed toward her, the captain close behind.

Mother Veronica shook her head slowly from side to side. Her eyes were still wide with the horror of whatever she had received from the King's mind.

"Such hate," she whispered. The words sounded as though they were strangling her. "Darkness. Black hatred. Two men . . . a room . . . Loneliness. Vengeance. Too much . . ."

She turned and fled into the turbolift. The doors closed behind her before Troi could follow.

The counselor glanced at the captain. "Go after her," Picard ordered. "Get her calmed down and try to find out exactly what she learned. Then join me in my ready room as soon as you can."

"Yes, Captain," Troi said as she stepped up to the turbolift doors and waited for them to open.

* * *

It was a little over fifteen minutes when Troi entered the captain's ready room. Will Riker was there, pursuing a conversation he and the captain had had before.

"I wish you would reconsider," Riker was saying.

"I couldn't change my mind even if I were inclined to do so, Will—which I am not."

"But, Captain, in light of the change in the King's attitude—"

Picard held up his hand and silenced his First Officer. "Enough, Will. Thank you for your concern, but it is unnecessary. You are a skilled commander and no one doubts your abilities. However, the King's recent words make the diplomatic aspect of this mission more important than ever. I have had more experience at treaty negotiations and that alone requires that I lead this Away Team."

"At least let me assign a security team to you."

The captain shook his head. "A security team might be interpreted as an insult against the government. I cannot take that chance. Now, if there is nothing further, Counselor Troi and I have a matter to discuss."

"Yes, Captain," Riker said a little stiffly. He turned on his heel and left the ready room. When the door slid shut, the captain met Troi's eyes.

"Sometimes," he said, and Troi could feel his patient amusement, "I think Commander Riker forgets I have led more than a few Away Teams in the course of my career."

Picard indicated that Troi should take a seat while he called Data over the comm link. "Mr. Data," he said, "what is our ETA to Capulon IV?"

"At our present speed, eight days, seventeen hours, twelve minutes."

"If we increase speed to warp seven?"

Data's pause was almost indiscernible. "Twenty-two hours, nine minutes."

"Thank you, Mr. Data. Make it so." Picard came over and took a seat next to Troi on the small sofa his office contained.

"Now, Counselor," he said, turning to face her, "I would like you to accompany me to the planet. I believe I will have need of your special insight. Since the King requested that the Little Mothers come to Capulon IV, I also think Mother Veronica should also accompany us. What is her condition?"

"She is very upset," Troi replied. "I couldn't get any more information from her than what she told us on the bridge."

"How are your sessions with her coming?"

"She has learned to use very rudimentary shields, but I'm not certain that will be enough."

"I feel it is imperative that we arrive at Capulon IV as quickly as possible. Is there any more you can do for her in the next hours?"

"I don't know, Captain. I can try, but it depends on Mother Veronica."

"Explain."

Troi shifted a little in her seat and crossed her legs. "In order to make any progress in so short a time," Troi said, "we will have to forgo formal lessons. I will have to pour a great deal of information directly into Mother Veronica's mind. You saw how upset she was, and there are other matters she still has not resolved. These are upsetting her, as well. I don't know if she will be willing, or able, to allow me the depth of telepathic link I will need."

"If you are not successful, will she be in any condition to go to the planet with us?"

"I believe she will go regardless of her personal

feelings, Captain," Troi said. "That is why she is here, and Mother Veronica has a very strong sense of duty."

"Please devote as much time to her as you can," the captain said. "Her presence could be important in our negotiations with the King."

At that moment, Joakal I'lium, true King of Capulon IV, lay curled into a fetal position in the corner of his cell. He had not moved in hours; he had barely eaten in days. His captivity was slowly eroding his strength. Each time Beahoram came to taunt him, Joakal found himself less able to fight off his depression. Beahoram had everything—he had Elana. This thought twisted round and round in Joakal's brain, draining the hope and the life out of him.

This time Joakal did not bother to move when he heard the key turn in the lock. What was the use? It was only his brother coming to gloat, to remind Joakal of all he had lost. Joakal pulled himself more tightly into a ball and ignored the sound of approaching footsteps.

A boot prodded him in the back. "Sit up," Beahoram ordered. Joakal ignored him. The boot came again, harder this time. Joakal suppressed a grunt as it connected with the tender area of his spine.

"Sit up I said, or I'll drag you up."

Slowly, Joakal uncurled. He turned over and pulled himself up until he was sitting with his back wedged into the corner of the cell.

Beahoram was not alone this time. Aklier was with him. Unable to bear looking at the triumphant sneer on his brother's face, Joakal fixed his attention on the Elder. The few times Aklier had come to the cell, he had not said a word. He had completed his errand and left as quickly as possible. But today, Aklier's eyes met

97

Joakal's with an expression of shock and regret. Maybe today, Joakal thought, he'll tell me why he has betrayed me.

"You haven't eaten, Brother," Beahoram said, his voice breaking the momentary sympathy between Joakal and the Elder. "I can't allow that. You might die while I still have use for you. I'll warn you once—either you eat on your own or I will force the food down you myself. Do you understand?"

Joakal nodded. "What is it you want?" he asked in a tired voice.

"*I* don't want anything, Brother. I thought *you* would want the latest news. I spoke with the captain of the Federation starship today. They'll be here in time for my coronation. But I'm not going to sign their treaty. There's another of your dreams gone, Brother."

Joakal raised his head and finally met his brother's eyes. They stared at each other for a few seconds. Then Joakal slowly shook his head.

"My dreams," he said. "What can you possibly understand of my dreams or of my life?"

Beahoram's eyes narrowed. His lips drew into a tight line before he spoke.

"Oh, I know your life," he said. "You have sat here in your palace with your servants waiting on your every whim, surrounded by luxury most people can't even imagine."

Joakal studied his brother's face, undaunted now by its likeness to his own, and he nodded. "You're right," he said. "I do live in a palace. But that's all you see, isn't it? You look at the clothes and the furnishings, and you think that's the life of a King. Well it's not."

Joakal slowly rose to his feet. He felt his own anger mounting. This was not the sudden burst of rage he had felt when Beahoram told him about Elana, a burst that soon burned itself out and left despair in its ash. This was a steady flame that gave heat to his soul and strength to his words.

"You say you saw your father work himself to death," Joakal continued. "Well so did I. I saw my father—our father—work and worry every day of his reign. His thoughts were always on doing what was best for the people the God had given him to govern. This power you crave isn't a gift. It's a weight. It's a responsibility, and it's as much a life of Service as that lived at the temple."

Beahoram snorted with laughter and Joakal realized his brother had not understood or believed a word he had said.

"Are you willing to give up any thought about a life of your own, Beahoram?" Joakal tried again. "That's what happens when you take the crown."

"A life of my own," Beahoram shouted. "What has having a life of my own ever given me?"

"It has given you the same chances it gives everyone."

"You're wrong," Beahoram snapped. "It has given me *nothing*. Well that's over. It's *all* mine now. You're very good at speeches, but none of your pretty words are going to rob me of my turn."

Beahoram turned on his heel and left. After a brief hesitation, Aklier also turned.

"Wait—Aklier, please," Joakal called after him. Slowly the Elder turned back around.

"Please, Aklier, tell me—how is Elana?" Joakal asked.

"She has disappeared. No one has seen her in weeks."

She's gone to the temple, Joakal thought. Beahoram won't have her after all.

The Elder had turned back around and was almost out the door. Joakal called to him again.

"Tell me why, Aklier. I thought you were my friend. I trusted you."

Once more the Elder turned to face the King, his eyes studying the haggard face.

"She would have been only two years older than you," he said softly.

"Who?"

"My daughter."

"Your daughter? Aklier, I don't understand. You don't have a daughter."

"You don't understand." Aklier's voice grew harsh and his eyes went cold as he spoke from that realm between anger and pain. "Beahoram is right. There is too much you don't understand about the lives of your people. Let me explain. Once my wife and I had a daughter, our only child. But she was born deaf and blind. By the law she was imperfect. Abnormal." Aklier nearly choked on the word. "The law said she could not live. I'm an *Elder,* a servant of the law. I had to leave my only child at the temple, knowing it meant her death. My wife, who had longed for a large family, refused to risk another child that way. The grief of it killed her. She wasted away, eaten up by the loss and longing. Beahoram understands. He understands in a way no one else on this world can, and he has promised that once he is *Absolute,* he'll do away with that law. To see that happen, I will do anything—even betray you."

"Aklier," Joakal said, "it's not too late. I was going to abolish that law, it and others like it. That's why I asked the Federation to come to Capulon—to help me make these changes. Beahoram is going to send them away. Aklier, listen to me."

Aklier looked slowly around the cell, then brought his eyes back to the King's face. "How can I believe you?" he said. "You'd say anything to get out of here."

Aklier turned abruptly and left, pulling the cell door closed behind him. As the lock mechanism clicked into place, Joakal slid slowly back to the floor.

Chapter Twelve

BY THE TIME Troi returned to her quarters eighteen hours later, she was exhausted. They had been eighteen long and grueling hours, working with Mother Veronica and trying to cram the essence of eight days worth of lessons, the amount of time Troi had thought to have with the nun, down into one extended block of information. Nor was Troi confident it had done much good. Whatever Mother Veronica had seen during that brief contact with the King's mind had reawakened all of her old fears of her psychic talents. It had been extremely difficult for Troi to establish and maintain the link necessary between herself and the nun.

All Troi wanted now, as she went into the bathroom, changed into her favorite pink nightgown, and released her hair from its usual arrangement, was sleep: deep, refreshing, uninterrupted sleep.

A few minutes later she crawled into her bed. As she stretched out under the cover, she felt the tension flowing out of her muscles. She gave a passing thought to the patients whose appointments she had been forced to cancel. Only Ensign Marshall was a worry.

I'll see if he can come for an appointment later today, Troi thought as she turned on her side and pulled the pillow more comfortably under her head. Then she remembered. I have to go with the captain today, she thought, down to the planet. Ensign Marshall will have to wait one more day. I'll see him as soon as we return.

Her thoughts were getting hazy. Warm, gentle darkness was spreading through her body and closing in on her mind. She slept.

The sound of the captain's voice pierced through Troi's comfortable veil of slumber. "Picard to Counselor Troi," he said.

"Troi here," she answered without opening her eyes.

"Counselor, we have just entered orbit around Capulon IV. We will be beaming down to the surface in thirty minutes. Will you inform Mother Veronica?"

"Yes, Captain," Troi said automatically.

"Very good. Picard out."

With a small groan, Troi opened her eyes and glanced at the chronometer. 15:37. Troi sat up and tried to clear the sleep from her brain. It's only been six hours, she thought as still weary in mind and body, she rolled from her bed and went to splash some cold water on her face, hoping to find the energy for the duties ahead.

"Computer, location of Mother Veronica?" Troi asked as she walked across the room.

"Mother Veronica is in Stateroom sixteen D."

She's in the chapel, Troi thought. I'll give her five more minutes alone with her prayers and then I tell her. I hope she feels more ready for this than I do.

Will Riker and Sister Julian accompanied Troi, Captain Picard, and Mother Veronica to the transporter room. While Troi and Picard stood on the platform and waited, Sister Julian bade Mother Veronica farewell with soft-spoken words of encouragement and a brief embrace. Troi hoped this show of affection would strengthen the nun through the forthcoming interview with the King.

"Energize," Picard said. Immediately the transporter beam locked on and the room dissolved in a curtain of kinetic molecular waves. A few heartbeats later, that curtain lifted and the three of them stood in a reception hall of the royal palace on Capulon IV. A few feet away, a delegation of Elders was waiting to greet them. As soon as the last lights of the transporter beam faded, one of the Elders stepped out from the group.

"Welcome to our planet, Captain Picard," he said as he touched three fingers of his right hand to the center of his forehead in salute. "I am Aklier of the House Ti'Kara. His Majesty, King Joakal, has sent us to escort you into his presence. If you will please follow me."

He's not at all pleased to see us, Troi thought. He's frightened that we're here. She quickly let her empathic senses scan the other three Elders, but from them she received only mild interest and none of Aklier's apprehension. She eyed the nervous Elder with interest. What is he hiding? she wondered.

The Elders turned to lead the way through the palace. Picard walked beside them, but Troi hung back. She wanted to stay near Mother Veronica in case the nun's reaction to the King was similar to what had happened yesterday on the bridge.

Troi watched Mother Veronica closely as they left the reception room and walked down the long corridors of the palace, looking for the first signs of wavering in the nun's control. But Mother Veronica did not spare Troi a glance. She kept her eyes fixed straight ahead; her mouth was drawn into a tight line and her hand clutched the cross on her breast as if it were a talisman.

Finally Troi looked around at her surroundings. Although she was used to living on a starship and having the galaxy displayed beyond the viewports, she found the size of the palace daunting. The corridor down which they were walking was lined with massive black wood doors, fifteen feet tall and ten feet across and carved with unfamiliar symbols. The walls were made from blocks of stone, as was the floor beneath her feet. Through the stone ran veins of a darker substance that shone with a pale green light and cast an eerie glow over the area that was not quite disguised by the white light that blazed from the chandeliers suspended from the ceiling.

The ceilings themselves soared thirty feet above Troi's head. She felt dwarfed by the dimensions and slightly awed by the aura of antiquity the palace exuded.

The corridor ended in a set of double doors, where two servants waited. They were dressed all in black except for the predatory bird stitched in crimson and gold on the right front of their tunics. At their touch, the huge doors swung in silently, more easily than Troi thought possible. Behind the doors waited the audience chamber and the King.

As she entered the chamber, Troi felt the immensity of the room overwhelm her. The ceilings were easily sixty feet tall, twice the height of those in the corridor, and the walls were four times that distance from one another. The very size of the room was oppressive. It was like entering a huge cavern. There were no windows to the outside, no flowers or pictures or brightly colored wall hangings, nothing to give a breath of freshness to the chamber. It gave Troi a headache and made her feel as if a weight was resting upon her chest.

Troi forced herself to look at the man toward whom they were walking. He sat upon a throne carved from the same green stone as the walls and perched on top of a dais of five steps. As they approached, Troi could see that the throne had been intricately carved in flowing geometric designs.

The King did not move as they neared him. His face wore a smile that did not reach to his eyes or mask his darker emotions.

He's furious that we're here, Troi thought as the King stood and walked down three of the five steps that raised his throne above the floor. Go carefully, Captain. He's a dangerous man.

"We were surprised, Captain," the King began, "when your ship informed us that you were in orbit around Our planet. We did not expect you yet. Still, accept Our welcome."

"Thank you, Your Majesty," the captain answered. He returned the King's smile, but to Troi the captain's voice sounded guarded. She wondered if he also felt that there was something hidden behind the ruler's words. "Please allow me to present one of my officers," Picard continued. "This is Lieutenant Commander Deanna Troi."

Troi took a step forward and bowed to the King,

noticing that the captain had chosen to use her rank rather than her professional designation.

"And this is Mother Veronica, Leader of the Little Mothers, whom Your Majesty requested come to your planet."

Troi felt a jolt of surprise and alarm crash through the King. His eyes narrowed as he looked at them. He doesn't remember sending for the Little Mothers, Troi thought. He doesn't know who they are.

Troi's eyes shifted to Mother Veronica. The nun was still clutching the wood cross she wore, as she had been since they materialized on the planet. Her face was taut with concentration. Troi hoped all the work they had done together in the past weeks, and especially the last eighteen hours, was coming to fruition. She tried to sense the nun's emotions, but Mother Veronica was closed to her.

The King inclined his head slightly in their direction, then returned his attention to the captain. "Now, Captain Picard," he said, "is there some reason you have chosen to arrive before the time previously arranged?"

"There is, Your Majesty," Picard replied. "In our last conversation, you expressed some doubts about the benefits of signing the treaty with the Federation. I took the liberty of arriving early so that we would have time to examine the treaty together and discuss your concerns."

"That was most considerate, Captain," the King said. "However, such a conversation is not possible today. We have, therefore, had guest rooms prepared here in the palace for you and your companions. We will meet again tomorrow."

The King turned away. He remounted the steps and sat again upon the throne, then motioned toward the waiting Elders.

"Aklier will show you to your rooms," the King said, waving his hand in the Elders' direction. "You may leave Us now."

Picard gave a curt bow. If the captain was irritated by this abrupt dismissal, he was too practiced a diplomat to let it show in his voice.

"I look forward to our meeting tomorrow," he said evenly. Then he turned and strode toward the doors. Troi saw the surprised Elder glance up at the man on the throne before rushing to follow the captain.

Troi and Mother Veronica fell into step behind them. Troi noticed that Picard looked neither right nor left as he walked, but held himself at attention until they were out in the corridor and the doors had once again swung shut.

As they started down the long corridor Troi could again feel the little tendrils of fear that wove themselves in and out of Aklier's consciousness. He began to wring his hands together nervously as he tried to find the right conciliatory words to offer the captain. Troi listened closely.

"I'm sorry if His Majesty seemed brusque," Aklier said, his words quick and breathless. "Please understand, Captain Picard. You have arrived unexpectedly, and at a very inopportune time. The King—all of us—are quite overwhelmed with the preparations for the coronation. Tonight is His Majesty's Vigil in the temple and tomorrow at dawn the ceremony for his Coming to Age will take place. It will be impossible for him to speak with anyone until after these have taken place. Please accept my apologies, Captain, and understand that we had not scheduled your arrival for several more days."

While he talked, the Elder led them down the long corridor, up a flight of stairs, and down another corridor to the appointed guest rooms. The doors were opened, revealing three magnificently furnished chambers. For the first time since leaving the *Enterprise,* Mother Veronica spoke.

She turned to the counselor. "Please," she said softly. "Stay with me."

Troi smiled at the nun, then turned to Aklier. "The third room will not be necessary," she said.

"As you wish," he said, giving Troi a slight bow. "Because of His Majesty's Vigil, there will be no formal dinner this evening. Your meals will be brought to you here. If there is anything else you require, you have only to ring and a servant will attend you."

"Thank you for your help," the captain said. "We will be eagerly awaiting the time when we can speak with His Majesty in greater depth."

The Elder sketched another bow, then turned and hurried back the way they had come. Once he was out of earshot, the captain motioned for Troi and Mother Veronica to join him in his room.

"Now, Counselor," he said once they were all seated. "What is your report?"

"The King is very arrogant," she said. "That is, perhaps, not unusual, but he is also very full of anger. He doesn't want us to be here, and neither does the Elder, Aklier. The other Elders and the servants we encountered were a little surprised by our arrival, but Aklier was near a state of panic, and the King was furious. There is something more, Captain. When you introduced Mother Veronica, the King was surprised. He doesn't remember sending for the Little Mothers. The sight of Mother Veronica frightened him."

"He has two minds," the nun said. Both Troi and Picard turned to look at her. Mother Veronica did not meet their eyes. She sat ramrod straight, her gaze focused on the distant wall, or on some ethereal point beyond seeing.

"What did you say?" the captain asked.

"Two minds—he has two minds," the nun repeated.

"Mother Veronica, look at me," Troi said. "Tell me exactly what you read from the King's mind. It is very important."

Slowly Mother Veronica turned her eyes to Troi's face. "I did what you said," she began. Her words were soft and hesitant, as if she had to search for each one before she used it. "I walled my mind against his thoughts. But some of them were too strong. Too strong," she repeated in a whisper, then grew silent.

"What were they?" Troi urged. "What did you learn?"

Again Mother Veronica looked, unseeing, at some distant point. "The King . . . his mind is dark, his thoughts . . ." She closed her eyes and shook herself. The breath she drew was uneven.

"The other mind is far away," she continued, without opening her eyes. "It is buried. There was light, but it is fading. That's all I learned," Mother Veronica said. "And I didn't want to learn that much."

Picard turned to Troi. "Counselor," he said, "can you explain that? Could the King be suffering from some sort of mental aberration?"

"Do you mean like schizophrenia? No, I don't think so, Captain. I would have felt that, and none of the reports sent by the cultural observers over the past few years have mentioned any unusual mental powers or conditions. But we know so little about the people of this planet, maybe there is a true psychological change that accompanies this Coming to Age. Maybe we've arrived during some sort of transition period."

"Well, whatever is going on here," Picard said, "I hope it will become clearer tomorrow." He tapped the communicator insignia on his uniform. "Picard to *Enterprise,*" he said.

"Enterprise. Riker here," came the almost immediate response. "I didn't expect to hear from you quite so soon, Captain."

"Our initial meeting with the King was rather brief, Number One," Picard explained. "It seems he will not have time for us until after the conclusion of the Vigil of his Coming to Age tomorrow morning."

"Do you want me to have you and the others beamed back to the ship?" Riker asked.

"No. The King has had rooms prepared for us here in the palace. I think it best if we use them. I'll report in after I have spoken with the King tomorrow."

"Aye, Captain. Riker out."

Aklier returned to the audience chamber. When he entered the room, Beahoram dismissed his attendants. "All except Aklier," he said as he turned to the Elder. "You will attend me as I prepare for my Vigil."

Aklier bowed low. "As you will, Your Majesty," he said.

The room emptied. Once they were alone, Beahoram stood and descended the steps of the dais. Aklier watched Beahoram begin to pace, walking back and forth while he slapped his right palm impatiently against his thigh. Then he stopped and ran both hands through his hair in a gesture so like his brother's that Aklier's breath caught in his throat. Beahoram turned on his heel to face the Elder. The look in his eyes made Aklier take a step backward.

"We've got to act quickly," Beahoram said, "or everything will be ruined."

"Why? Nothing has really changed. Isn't it better to proceed according to plan, especially now that the Federation people are here?"

Beahoram again studied the Elder. Aklier felt his heart begin to pound as the younger man's eyes narrowed.

"You're a fool, Aklier. *Everything* has changed now that the Federation people are here. That one in the brown robe—"

"Mother Veronica," Aklier supplied.

Beahoram nodded. "Mother Veronica—she's a danger to us. I don't know how she did it, but I could feel her mind touching mine. Why didn't you tell me my brother had sent for these Little Mothers?"

"I didn't know. Joakal was full of plans for after he became *Absolute*. He would hint at them, but he never discussed them—except, perhaps, with Elana."

"Well, it's too late to do anything about that now," Beahoram said as he began to pace again. "The Federation people *are* here and we have to act. The other female, the one with the dark eyes, she's a threat to us as well. When she looked at me, I could have sworn she was reading every secret I have. We're too close to success to take any chances. They have to be eliminated before the coronation."

Aklier gasped. "We can't . . . kill them. The people on their ship . . . the whole Federation—"

"No, we can't," Beahoram said. He resumed slapping his thigh, as if the action helped him think.

Finally he said, "Tonight, when they call for their evening meal, make sure that there is something to make them sleep added to their wine. Something strong, so they'll stay asleep for hours. Then, after moonset when most of the palace is asleep, have them

112

carried to my brother's cell. They can stay with him until after the coronation. Once I am crowned, their own laws will keep them from interfering."

"How can I . . . who do I . . . ?" Aklier stammered.

Beahoram snorted with disgust. "Must I do all your thinking for you? There are always corrupt servants. Find them and use them. You'll have to do it. I'll be at my Vigil."

"I'm supposed to attend your Vigil with you."

"That doesn't matter. If someone does come through the temple, it's me they'll be looking for, not you. It will be easier for you to slip out during the night than for me to do it. I have to stay where I can be seen by any of the Servants that might pass through the temple during the night. Now go, Aklier, and hurry. Be back here before sundown."

Aklier bowed and left Beahoram's presence. Once the Elder was out in the corridor, he leaned against the wall and waited until his heart ceased pounding. He lifted a hand to his forehead, to wipe away the beads of nervous sweat that had gathered there, and noticed that his fingers were shaking.

Nothing was working out the way he had anticipated.

Chapter Thirteen

THE FIRST OF Capulon's two moons was well into the
sky and the second had just become visible when the
sun touched the far horizon and sank slowly from
sight. All of the Elders from the Council, except for
Aklier, and thirty of the senior temple Servants,
headed by Faellon, lined the corridor outside the
King's private chambers. At the moment the sun
disappeared, the Chief Servant knocked on the King's
door. Immediately, it swung inward and Aklier stood
framed in the doorway. A few steps behind him was
the King dressed all in white, without jewels or
adornment of any kind except the long crimson
overcloak draped around his shoulders to protect him
from the chill of the temple.

"It is time," Faellon said and he turned away.
Aklier and Beahoram followed Faellon past the rows
of witnesses that closed ranks behind them as they
passed.

When they reached the head of the column, Aklier stepped into line and let Beahoram take the place beside Faellon. There were now sixty of them—thirty Servants of the God, thirty servants of the people—twice the sacred number to walk the King to his Vigil.

"O, Light of the God," Faellon intoned, "shine on us that we do not stumble in darkness."

With one accord, the line began to move. It was a colorful procession: the Servants in their long hooded robes of deep green, like a row of emeralds on the move; the Elders dressed in the finery of their Houses, a kaleidoscope of fabrics and hues; and the King leading them in shining, unspotted white and deep crimson.

The boots of the Elders pounding on the stone floor drowned out the sound of the soft-soled slippers of the Servants as they passed out of the palace and into the blue and purple shadows of gathering twilight. The people they passed as they crossed the city square all stopped to watch. Some touched their foreheads in a three-fingered salute, others fell to their knees; all watched the procession with the joyful, hope-filled hearts that their young King had long ago inspired.

The long line at last reached the temple and mounted the steps. When Faellon reached the four pillars that guarded the temple doors, he raised his hands beseechingly toward the sky.

"Look favorably upon our doings here, O Great God," he called in loud and dramatic tones. "Guide and protect us as we enter your temple, following the Laws revealed to our forebearers."

He lowered his hands and led the procession through the doors and down the long nave. He stopped before the altar. After a deep bow in its direction, he turned and motioned for the King to kneel. Two by two, the rest of the column came forward. The Elders slipped reverently into the empty pews; the Servants, after a bow to the altar, each turned to the side and marched to the rear of the temple, climbed the hidden stairs, and joined the rest of the temple population in the railed loft. From there they would watch the proceedings and sing the responses to the sacred ceremony that began the Vigil for the King's Coming to Age.

Once everyone was in place, Faellon turned back around and mounted the six steps to the altar. He bowed in obeisance to his God, kissing the cold stone before him. Then he lifted the golden bowl and raised it high over his head.

"We are empty, Oh God, without you," his voice rang out.

"Come, fill thy people," sang the response.

"We seek thy Virtues."

"Come, fill thy people."

"Guide us to Wisdom . . ."

Faellon sang through the Litany of Invocation; the responses echoed back each time until the temple seemed filled with a single cry. When the litany ended, the Chief Servant turned and brought the golden bowl to the kneeling King. He placed it in the outstretched royal hands.

"Youth passes from you this night," Faellon said. "The burdens of manhood come with the sun. Let this sacred bowl be your model. As you kneel here in the God's holy temple, empty your heart and mind of all things past. Become as receptive as this waiting bowl. Only then can the God's Wisdom fill you—only then will you be ready for the burden of your future, for you must rule not in your own wisdom, but in the God's."

Faellon placed his hands briefly on the King's head

116

in blessing. Then he turned away—the ceremony had ended; the Vigil had begun. All of the Elders except Aklier, who was to witness the Vigil, stood and filed from the temple. The Servants did the same. Not a word was spoken, and soon there was left only Aklier kneeling in the front pew and the young King kneeling before the altar, staring into the depths of the golden bowl.

Minutes passed by. The silence deepened. Finally Beahoram placed the bowl on the floor, sat back on his heels and sighed. Then he turned to the Elder.

"Is it arranged?" he asked.

The sound of Beahoram's voice startled Aklier from his private realm of regrets. "It's arranged," he confirmed without looking up.

"Good." Beahoram stood and stretched. "This is going to be an interminable bore," he said. "I wish I'd thought to bring some food."

Beahoram came over and sat in the pew next to Aklier. He propped his feet up on the rail in front of him. "Do you have your flask?" he asked. "Give it to me."

Aklier reached into his pocket and withdrew the silver flask that was filled with the strong amber wine he had planned to drink to fortify himself before this night's business. Reluctantly, he handed it to Beahoram.

Elana had sat among the Servants during the ceremony, and with them she had left the temple. But now, alone, she returned. Although Joakal had changed in some unfathomable way into a person she could never marry, the sight of him kneeling before the altar stilled some of the aching loneliness that had filled her these last weeks. Her eyes, and her heart, were hungry for the sight of him, and she crept silently back to the loft where she could watch him undetected.

He was not kneeling, as when she had last seen him. Joakal, who had always shared her love and reverence for the God, was lounging in a pew, his feet propped up, disdainful of where he was. She saw the flash of silver in his hand as he raised the flask to his lips; he was drinking, here in the God's presence. The sight almost made Elana cry out.

Elana felt darkness close around her and settle somewhere in the region of her heart. Over the last weeks she had almost—almost—convinced herself that Faellon was right and she had misjudged the change in Joakal. But here was irrefutable proof.

She raised a hand to her mouth and bit hard on one finger, trying to stifle the sob that was collecting in her throat. Part of her wanted to run away, to leave behind the pain of what she was seeing. Another part of her, the part that had so hungered for the sight of Joakal, begged her to stay a little longer. As she battled between desires, some of the conversation filtered up to her from below.

"Do you have the sleeping drug?" The words were faint but clear; the voice was Joakal's, and yet it was harsher than Elana ever remembered it sounding.

"Yes" was the reply. Elana recognized Aklier's voice.

"Who did you find to help you?"

"Do you really want to know? If you're in ignorance, no one can blame you, should something go wrong."

"If I don't know, Aklier, I'm at the mercy of others. I'll never be that again. Tell me."

Elana leaned forward to listen more closely, her tears banished as she concentrated on the faint words.

"Tymlan is the servant who will bring their meals. He hates his work in the kitchens. I've promised him enough money to buy a commission into the palace guards. All he has to do is deliver the trays. I'll put the drug in their wine myself."

"And after they're asleep—who is to carry them to my brother's cell?"

"Tymlan, myself, and Benget, the captain of the guard of my House."

"What did you promise him?"

"My niece—her hand and her dowry. He's a very ambitious man."

"Will that be enough to ensure their silence?"

"Yes. I made it very clear that I would not be subject to future threats and that if they talk, they die."

"Very good, Aklier. I wasn't sure you had the stomach for this. I'm glad I was wrong."

Suddenly there was a burst of harsh laughter and it stabbed Elana's heart to hear it. Then the laughter faded and the words continued.

"Won't Joakal be surprised when these Federation people are brought to his cell? I wish I could be with you to see my brother's face as he sees the foundation for all of his dreams of the future lay in drugged bundles at his feet. He wanted to talk with them. Now he can talk all he wants until after the coronation. Once I'm crowned and the power comes to me, I'll need everything I can learn from Joakal's mind, every plan and dream, every nuance of memory. After I'm done, he might not have enough mind left to talk, let alone to dream and plan." There was another shorter burst of laughter. "I've won. Nothing can free Joakal now. I've truly won."

Elana sat back, stunned. This man who wore the

King's robes, who spoke with the King's voice—this was not Joakal!

The darkness that had enveloped her lifted. The stranger whose lips had fastened on hers so greedily was Joakal's brother, and he was bent on revenge of some kind. She did not know how such a thing could be, but she knew this man was wrong. Someone could still help Joakal. She could—she would. Somehow. She leaned forward and listened again.

"You'd better go now," the not-Joakal said. "Use the rear entrances and be certain you're not seen. Once it's done, come back here. I want to know everything."

Elana saw the Elder stand and head for the side entrance to the temple. She sprang to her feet, thankful for the soft-soled slippers and the dark green robe that would allow her to move noiselessly and hide in the shadows.

While Aklier walked toward the side door, Elana glided down the loft stairs and out the main entrance to the temple. The evening air was chilly after the warmth of the loft and she shivered slightly. She pulled the hood of her Servant's robe over her blond hair as she began to run down the temple steps and around to the side of the building, trying to keep to the dark areas and praying that the light of the moons would not reveal her.

She saw Aklier emerge. Like herself, he also preferred the shadows, but he did not move silently. His boots scraped and pounded on the stone alleyways the material of his clothing hissed as it rubbed together. Elana found the noise comforting; it made him easy to follow and covered any sound she might accidentally make.

She followed him around the backs of the buildings until he reached the courtyard of the palace. The open area where she had so often walked hand in hand with Joakal no longer seemed like the beautiful setting so fond in her memory. The patterned stones of the courtyard had become a hazard to her purpose, for they reflected the light of the moons and illuminated the area too brightly for her to cross unseen. She would have to wait until Aklier had entered the palace before she moved. O, Great God, she prayed, please let this work.

Aklier stepped out of the shadows and began to walk boldly across the courtyard. Of course, Elana thought, who would dare to question an Elder? She watched until she saw him finally reach the palace, open the door, and step inside.

Elana took a deep breath and began to run, still wordlessly praying for the help of the God. She reached the door and paused a moment until her breathing returned to normal. Then she, too, entered the palace.

She was by the back stairs that led from the kitchens to the rest of the palace. Below her, she could hear the cooks and servants talking and the occasional clatter of dishes and pans. Aklier was nowhere to be seen, nor did Elana know where to look for him. She tried to guess which of the many guest rooms might have been given to the Federation people, but the palace was large and she quickly gave up. Instead she climbed the stairs to the next floor, entered the first room she reached, and, leaving the door slightly ajar so she could see the stairwell, sat on the floor to wait. The servants would have to use these stairs when they carried the dinner trays, and Aklier would have to meet them—somewhere.

Seconds stretched into fruitless minutes of slow-passing time. Elana began to ache with frustration. Now that she knew the truth, she wanted to be up and away, working to free her beloved. But there was nothing more at the moment she could do, and she forced her impatience back under control.

Finally, Elana heard voices on the stairs. She raised herself to her knees, straining to hear over the sudden pounding of her heart.

Two servants passed carrying large, laden trays. Aklier was not with them. Elana stood and followed, carefully staying several paces behind, hidden by the bend in the stairs and the indifference of the servants.

At the second floor the servants turned into the corridor. Cautiously, Elana moved her head around the opening that led from the stairwell. She saw Aklier waiting for the servants in front of guest rooms a third of the way down the hall. Again Elana slid to the floor and watched from where she would not be seen at eye level.

Aklier greeted the servants, then took the tray from one of them and dismissed him. He turned back around and started to walk toward the stairwell. Elana felt a surge of panic. Where could she hide? Quickly she stood and ran up the stairs to the third floor and waited. She counted slowly to one hundred and back again, giving the servant time to return to the kitchens before she climbed back down the stairs.

She took up her vigil in time to see Aklier hand a small purse to the remaining servant. Then he knocked on the door to the guest rooms and went inside.

Elana sat back and let the air slowly from her lungs. Should she go to the Federation people and warn them of Aklier's duplicity? They did not know her; why should they believe what she said? Should she hurry back to the temple and try again to convince Faellon? Elana shook her head; the Chief Servant had already made his position clear and changing his mind, if possible at all, would take too much time. And, most important to Elana, neither of these actions would lead her to Joakal. Elana knew her only choice was to stay close to Aklier.

She heard the Elder's voice again as he bade goodnight to the palace guests. Elana stood and rushed back to the room on the first floor where she had watched for the Elder. Soon he and the servant came down the stairs. They paused briefly by the door that led to the courtyard, and Aklier whispered some words Elana could not hear. Then the servant turned away. Aklier opened the door and stepped out into the night.

He's going back to the temple, Elana thought. She would give Aklier time to cross the courtyard, then she would follow. She would return to her place in the loft and there she would wait and watch and listen until she found a way to free the man she loved.

Picard, Troi, and Mother Veronica dined together in the captain's rooms. Aklier had apologized for the simple dishes, but their meal was a mini-feast of roast fowl in thick, spiced sauce, three bowls of colorful steamed vegetables, freshly baked bread, two cheeses, and a small basket of fruits, all served with a decanter of sweet, golden wine.

Troi found the sauce on the fowl to be too rich for her taste, but the vegetables were delicious and crisp. The bread was hot, flavored with little red seeds, and the cheeses—one tangy, one smooth and soft—went well with the fruit.

She noticed that like herself, Mother Veronica ate none of the meat, but the captain attacked it with gusto, saying it reminded him of a dish his mother used to make. The conversation during the meal was pleasant and informative, centering on the work of the

Little Mothers. As the meal drew to a close, Troi found her eyelids growing heavy and she had trouble concentrating on the words of her companions. She saw the captain stifling a yawn.

"I think, Captain," she said, "that it is time Mother Veronica and I went back to our rooms. We're all tired."

"Hmm . . . yes, Counselor," the captain said around another yawn. He stood; the women did the same. "Thank you for joining me. It has been a very enjoyable evening."

"Good night, Captain," Troi said.

As Troi turned toward the door, she heard the nun mumble a good-night, but her words were indistinct. Troi looked at her and saw that Mother Veronica's cheeks were flushed and her eyes slightly glazed.

Troi thought about the wine. It had not tasted that strong, but it was also not the synthehol she was used to drinking on the ship—and neither she nor Mother Veronica had had much rest in the last twenty-four hours.

By the time they reached their rooms, Troi noticed that the nun's step was unsteady as she walked over to the bed and dropped heavily to her knees. Troi grabbed the nightclothes she had had beamed down from the *Enterprise* and went to change as Mother Veronica bowed her head and began her evening prayers.

With each passing second, Troi found her movements becoming slower and more difficult. By the time she reentered the sleeping area, dressed in a pale pink nightdress and her uniform draped over her arm, it was a struggle to keep her eyes focused. The bed across the room looked miles away.

Troi saw that Mother Veronica had fallen asleep where she knelt, her head on the mattress, her arms outstretched as if in supplication. Troi dropped her uniform onto a chair and started to cross to the nun and help her into bed. She took a step; her balance became a precarious thing. She could barely . . . put one foot . . . in front . . . of the other. . . .

Troi fell, unconscious, to the floor.

Chapter Fourteen

FIVE THOUSAND KILOMETERS above the planet's surface, the USS *Enterprise* maintained her synchronous orbit with exact, unperturbed efficiency. It was ship's night and the computer had lowered the lighting throughout the corridors and public areas, in simulation of the hours after sunset. Beta-watch, the 4:00 P.M. through midnight shift, was nearing its completion and still Will Riker, temporarily in command of the *Enterprise,* could not sleep.

He walked down the dim corridors on his way to Ten-Forward, fighting the urge to return to the bridge. Although, being in command, he was technically always on duty, his next watch was not for another ten hours. His presence on the bridge now would be an unwelcome intrusion, a signal of his lack of confidence in the officers stationed there.

Riker's trouble was not with the duty roster, or with any one on board. None of his activities this evening, not even the hour he spent playing his trombone, had been able to pull his thoughts away from Picard and Troi on the planet below.

Riker was never happy when the captain decided to lead an Away Team, even when the mission appeared to be as peaceful as their present one. The captain's safety was Riker's responsibility and part of his duties as first officer. Despite Riker's casual friendliness, which had made him so popular with the crew, despite the quick, disarming grin that he wore so easily, William T. Riker took his duties very seriously.

Riker reminded himself once again of the captain's expertise at diplomatic negotiations. If trouble does arise, Riker's thoughts continued, he knows how to handle himself. Jean-Luc Picard hasn't always been a captain, after all. He has faced his share of danger and survived.

But knowing these things did not alleviate Riker's uneasiness. He still worried, like the old mother hen Picard had once called him.

Well, cluck-cluck, Riker thought wryly. He ran his right hand over his mustache and beard in the gesture that had become so habitual he was no longer aware of it. As he stepped onto the turbolift and gave his destination to the computer, he hoped Guinan would have something to say that would set his whirring thoughts to rest.

Will Riker was not the only one on board who wanted to have a few words with Guinan. Data was already in Ten-Forward. It had, in many ways, been a confusing two and a half weeks for the android. In his search for spiritual understanding, everyone with whom he had spoken so far had had something different to say.

He had spoken with many crew members besides

127

Worf and Geordi. Not everyone he spoke to claimed to have any religious beliefs; some, in fact, were quite adamant that they did not. Others spoke of religion and religious practices in terms of family history and traditions rather than personal beliefs. They reminded Data of something Keiko and Miles O'Brien had said shortly before their wedding.

Keiko's family still followed the Ryobu-Shinto traditions which united the earth mysticism of the Shinto with the teachings of Buddhism. O'Brien's heritage was Irish Catholic. Data knew that historically these two religions were opposed, sometimes violently, to one another, yet rather than be disturbed by the differences, as their ancestors would have been, Keiko and Miles O'Brien welcomed the diversity and claimed it added a richness to their marriage. Data wished Keiko and Miles were still on the *Enterprise* so that he could discuss this further with them.

Data had also spoken with Beverly Crusher. Her opinions reflected her idealistic and passionate love for all life-forms, but they were as personal and elusive as Geordi's. Then Data had talked to others, including Yeoman Joshua Stern who followed the ancient Earth religion of Judaism, and with Chief Thomas Greycloud whose heritage was Amerindian of a tribe called Sioux. Each of them had shared with Data some of the rich tapestry of legends that made up the history and definition of their cultural backgrounds.

Data found both the disparity and similarities a fascinating study, but none of the vast influx of information he had gained from his readings and from contact with his crewmates had provided any form of personal enlightenment.

When Data took a place on one of the bar stools, the hostess of Ten-Forward was serenely wiping the already immaculate bar. Guinan put her cloth away and came to stand before him.

"I was wondering when you'd get around to me," she said.

"I beg your pardon?"

"Data, everyone on ship knows about your current —quest." Guinan's mouth quirked quickly toward a smile and back again. "Some find it admirable, others find it amusing. I think it was inevitable and I was wondering when you'd get around to asking me."

"I have many questions."

"I know."

"And you do not mind answering them?"

"No."

"Thank you," Data said. "I have sensed a certain hesitancy from many of the people I have talked to."

"That's only natural, Data."

"Why?"

"Because most people, even those who follow an established tradition, spend much of their time trying to reconcile belief with experience."

"And you do not?"

Again, the half-smile danced across the mouth of the enigmatic alien. "Yes I do," she said. "I've just had a little more time and practice. So ask me your questions."

"Do you believe in God?" Data began.

"Yes."

"Which one?"

"There's only one, Data."

"In the last several days, using the computer at top speed, I have read all of the major writings on the myths and religions of Earth. I have also read many of the Vulcan teachings and most of the writings from Betazed. I have encountered the names of several thousand deities."

"No, Data. There has been only one."

"If there has been only one, how do you explain the multitude of definitions and practices, each claiming to come from divine inspiration?"

Guinan clasped her hands together and studied the android. Data, to whom impatience was null-programing, waited while the bartender chose her words.

"You've missed the point," she said at last.

"I would appreciate it then," Data said, "if you could explain—the point—to me."

"The point, Data, is that this—*something*—this power we name God—and God is a good name; short, simple, easier to say than many—is beyond our definitions. Whether you call it a force or a being, whether you make it male or female or androgynous, whether you break its characteristics into a thousand different aspects or gather them together into one all-powerful being, God—true God—is beyond all that."

"Then no one is correct in his beliefs."

"On the contrary, Data, everyone is correct."

"Then how does one choose which expression of beliefs to follow?" Data asked.

"Like the rest of us, Data, you'll just have to follow your heart."

"But, Guinan—I have no heart."

This time Guinan's smile was not fleeting. "Oh yes, you do, Data," she said.

Data looked puzzled. "I am a constructed being made up of component parts of—"

"You have a heart, Data," Guinan repeated. "Not a muscle in your chest, but a heart."

"I do not understand."

"Let me ask you a few questions, Data," Guinan said. "If Geordi were in danger and the only way to save him would mean the end of your existence, would you do so?"

"Yes, but that—"

Guinan held up her hand. "What about Worf, or Picard, or any of us?"

"Of course, but—"

"When Keiko and O'Brien were having trouble on their wedding day, did you put aside your own interests and try to help them?"

"They are my friends."

"When you rescued the little girl, Sarjenka, and talked the captain into using the ship's resources to relieve the tectonic stresses that were tearing her planet apart, she was only a voice over subspace."

"She needed our help."

"That's my point, Data. I've never known you to turn away from anyone. That's love, Data, that's heart. You're mistaking the emotion, the warm, fuzzy feeling of being in love, for the reality. Love isn't just about emotion; it's about choices and action. That's why I say you have a heart, and like the rest of us, you just have to learn how to recognize what it's telling you."

"How?"

"No one can answer that for another individual."

"Thank you, Guinan," Data said as he slid off the bar stool. "You have given me much to consider."

"One more thing, Data," Guinan said. "In all the reading you've done, have you come across the teaching that man—sentient life—was made in the image of God?"

"In several different expressions and philosophies."

"You'll come across it in countless more. If man was created in the image of God, and you were created in the image of man, aren't you part of God, too?"

With a smile, Guinan picked up her cloth and began

again to wipe the bar. Data cocked his head slightly to one side, his positronic brain pondering her final question on several levels. Behind him, Data heard the door open and recognized the sound of Commander Riker's footsteps.

The Captain Pro-tem slid onto a stool two seats down to Data's left. Data watched as once more the *Enterprise*'s favorite hostess put her bar cloth away and went to stand in front of her troubled customer.

"What would you like, Commander?" she asked.

"Actually, Guinan, I'd just like to talk."

Guinan turned and gave Data a small Mona Lisa smile. Then she leaned on the bar in front of Riker and said, "Sure, Commander. Anything particular on your mind?"

Chapter Fifteen

IT WAS THE PAIN in her head that finally reached through the heavy fog that enveloped Troi. Even lying still, she felt as though a hundred horses were galloping through her brain. At first that was all she could feel. Even the slight movement of breathing was torture. Then, slowly, she became aware of the other sensations in her body. Her tongue felt thick and her mouth felt as if it had been filled with a wad of cotton. And she was cold. The floor beneath her was not covered with the thick carpet she remembered.

She lay there, unable to move yet, and tried to piece together the last events she could recall. Dinner with the captain, the wine, Mother Veronica asleep by the side of the bed . . .

Troi heard a groan next to her. The captain? She opened her eyes, and although it made her feel as if sharp knives were being stabbed into her brain, she kept them open until she could focus and look around.

She was lying on cold, hard stone. It was every-where she looked: floors, walls, ceiling. It was the same luminous green stone she had seen in the corridors and audience chamber. Its pale light cast a sickly hue through the room and over the faces of her companions lying on the floor next to her.

Moving with care, Troi eased herself into a sitting position. The movement caused the room to spin. She raised cold, shaking fingers to her forehead and fought back a wave of nausea. Beside her, the captain moaned again and started to sit up.

"Go slowly, Captain," she warned him.

"Counselor?" His voice was hoarse. Troi saw the muscles in his jaw working as he clenched his teeth and forced himself to sit. He opened his eyes to a narrow slit and looked at her.

"What happened?" he asked.

"I think we were drugged."

"You were," came a man's voice from the far corner. Troi turned her head. Too quickly; instantly she regretted the movement.

"Who are you?" she heard the captain demand while she waited for the second wave of nausea to pass. There was a burst of laughter from the same corner. Even in her current impaired state, she could sense the hysteria and the surges of bleak despair that swelled through the laughter.

Troi again opened her eyes; they focused more easily this time and she saw the man crouched in the far corner. He looked like a nightmare version of the King.

His laughter subsided. "I," he said, "am Joakal I'lium, King of Capulon IV."

"You're the King?" the captain said. "Then who—"

"My brother," he said. "A twin I never knew existed. He decided it was his turn to rule. So, with the help of a trusted friend, he took me prisoner. He usurped my place and I am left with only this cell for a kingdom."

While their new companion was talking, Troi noticed the captain reach up toward the left side of his chest, as though to tap his communicator and signal for help. But, like Troi, Picard had changed into sleeping attire before the drug had knocked him out. They had no communicators with them; there would be no easy rescue.

The captain struggled to stand. Troi saw the color drain from his face and he swayed unevenly on his feet. She automatically reached out to help him, but again a wave of nausea gripped her. Picard waved her away. He began to stumble about the circumference of the room, his hands searching the walls.

"There is no way out, Captain Picard," the King said. The captain shot him a startled glance and the younger man nodded.

"Yes," he said. "I know who you are. I was informed of your identities when you were dumped here. You're wasting your time. I've pushed and pulled on every stone. I've rattled the door a thousand times. We are all—guests—of my brother until he decides otherwise."

On the other side of Troi, Mother Veronica at last began to stir. The counselor quickly switched her attention to the nun. She crawled over to Mother Veronica's side and began whispering to her, reassuring her through the first painful moments of awakening.

Picard finished his inspection of the cell. He came

over and lowered himself to the floor beside Troi, who was helping Mother Veronica to sit upright. The nun's eyes were closed and her face was ashen.

"Are you all right?" he asked. Troi nodded. "And Mother Veronica?"

"She will be. Although she drank very little of the wine last night," Troi said, "she ate almost nothing. That's why the drug has hit her so hard."

Picard nodded curtly before he turned to Joakal. "I want to know everything," he said in a firm voice of command.

The King shrugged. "I'll tell you what I can," he said. "I don't know for certain how long I've been here or what has happened in my absence. I've been here weeks, I'm sure—weeks of being locked alone in this room . . ." his voice trailed off. Then after a moment his whole body shook sharply. He pulled himself back to the present and told his listeners of his capture, of the visits Beahoram had made to the cell, and of Aklier's betrayal.

"You keep mentioning your brother," Picard said when Joakal had finished. "The twin of whom you had no prior knowledge. Explain."

Again the captain's voice allowed no argument. "To understand that," Joakal answered, "you must understand the ways of my people."

"We have to understand," Picard countered. "We have to know everything you can tell us if we're to find a way out of here."

Joakal jumped to his feet. "There is no way out!" he shouted. He paced a few steps back and forth, running his hands through his lank, matted hair.

"You may have given up," Picard said. "But we haven't."

The King stopped pacing. He stood absolutely still

for a moment. Then he shrugged again and sat back down.

"It will pass the time," he said, more to himself than his companions. For another long moment, the King was silent. Troi wondered what he could say that would shed some light on their situation.

"Our ways," he began. "Our society and laws are based upon what we believe to be the Will of our God. This is the first thing you must understand. Everything we are has been shaped over the centuries by our faith. The oldest teachings of our faith tell of a time when the God walked upon this planet and had direct communion with the world he had created. All was peace then, the Teachings say; all was in harmony. The world remained this way for untold ages, until the God returned to his place beyond the heavens. He left the people of this world to be the caretakers over his domain."

Joakal stopped and looked again at the faces of his listeners. Troi felt the intensity behind his scrutiny, as if he was trying to measure how much of what he had just said they could accept. His expression was serious and the look in his eyes was almost beseeching.

Captain Picard gave him a small nod. "We have such a legend on the planet that is my home," he said, "and we have encountered similar ones many places throughout the galaxy."

"Ah—then you know of the God." Joakal gave a smile that wiped some of the weariness from his face. "I am glad."

Troi was struck by this expression of faith. These simple words sounded naive in the light of a universe filled with science and technology, but simple words, words like love and hate and mercy, often carried the greatest power. Was that also true of faith? she wondered. Was a simple faith also the strongest?

Joakal took a breath and continued. "The legends also say that before the God departed from our world," he said, "he granted a gift to the people here. He opened our minds to one another, in a gift the ancient writings call Mind-share. We are told that we were given this gift in order to protect the world over which we were left in charge.

"But without the God among us, the peace did not last. Over the ages we ceased to be one people and one world, united in our service to the God and our care of his creation. We became divided into a multitude of little kingdoms, each vying for dominance over the others. Over the centuries, science took the place of religion. Our technology grew and soon wars came and went and came again. Each time they were more devastating. Soon we were using our scientific knowledge that could have done so much for this world to build weapons capable of killing millions."

Joakal stopped again and rubbed a hand over his eyes. "Then the final wars came," he said after a pause, "wars of a terror worse than death. They were a hundred generations ago. Although our science had a part in them, the most devastating weapon came from within ourselves. These were the Mind Wars and they were fought with the very gift the God had given us for peace."

Joakal sighed and leaned his head back against the wall, keeping his eyes closed. "The old histories tell of the terror of those years," he continued. "Terror-filled years. The gift of Mind-share had been turned into a weapon from which no one was safe. Thoughts and plans could be ripped from the mind of an enemy. The weak could be forced to serve the more powerful; even their bodies could be manipulated against their wills. Peace-loving people were turned into puppets of destruction. The wars dragged on for over a generation.

Then, suddenly, the power began to fade. Children began being born without the ability to Mind-share. The God had stripped his gift from us.

"Now a new fear took over—fear of the God and of his anger. The people abandoned the sciences, maintaining only those, such as communication and transportation, basic heat and water sources, necessary to keep the planet from total collapse. People flocked back to the old temples. They begged the Servants to help them find the way to appease the God. Sacrifices were made. Kingdoms toppled until we became a united people again. But it was not enough; the gift did not return to us. Stronger measures were called for and new laws were passed, decreed by the King, sanctioned by the temple. These laws demanded that all that was not perfect be eliminated from our society. Nothing was exempt, not even our children. Any abnormality, and that includes the birth of a twin, was to be left on the temple steps to die. *This* was our offering to appease the God. It was pronounced the only way to display the depths of our faith, and our repentance."

For several seconds the only sound in the cell was the harsh breathing of its inhabitants. Joakal opened his eyes and met those of his listeners. Troi knew how stunned the King's last words had left her. She looked and saw her feelings mirrored in her companions' faces, Mother Veronica's in particular. The pale cast to her cheeks and the fever brightness of her eyes was more than the residual effects of the drugged wine; it was horror at what she was hearing.

"And this law—" the captain began.

Joakal nodded. "Is still in effect. Oh, we have ceremonialized it. The infants are not now left to die on the temple steps. They are euthanized gently and buried in special crypts below the temple—returned

139

to the God, it is said. But this is the reason I asked the Little Mothers to come to Capulon IV. I wanted them to help me abolish this law and others like it that have kept this world from moving forward. Now it's too late."

"This—law—was not mentioned in any of the reports on your culture," Picard said.

"Would you, Captain, allow such a thing to be known about your people?" Joakal asked. "Would you even speak openly about it among yourselves, except in the most general terms? When your observers heard the term 'returned to the God,' do you believe they thought more than that the child had died? But you asked how Beahoram fit into this. He was the second to come from my mother's womb. He was supposed to die. Instead, he has come back to take my place and my future, and soon there will be nothing anyone can do to stop him."

"Why?" the captain asked harshly. "Why can't you fight him, stand up for yourself and claim back—"

Joakal again barked out a laugh. It was filled with bleak, sardonic humor. "You don't understand, Captain," he said. "The gift of Mind-share has returned in a very small measure. It is very rare among the population and it never comes with the power of the ancient times. But it comes often enough for the people to keep hoping. That is what has continued to give this law its hold over my people."

"When does this gift show up and to whom?" Picard asked. "Is there any way of predicting it?"

The young King shook his head. "Usually, if someone feels any stirrings of the old gifts within them, he or she enters Service at the temple. But not all the Servants claim to possess these gifts, and even in the ones who do, it is very weak.

"What does this have to do with Beahoram?"

"The first of my House, after whom I am named, was a Chief Servant here in this city. Then one day, when he was at the altar, something happened to quicken his mind and return to him all of the old gifts. The writings do not tell us exactly what happened, they say only that the God entered him. He was proclaimed King and *Absolute*. My House has ruled ever since. Each time the King has been crowned to *Absolute*, the God has entered him in the same way. The *Absolute* is the only one to whom the gifts of the God are again granted in full."

Joakal stopped. He turned his face toward the ceiling, his eyes closed tightly against his despair. "I was to be the thirtieth generation of I'lium Kings," he said. "The sacred number fulfilled, and in that fulfillment I was going to guide my people forward. A new age—that was my dream. Now it will be Beahoram who rules instead."

Troi had sat quietly during the King's long recitation, riding the Gordian knot of his emotions as they mutated through shadings of despair to resignation to troubled conviction and back to despair. As he said his last words, she sat forward, her eyes blazing with sudden insight.

"Captain," she said, "it all makes sense now."

"What, Counselor?"

"Everything—the feelings of anger and arrogance I received from Beahoram, the two minds that Mother Veronica sensed. Joakal, here, is the other mind."

Troi raised herself to her knees, eager to make Picard understand. "Don't you see, Captain?" she said. "Beahoram is a telepath. Joakal is, too. I'm certain that most of the people of Capulon are telepathic, but with abilities locked behind shields no one remembers how to lower. In wars such as Joakal has described, only those who could learn to shield their minds would survive. This ability would be passed on from one generation to another until it became . . ." she searched for the word, ". . . instinct, a product of survival. Those who then learned how to release their psychic talents would appear amazingly powerful—God-embodied."

The captain's eyes were fixed on her and Troi could almost see him quickly sorting through possibilities. "Why would this happen when the King is crowned?" he asked.

"Joakal said that many of those who enter Service have rediscovered their psychic identities, at least in part. It's my guess that during the coronation, when the King is the willing focus of so much psychic energy all united to the same purpose, it acts as a trigger and unblocks the King's own talents."

"Could you and Mother Veronica do the same thing for Joakal—here, now?"

"I don't know, Captain," Troi answered. "I'm willing to try." She turned to Mother Veronica, but the nun shrank back.

"No," she whispered. "I . . . I can't."

Troi glanced at the captain. "Let me talk to her," she said.

Picard nodded and went to sit by the King, giving the women as much privacy as the situation allowed.

Joakal did not open his eyes. "It won't work," he said as the captain sat down.

"How do you know?"

"Because it is a gift from the God, and you are not his Servants."

"Mother Veronica is. Her life and the lives of the others like her, her work and her Order are all dedicated and vowed to the service of God."

"Is it the same God—the true God?"

Picard was suddenly reminded of his Second Officer. Had Data found his answers to questions such as this? Picard knew his own, and he gave a little smile.

"Is there more than one truth?" he asked. "And isn't all service to the truth rendered to the same place?"

"A wise answer, Captain," Joakal said, the hint of a smile appearing on his face. "Perhaps this will work, after all."

It was just after dawn. The members of the Council of Elders, the Gentleborn who were in the city for the King's coronation, and many high-ranking officials and merchants were gathered at the temple to witness the final ceremony for the King's Coming to Age.

Elana sat once more in the loft surrounded by the other Servants. Below her, the rite was just drawing to a close. The man she now knew to be Joakal's brother had received his knee-length Vest of Manhood. But to Elana, the deep crimson color made it look like a cloak of blood, Joakal's blood, overlaying the purity of the white clothes in which Beahoram had kept his Vigil.

Faellon's hands were lifted high in the final invocation. Elana was not listening; she was watching Beahoram and Aklier. In the darkest hours of the night, after the first moon had set and the small, second moon was in its descent, she had followed Aklier once more to the palace where she had seen him and his hirelings carry the inert bodies of the Federation people from their rooms. She had tried to pursue, but she soon lost sight of her quarry in the maze of palace corridors and back stairs. Elana was determined not to let that happen again. Today, tomorrow, however long it took, she would keep dogging their movements until they led her to Joakal.

The drone of the Chief Servant's prayer ceased. Before he could dismiss the assembled officials, Beahoram raised himself from his knees, interrupting the rite before its completion. He turned to face the half-filled pews.

"My people," he said, raising his voice to carry through the building. "My friends, the long night of my Vigil has ended. With it has gone the years of my youth. My Vigil was not an easy one. During the hours I knelt before this altar I had not only my own future to lay before the God, but the future of this planet. We are at a crossroads. The decision I soon must make will affect all of the generations to come.

"As you know, a starship is in orbit around our world. In the palace, representatives from that great organization, the United Federation of Planets, wait with a treaty for me to sign. All through my long Vigil I asked the God for guidance and for Wisdom in this decision. Only one answer came to me. I believe it came from the Voice of the God."

Beahoram paused, letting the words sink into the minds of his listeners. They must believe his next command to be a divine directive. He waited a few seconds more.

"This is the answer the God has given to my long hours of imploring: the coronation must not wait. It must take place this afternoon, in the third hour after the sun has reached its zenith."

Again Beahoram paused, this time to let the murmurs of shock and surprise that swept through the temple crescendo and die away.

Behind Beahoram, Faellon gasped. "But, Your Majesty, that is only nine hours from now. We cannot prepare."

Beahoram turned and looked at the Chief Servant.

"You must," he said. He turned back to the waiting crowd.

"I know it will be difficult for all of us to be ready in so short a time," he continued. "I understand all of the work it will involve. But I cannot deny or reject the Voice of the God as it came to me. I stand before you now as a man, ready to take up the heavy weight of the crowns and robes and to be your *Absolute*. Yet, I would willingly wait for the appointed time, had an authority greater than mine not demanded otherwise."

Beahoram turned to the altar and knelt in an attitude of humility. After a stunned moment, the Chief Servant hurried to the King to pronounce the final blessing and dismissal. He held his hands out over the people.

"Go in the Light of the God," he said. "Walk in Peace and Wisdom—and may the God strengthen us all."

Faellon turned back to the altar. Out in the nave of the temple, those who had come to witness the ceremony rose from their seats and filed toward the great doors. There was no idle chatter. Their minds were too paralyzed by Beahoram's announcement and all it would mean.

Up in the loft, the Servants rose as well. All except Elana. Nine hours, the thoughts shouted in her brain. Nine hours, and before that time had passed, she must find a way to stop this coronation.

She must find Joakal.

Chapter Sixteen

It took Troi several minutes to persuade Mother Veronica to help her try to reach the hidden recesses of King Joakal's mind. The counselor knew she needed the help; she had no chance of succeeding in this type of endeavor alone. Yet, as she remembered Mother Veronica's past, Troi also understood the nun's hesitation and tried to go gently as she explained to Mother Veronica what it was they needed to do.

Now Troi, Mother Veronica, and Joakal sat in a tight circle, holding hands. Their eyes were closed and their faces drawn up into frowns. Especially Troi's. She had used several different techniques she had learned during her years of training on Betazed to try and reach the hidden depths of the young King's mind. So far she had had no success. For the first time in several years Troi wished for full telepathic talents.

Although Mother Veronica had agreed, albeit reluctantly, to allow Troi to establish the link with her mind once more, and the nun's psychic strength was augmenting Troi's own, Mother Veronica was untrained. They could not work truly in tandem. There was a part of Mother Veronica that was holding back. At times her personal horror at using her mind to invade that of another being, however willing, was so strong Troi found herself having to struggle through a backwash of Mother Veronica's emotions while still trying to find the way through Joakal's mental defenses.

Finally, Troi sighed. She released her hold on the hands of her companions and opened her eyes. The captain sat a few feet away, watching them and willing them to succeed. Troi met his eyes and she shook her head in answer to his worried expression.

"I'm sorry," she said. "Joakal's shields are too strong. And they are shields, Captain. Now that I've touched them, I have no doubts."

"But I did feel something," Joakal said. He searched for the right word. "A . . . a stirring, or something."

"Counselor?" the captain asked.

"Perhaps, sir," Troi answered, carefully keeping her voice neutral. She had felt no such response, but this was the first time since they had awakened in Joakal's presence that she had sensed any positive emotion in the young King.

"Maybe after we have rested," she continued, "and any lingering effects of the drug have worn off. . . ." She let the statement remain unfinished; she did not want to deny their hopes or raise false ones.

Again the captain's eyes met hers, and she knew he understood exactly what she had not said, and why.

"Very good, Counselor," he replied aloud. "And you're right, of course. I know that I, for one, still have a pounding headache."

"Someone should bring some food soon," Joakal said. "My captivity may not be in the most comfortable surroundings, but Beahoram is quite insistent that I do not starve."

Picard nodded. "Then I suggest we all try to rest until the food arrives."

Their little group broke up. As Troi looked for a way to be comfortable on the cold stone of the cell, Joakal retrieved the blankets he had been given for warmth. He stood and shook one, then spread it on the floor.

"Please," he said, gesturing that Troi and Mother Veronica should use it. Then he handed Troi the other blanket for a covering. Troi was grateful. The material of the nightdress she was wearing, while comfortable to sleep in, did not give her much protection from the chill air of the cell. Mother Veronica was still in the habit and veil she had been wearing when she succumbed to the drug in their wine. She did not seem to notice the cold and Troi envied her the heavy material.

"Thank you," Troi said and she smiled at the King as she moved onto the warm thickness of the blanket. Mother Veronica joined her, and Joakal took a place next to where the captain sat with his back against the wall, his arms folded across his chest and his eyes closed.

"Perhaps," the captain said without opening his eyes, "while we rest, you could tell us more about your world and your people."

"Of course, Captain," Joakal replied. "What would you like to know?"

"I leave that to you. Any information will be helpful."

Troi watched the young King's face as he tried to decide what to say. Her foray into his mind had made her sensitive to the nuances of his emotions and she knew how deeply he was hurt by his captivity. But now, she also knew the resilience of his spirit. Earlier, Joakal's depression had been pervasive, a black melancholy held off only by occasional flashes of anger. Now that he was no longer alone and a single thread of hope had been offered, slender though it was, he had banished all thoughts of defeat.

As she closed her eyes, Troi shifted her attention to Mother Veronica. Troi could feel the nun's weariness in both body and mind. The recent upheavals to her life were taking their toll on the nun. Yet she, like the King, possessed an inner core, a center of strength that was both tough and pliable. Troi had felt it often during their work together on board the *Enterprise*. She had felt it again here, when the nun struggled to overcome her personal repugnance and yield control of her telepathic abilities to Troi. That she had not always succeeded was irrelevant.

Troi heard the rustle of cloth as Joakal shifted his position, ready now to speak. "Much of what I could tell you," he began, "you have doubtless already learned in preparation for coming to Capulon IV. I would have in your position, and I am certain you are no stranger to the necessities of diplomatic encounters, Captain. I assume, therefore, you know the statistics on our industries and agriculture, our population dispersement, socio-political hierarchies, basic religious observances, and social customs. Am I correct?"

"You are," the captain replied.

Joakal shifted positions once more. "I have already told you that our society is based upon the dictates of our religion. Harsh as some of those ways are, we are not an unfeeling people. We are a people dedicated to

149

the Virtues of Wisdom. Before the door of every temple are four pillars. They represent the four faces of Wisdom: Patience, Honesty, Mercy with Justice, and Faith. The pillars themselves are called the Guardians of the Virtues and they are there to remind us of what we seek and what we value.

"My ancestor whom I have already mentioned to you, Joakal I'lium the First," the present Joakal continued, "was a great King, a King who had gained Wisdom. He is the example to us of what we strive to become. Of the many stories that have survived the generations since his reign, my favorite is this one:

"There were two bakers in the royal city. They were both of fine old families. They both had well-established shops where each was reputed to bake and sell the finest goods in the world. A rivalry grew up between them. They decided to have a contest for the title of best baker and they asked the King to be the judge.

"On the day of the competition the two bakers arrived at the palace to use the royal ovens and await the King's decision. They baked all day, using secret recipes and skills they had developed over the years of their rivalry. Then they presented the products of their labor to the King.

"The room was filled with spectators as the King began to eat. He sampled first one item then another, praising their virtues of taste, aroma, and texture. He tasted dozens of different breads and rolls and cakes and pies and pastries until he could eat no more. Then he went to his throne and sat in silence, contemplating his judgment. The minutes stretched on until finally the contestants could wait no longer. Tell us, they begged him, tell us who is the greatest baker.

"King Joakal looked up. He was frowning and

unhappy. 'Today,' he said, 'I have tasted delicacies such as I thought could only exist in dreams. The God, himself, must be tempted to come and walk once more among us so that he might smell these smells and taste this food. But, I cannot name either of you the greatest baker. Each of you has qualities the other lacks. It is the one who can combine these talents who will be without peer.'

"The bakers hung their heads and went away. But within the month they had opened a shop together. Once they realized they had things to learn from and to teach each other, their past rivalry died away—and the city reaped the benefits of their new partnership."

Lying on the soft blanket on the floor, Troi listened to the King's tale. His low, polished voice relaxed her like a lullaby sung to a tired child. As he finished speaking, she felt herself drifting toward the place where sleep hovered, waiting to drop its mantle of dreams across her willing mind.

Anger blazed. It flared with pyrotechnic fury behind Troi's eyes and seared the slumber from her mind. She came awake with a start. Beside her, Mother Veronica moaned in agony. Troi put a hand on her arm.

Shh, she thought to the nun, making use of the light, familiar link they had used during their long hours on the *Enterprise. Let me listen.*

Cautiously, Troi opened one eye. Both the captain and Joakal were on their feet, confronting . . . Troi shifted her glance . . . Beahoram. Standing so near Joakal, the mirror likeness of them was even more striking. But the emotions, the inner qualities of mind and soul that Troi could perceive, were as different as their faces were the same. And Beahoram's voice, when he spoke as he was speaking now, had an edge to

151

it Troi had never heard from Joakal, not even when she had first awakened in this cell and felt his utter despair.

"Your threats do not concern me, Captain Picard," Beahoram was saying. "Neither does your Federation. I know about your Prime Directive. Once I am crowned, I will be the legal ruler. By your own laws and oaths, you cannot interfere with this culture if I choose to order you to leave, which I will. But in fact, Captain, I am grateful that you are here, grateful enough that I will let you live. But don't presume too far upon that gratitude. For now, your presence has given me the excuse I need to move the coronation forward. In just a few hours I will be crowned the *Absolute* of Capulon IV."

"You . . . you can't do that," Joakal stammered.

"Oh yes I can, Brother," Beahoram said, his eyes narrowing as he looked at Joakal's face. Another wave of anger, tinged black with hatred, surged from Beahoram and crashed through the room. "I have claimed to need the full Wisdom of the God in order to decide whether or not to join the Federation. No one has dared to challenge this claim."

Beahoram turned back to Picard. His voice took on a silken formality that was more chilling than the obvious enmity with which he spoke to his brother.

"Of course," he said. "I will not be able to release you and the others until after I have divested my brother of the contents of his mind. After that is accomplished, I doubt there will be enough left of him to be worthy of your support as a ruler, even if you were so allowed by your Federation laws."

"Beahoram," the captain snapped, "what you're planning is no different from murder."

Beahoram laughed; it was a cruel, dark sound.

"Murder? No. Justice—a life for a life. My past, my rightful life here at the palace as the son of a King, was robbed from me. Now his future will be taken from him. It is Justice—and soon, Brother," Beahoram said, looking again at Joakal, "soon I will have everything."

Beahoram turned on his heel and strode to the door. When Troi heard it clang shut, she sat up. Picard and Joakal turned to her. The young King's cheeks had become ashen and she felt the slow coil of terror that was winding its way through his mind.

"Beahoram believes what he just said, Captain," Troi told them. "He believes that what he is doing is some strange form of justice. Beahoram's need for vengeance is so strong that it has become his entire identity. His mind is so twisted that he cannot see beyond his own plans. He doesn't care who pays the price for him to get what he thinks he deserves."

"Whatever Beahoram's motives," the captain said, "we cannot just sit here and wait. Are you and Mother Veronica sufficiently rested to try again to . . . what did you call it . . . unlock Joakal's abilities?"

Troi turned to the nun. Mother Veronica, like the young King, was white-faced and shaken. The force of dark emotions that had brought Troi awake had screamed painfully through the nun's mind.

Suddenly, there were soft, shuffling sounds from outside the cell and a woman's voice was whispering Joakal's name. He ran to the door.

"Elana," he cried out. While the others watched, Joakal tried, unsuccessfully, to fit more than his hands through the bars of the small window in the cell door. Dainty, white hands came up to meet his and their fingers caressed. Troi smiled at the sudden burst of joy that filled the room.

153

"Joakal." The woman's voice was full of happy tears. "I found you. The God be thanked . . . I found you at last."

"How? Elana, tell me what's happened. How did you—"

"Oh, Joakal, did you think I wouldn't know that *he* was not you? I came back early. I went to see you and to tell you that yes, I wanted to be your wife. But it wasn't you!" Her voice wavered on the last word, as if the pain of that meeting was still fresh. There was a pause, then Elana's voice began again, strong and clear.

"I went to the temple," she said. "I tried to convince the Chief Servant that something was wrong, but he wouldn't believe me. I've been in retreat at the temple, and I thought and prayed and tried to understand why you had changed. Then last night your brother had his Vigil—your Vigil. I stayed in the temple loft. That's when I learned the truth of who he is and what his plans are. I've been searching for you ever since. I love you, Joakal."

"Elana . . . I thought I'd lost you forever. That was the cruelest pain of all." Again his hands sought closer contact.

The captain cleared his throat. "Excuse me, Your Majesty," he said, addressing the King formally. "Time is short."

Joakal released one of Elana's hands and turned. "Of course," he said as he motioned for Picard to come to the door. "Captain Picard, this is Elana, First Daughter of the House E'shala."

"A pleasure, ma'am—circumstances notwithstanding," Picard said summarily, trying to think of a way to bring Joakal's mind back to their present problem.

Elana did it for him. "Joakal," she said, "your brother has moved the coronation to this afternoon."

"I know—he was here. We have to find a way out of this cell."

"Tell me what to do."

Joakal ran his free hand through his hair, then down across his beard as he stood thinking. Picard stepped closer to the cell-door window.

"Do you think you could get to our rooms?" he asked Elana. "Our uniforms are there, and our communicators. With them, we could contact our ship and they would send help."

Elana shook her head. "There are too many people, too much activity now. My presence there would be noticed."

"Is there another communications system somewhere in the city that you could use safely?"

Elana thought for a moment. "I have friends in the city," she began. Then she shook her head. "No, their systems would not be strong enough. The only ones that could reach your ship are in the palace—and the temple."

Elana's face grew animated. "Faellon has one in his office," she continued. "With the coronation only a few hours away, they're so busy at the temple I should be able to use that one unseen."

"Good," the captain said, taking command. "Now listen carefully. The name of my ship is the *Enterprise,* and my First Officer is Commander Riker. Tell him where we are and that we're being held captive. He'll know what to do. Keep your conversation short and don't take any risks you don't have to. You're our only contact with freedom. And thank you."

Picard stepped away from the door to give Elana and Joakal what privacy he could. While they whispered intimately for a few minutes longer, Picard came to sit beside Troi and Mother Veronica. He noticed Troi was smiling.

"Counselor?" he asked.

"Their joy is quite infectious," she explained. "They truly love each other."

"The galaxy would be a much easier place in which to exist," Mother Veronica added, "if all minds were as filled with such loving thoughts."

Troi nodded. Then her smile faded as she turned to the nun. "All the work we did," she began. "Your shields—"

Mother Veronica shook her head, her expression touched with weariness. "I can block out the worst of it," she said. "But some thoughts are too strong. Beahoram's hatred of his brother and his need for revenge—it almost overpowered me. Joakal and Elana's love—the strength of their feelings is like sunshine, with warmth to touch even the shadows."

"Let us hope," the captain said, "that it will bring a little light into our situation, as well."

Chapter Seventeen

ELANA ENTERED THE TEMPLE once more. She slid into a back pew and knelt there in an attitude of pious meditation. Although her thoughts automatically issued half-formed prayers for guidance and success, her eyes were busy furtively assessing the activities of the other Servants.

All around her they were preparing the temple for the coronation. From the steps outside the great doors, throughout the narthex, the loft where the Servants sat, the long central nave with its multitude of pews and kneeling benches, and the center aisle that led the way to the elevated great altar; all these had to be cleansed and purified before the solemn ceremony this afternoon.

The ancient paraments and antependia had to be pulled from their places of storage, shaken, aired, and pressed before they could be used upon the altar. The long banners decorated with the colors and symbols of the thirty Gentle Houses must be unrolled, checked, and hung from the ceiling, fifteen to a side, to line the walls of the interior of the temple. Then, finally, the royal vestments and regalia, the sacred implements of crowning, had to be prepared and laid out in readiness for the ceremony.

While the other temple inhabitants scurried on their tasks, Faellon was busy caring for the altar itself and for the sacred bowl. These, too, must be cleaned and polished, but only by the Chief Servant's hands. Elana was relieved to see Faellon occupied and away from his office.

Breathing one final prayer for success, she rose from her knees and began walking toward the transept at the head of the nave, the left arm of which led off to the Servants' quarters, and to Faellon's office. She dodged around the other Servants who were bent to their labors, and tried hiding her growing nervousness behind smiles and nods and greetings.

The long aisle felt endless as she walked. Yet, too soon, Elana found herself at the end of it, standing before the high altar. Automatically, she bowed and made her obeisance to the God. When she straightened, she found Faellon's eyes upon her.

Immediately, Elana's mouth went dry. Her heart began to race. It thudded in her chest and sent the blood pounding in her ears until she was certain Faellon must hear it, too. But he only smiled and, with a nod, returned to his work.

It took Elana a full two seconds to realize he had looked away. She swallowed back a cry of relief and concentrated on keeping her posture relaxed as she turned to the left and headed for the small side door. Her feet wanted to run; her brain screamed at her to hurry, but Elana forced herself to walk slowly, calmly, pretending she had nothing more on her mind than reaching her own room for a time of meditation.

But once Elana passed through the door and it had closed behind her, a sudden fit of shaking gripped her. She leaned back against the wall before her knees could buckle, grateful for the solid support of the stone.

The door to Faellon's office stood a few feet away. Elana eyed it suspiciously, as if it alone had the power to defeat her. For the first time in her life, Elana was truly frightened—for herself if she were caught; for Joakal, and for the people of this planet. What future did any of them have if Beahoram was not stopped?

Elana took a deep breath and, gathering her courage around her like a cloak against the night, she entered the Chief Servant's office.

The room seemed bigger without Faellon sitting behind his desk, and much, much more silent. Elana found she was holding her breath. She let it out with a rush and hurried to the communications console.

It was different from any system she had seen before. Elana sat down in the Chief Servant's high-backed chair, propped her chin in her hand, and studied the controls, trying to find the way to make the system come to life.

Precious seconds changed into minutes that slipped away unnoticed while Elana studied the board. Finally, she thought she knew how to turn the console on, but beyond that she was stymied. There were fourteen buttons grouped under the label "Temple," six under "Palace" and eighteen marked "City." But in the center of the board were twenty-seven buttons—Elana counted them—under no heading at all.

What are they for? Elana wondered, her frustrations mounting and mingling with the urgency that continued to gnaw at the back of her mind. What if I press the wrong ones? Will alarms sound? Guards come running? Doors automatically lock?

Did she dare to take the chance?

Did she dare not?

Elana chewed the corner of her lower lip. She knew that time was passing and with each moment of hesitation, the danger increased. She must act—for better or worse, she must act now.

Her hand had only the slightest of tremors as she touched the button at the base of the console that she hoped was the power switch. The viewscreen filled with light and Elana breathed a silent thank you to the God. That had been her only sure move; from here on it would be by trial and error, pressing buttons at random and hoping she could disconnect before she was discovered. She would have to continue that way until she made contact with the Federation ship.

Elana closed her eyes. The picture of Joakal's face as he looked out at her from behind those bars took shape. She felt again his fingers entwined with hers as he whispered that he loved her—words she had given up hope of hearing again. The memories strengthened her and she reached again toward the console.

"Elana!" a voice snapped. "What are you doing?"

Elana looked up. Faellon stood in the doorway, surprise slowly turning to anger across his usually placid features.

"What are you doing?" he demanded again as he stepped further into the room.

Elana felt the blood drain from her face. The hand that had been stretched toward the console flew to her mouth. She stood. The chair grated across the floor, loud in the tense silence.

"I . . . uh," Elana began. Faellon came toward her. The door swung shut behind him, carried by its own weight. As the Chief Servant approached, Elana stepped backward until she felt the edge of the chair behind her knees. She could retreat no further, nor would she. For Joakal's sake, she swallowed her fear.

"Faellon," she said, her voice sounding stronger than she felt. "You have to listen to me. The man who claims to be the King, the man you're planning to elevate to the highest and most powerful position on our planet, is a liar. He is not Joakal. He's Joakal's brother—his twin."

Faellon stopped a couple of feet in front of Elana. The expression on his face changed again. Anger faded, to be replaced by a look of deep sadness. He shook his head slowly.

"My dear child," he said, "I thought your time among us had eased your burden and that the God had healed you of your delusions. Now I see that is not so, and I am sorry."

"No," Elana cried. Desperation made her voice more shrill than she intended and she lowered it.

"Faellon," she began again, "I'm not deluded. I've seen Joakal, the real one. He's being held captive in a cell below the palace. The Federation people are with him. They're being kept there by Joakal's brother until after the coronation."

"And then what, Elana?" Faellon asked softly. "What does this brother then plan to do?"

Elana knew then that Faellon did not believe her, but she continued anyway, hoping to somehow convince him that she was telling the truth.

"He plans to strip away Joakal's mind and take his place as *Absolute*."

Again Faellon shook his head. The sadness in his eyes deepened. "Elana," he said softly. "There are no twins on this world—and the power you fear, the power to take another's mind, is among the abilities which the God, in His wisdom, has taken from our people. Even the *Absolute* no longer possesses such power."

"But Faellon, I heard—"

Faellon held up his hand to silence her. "I did not know the depth of your sorrow when you came to us," he said. "I blame myself that I did not realize how unsettled your mind had become. I should have done more to help you."

Keeping his eyes locked on Elana's as if willing her not to move, Faellon reached down and pressed one of the many buttons under the "Temple" heading. A few brief moments later the door to his office again opened. Two of the male Servants stood there.

"I'm sorry, Elana," Faellon said. "But this is for your own safety."

He made a motion with his hand. Elana looked up and saw the Servants coming toward her.

"No—wait! Faellon, I can prove what I'm saying."

The Servants kept approaching. They came around the desk. Elana backed away from them, and ran into Faellon. His hands closed around her arms, pinning her to him with more strength than she would have thought the Chief Servant's old and frail body possessed.

"Take her to her room," the Chief Servant ordered. "And make certain that she remains there. The mind of our dear Sister in the God has been disturbed and we must protect her from herself."

The hands of the other Servants locked on to Elana's arms. Faellon released her and she was pulled, gently but inexorably, toward the door.

"Faellon—please, don't do this," Elana cried. "Listen to me. Come with me and let me prove what I'm telling you is true."

"After the coronation, my child," Faellon said as

Elana neared the door. "We'll talk more then. And I promise, we will find a way to heal you. You must have faith, Elana."

Elana closed her eyes and hung her head. For the moment she was defeated, but only for the moment. She would not give up.

She raised her head and met Faellon's eyes. "You're wrong," she said as she felt one of her captors open the office door. "You're wrong about everything. You say I must have faith. Well, I don't want it—not your kind of faith. Your *faith* has blinded you to *Truth.*"

Then she was pulled through the doorway and out of Faellon's office.

Once the door had shut, the Chief Servant sat down heavily in his chair, shaken by the encounter. How could he have been so blind to her condition? he wondered. He had thought it only the distressed imaginings, the self-delusions that too often come with intense and unrequited love. He had encountered such often enough in his role as Chief Servant of the largest temple in the land. Many people came to him for counseling and other reasons, and he usually was able to help them.

But Elana—this was something more. What mischief had she been up to here in his office? What had she been trying to do? Faellon stared at the communications console as if it could give him the answers he needed. The screen was still lit, but there was no indication of whom Elana had been trying to call, or for what purpose. Faellon depressed the power button, turning the screen off, and sat back in his chair.

Where had Elana come across such ridiculous stories? Faellon wondered. A twin brother of the King. There were no twins, not alive. The Law strictly forbade it. The Law—that must be where Elana found the idea. Faellon knew that Joakal had spent much of his time in these last years poring over the old texts. The Chief Servant had even provided many of the more ancient and obscure ones for the King to read. Elana must have read them, too, and somehow the idea of a twin had implanted itself in her subconscious mind, providing the reason for what she saw as the King's changed behavior.

The mystery solved, at least for now, Faellon ran a hand across his tired eyes. There was still so much to do. He had only come into his office to signal for more cleaning supplies to be brought up from the temple stores. As he reached out to depress the intercom to the Cellarer's office, he felt the weight of his years settle a sudden burden on his back.

I'm getting too old for any of this, he thought. Too old and too tired. I can no longer Serve as I should. One more duty and then I'll name my successor.

Faellon closed his eyes and leaned his head farther back against his chair. A smile spread across his features, softening the worn lines in his face. After tomorrow, he thought, I'll retire to quiet Service at the temple near my childhood home. The North-march is so beautiful this time of year and I'd like to see the waterfall of Ennys again. . . .

Will Riker sat fidgeting in the command chair on the bridge of the *Enterprise*. Midmorning had come and gone and neither the captain nor Troi had reported in yet, nor had they responded to any attempts to contact them. Mother hen or not, Riker was getting impatient.

"Lieutenant Worf," he called to his Chief of Security, who also manned communications. "Hail the palace. Let's see if we can find out what's going on."

"No response, sir," the Klingon said a moment later.

"Keep trying, Lieutenant."

"Aye, sir."

Riker frowned. This was not like the captain, and Riker did not like it. No, he did not like it at all.

"I am finally receiving a response from the palace, Commander," Lieutenant Worf announced a few minutes later. Riker nodded and stood, unconsciously mimicking the captain's habitual tug at his uniform top.

"On screen, Lieutenant," he said. Immediately the now familiar view of the planet was replaced by the head and shoulders of a man, several times larger than life.

"I am Commander William T. Riker, on board the USS *Enterprise*," Riker announced, unintimidated by the giant size of the vision before him. "I am trying to contact the members of our Away Team that beamed to your planet yesterday afternoon."

"Greetings, Commander. I am Aklier, Elder of the House Ti'Kara, member of the Ruling Council. I apologize for the delay in answering your summons, but I have only just been informed that your communications system has been signaling for some time."

"Apology accepted," Riker replied, keeping the impatience he felt from his voice. "As I said, the reason we are calling is to try and reach our captain. He failed to report in this morning."

"Quite so, Commander. The reason for the delay in answering your call and the reason you have not heard from your captain are no doubt the same. Today at dawn, our King's Vigil for his Coming to Age concluded and the ceremony for his entry into True Manhood took place at the temple. No communication devices are allowed within the temple where they might disturb the worshippers from their meditation on the God. If your captain and the rest of your—

Away Team did you call it?—attended the ceremony, they would not have been able to contact you."

"When did this ceremony end?" Riker asked.

"Why, only a short time ago, and things have been in turmoil ever since."

"It is most unusual for the captain not to have contacted us as soon as the ceremony ended. With your permission," Riker continued, "I would like to beam another Away Team to the palace and verify the safety of our people."

"Commander," Aklier replied, sounding shocked, "Capulon IV is a peaceful planet. I assure you that no harm has come to your people. As for more members of your crew coming here, I'm afraid that is quite impossible. As I said, things are in turmoil here. By a divine command which came to our King during his Vigil last night, the coronation has been moved to this afternoon. His Majesty must be empowered with the full Wisdom of the God to resolve his uncertainties over the treaty with your Federation. I know this was a concern of your captain's. Your people are probably closeted with the King now, discussing the treaty, and have not had the chance to return to their rooms and retrieve their communication devices. If you will be patient a little while longer, Commander, I'm certain everything will be explained."

"But, Elder Aklier," Riker said, "surely two more of our people would not cause any more upset to your preparations."

"I'm sorry, Commander Riker. The palace is very large and they would have to be guided. We cannot spare anyone at the moment. Furthermore, if your people are with the King, as I believe, they cannot be disturbed without offending His Majesty. Now, if you will excuse me, Commander, I have duties to which I must return. Good day, Commander."

166

The large viewscreen went blank. Then the sight of the planet loomed again, contact with the surface broken. Will Riker sat back down in the center chair and scrubbed his hand across his lower face, stroking his beard contemplatively.

It all sounds so plausible, he thought, and I don't believe a word of it.

Cluck-cluck.

Chapter Eighteen

AFTER SEVERING COMMUNICATION with the Federation ship, Aklier fled to his rooms within the palace. He hid there throughout the day. Although he knew that he should be overseeing preparations for the coronation and for the banquet to follow, he could not bring himself to face the people of this world, the people he was betraying.

Now the final hour had arrived. Too soon, Aklier knew, he would be called to the procession that would escort Beahoram to the temple and the ancient rite. Too soon, Aklier would have to play his final part in seeing Beahoram crowned *Absolute* and making him the God-embodied to his people.

But Aklier felt none of the satisfaction he had expected this moment to bring. There was no joy, no sense of accomplishment anywhere in his mind or soul. Instead, as he continued to wait in his palace apartments so near to the King's, Aklier paced the thickly carpeted floor. His troubled thoughts allowed him no peace.

Aklier sank into a chair and covered his face with his hands. He had known from the start that Beahoram was different from Joakal, but his blindness to that difference had been misplaced and self-imposed. In his desire to see that hated law abolished, Aklier knew he had closed his eyes to too much.

He raised his head. On the table next to him, he noticed the goblet of wine he had poured himself hours ago and then forgotten. He reached out and grasped it, raised it to his lips, and drank to ease not the thirst of his body, but of his soul.

Aklier lowered the goblet from his lips, but the thirst remained. Doubts assailed his mind in new and torturous ways. Had Beahoram always been as cruel and hard as he had become lately? Aklier wondered. A month ago, he would had said no, but now he was not so sure.

Aklier remembered how he had first seen Beahoram sixteen months ago during a visit to Port Ceevat in the west. The Elder had been there to supervise the off-loading of cargo due for the King's household, and Beahoram had been working on the docks. Aklier had recognized him immediately and the sight of him had brought to mind the long-forgotten incident of Joakal's birth. Piecing together what must have happened, Aklier had arranged to meet with the young dock worker whose face was the mirror image of the King's.

Or he thought he had arranged it. Now he wondered. Beahoram had been willing enough for the meeting to take place, and he had known the story of his own birth. What was more, though at the time Aklier had been too involved in the conception of this plot, too caught up in the sudden possibility of attaining his long-desired goal to notice it, Beahoram had known about both Aklier's daughter and his wife.

Again his new doubts whispered. Had Beahoram engineered their meeting after all? He had certainly made himself conspicuous throughout the day. If I had not reacted, not sought him out, Aklier wondered, would he have found some other way for us to meet? Were all the words and actions I believed to be commitment to a cause mere manipulation? Why else would he have known about my past? Countless people all across the planet have had to sacrifice their children to the law and to the God. Why else should Beahoram know about my personal tragedy?

Aklier stared at the near empty goblet in his hand. The sip that remained in the crystal cup was deep red—blood red. Soon he would have blood on his hands. No, it was there already. There was the blood of his daughter, whom his hands had carried to the temple and to her death. It did not matter that the law of this world had required it. The blood remained. And there was the blood of his wife, who had died of grief and hopelessness. To those he had now added the blood of betrayal, and of blasphemy against the God.

The thought chilled him. If the God would not forgive him, he would be banned from the afterlife and eternally cut off from everyone he had ever loved. He would never be reunited with his wife and child.

Aklier threw the goblet from him. It crashed into the wall and splintered, and the red wine trickled slowly down the wall.

Aklier lunged to his feet and turned away, but the bitter aftertaste of the wine remained in his mouth. More bitter were the thoughts that continued to tumble through his brain.

I have betrayed my King and my people, Aklier

thought as he took a few stumbling steps. I have betrayed my faith and my God. He stiffened his back for a moment; I would do it again, he told himself. I would do anything to rid this world of that foul law. To keep my promise to Ilayne, I would willingly suffer the eternal blackness.

Then his doubts crept back and his shoulders once again drooped. What, the voice of his uncertainties whispered, what if Beahoram is lying? What if he is only using you to gain the throne, and he has no intention of keeping his promise? What if all you have risked means nothing, after all?

Aklier did not want to listen to these thoughts. It was all too possible. Decades embedded themselves into the lines on Aklier's face. Suddenly he looked like an old, old man.

If only I had trusted in Joakal's goodness, he thought as he again began to pace around the room. I should have gone to Joakal and talked to him. He would have listened. I was his friend.

Aklier turned his face toward the ceiling. He shut his eyes tightly, trying to squeeze away the pain he felt in his soul. Oh, Joakal, why didn't you discuss your plans with me before I met Beahoram instead of later? Why didn't you tell me before you were down in that cell? You said you had help coming, but how could I believe you? I thought you were trying to talk your way free. Then the Federation people showed up and they had the Little Mother with them. I should have trusted you, Joakal. I should have known you wouldn't lie to me.

Aklier paced around the room a few more times. He knew he was trapped by his own choices. He was as much a captive as Joakal.

Aklier stopped. A plan, a sudden breath of hope

blew through his brain and he held himself still, afraid that any movement might make it disappear. His hand went to the deep pocket of his pants and he felt the weight of the extra key Beahoram had given him.

I'll go to the cell, he thought as he swallowed down a gulp of air. I'll go to the cell and release them, then I'll offer myself up to Joakal's mercy. He'll understand. I didn't want him harmed—I never wanted anyone harmed. I just wanted . . .

There was a knock on Aklier's door. His breath caught in his throat and his new purpose fled.

He turned. With heavy, weary footsteps, he crossed to the door and opened it. A liveried servant stood there.

"The procession is forming, Elder," he said respectfully. "Your presence is required."

Aklier nodded. Too late, his thoughts whispered in rhythm with his heartbeat.

Too late. . . .

Beahoram stood in his apartments, his arms outstretched while his dressers added the last refinements to his attire. As for his Vigil, he was dressed in white. But this was no simple tunic and pants of bleached cloth. The clothes he wore today were of brocade woven of shimmering silk, with the predatory bird that was the symbol of his House worked white-upon-white into the weaving. The buttons that ran in a line down the front of the tunic were diamond-encircled rubies. More rubies sparked their particular fire at his cuffs and around the base of the stiff high collar, and his boots were of soft red leather.

One dresser knelt before him, wrapping a crimson sash around Beahoram's waist. Another stood a few feet away, waiting to fasten the long cloak of white

172

brocade, on the back of which the same predatory bird had been stitched in gold and inset with rubies for the beak, eye, and talons, about Beahoram's shoulders. A third stood in the corner, carefully cradling the ancient golden Circlet of Kingship with its single bright ruby that would grace Beahoram's head as he entered the temple. Once these final embellishments had been added to his attire, the dressers stepped back to let Beahoram view himself in the long mirror.

Beahoram could not suppress the smile that came to his lips. He looked majestic. He looked every bit the part he had assumed and was now to become in fact. No one would think to question or doubt him. Everything he had dreamed of, everything he had planned and worked for, was his now.

There was a discreet knock on the door. Beahoram nodded and one of the servants who had dressed him went to answer it. Another servant, young and liveried, stood in the doorway.

"The procession has gathered below, Sire," he said with a deep bow, "and they await your presence."

"Very well," Beahoram answered and he turned to follow his guide into the corridor.

The servant walked before him down the long hallway to the top of the great stairs. Then he stood aside to let Beahoram descend alone.

Beahoram walked slowly. The long train of his cloak fanned out across the stairs above him. The silk of his brocaded clothing and the jewels studded about his person all flashed in the bright lights of the hall. One by one, the Elders turned to him, then dropped to one knee and bowed in deep obeisance.

Beahoram stood on the stairs, gazing in triumph at the sea of bowed heads. In their hands he saw the swords and scepters, robes, stoles, chains, and crowns with which he would soon be invested. His thoughts soared. They leapt and reeled and laughed.

He had won.

Troi could not feel her body, nor could she feel the hands she knew were clasped tightly in her own. The only reality now, and for these last few hours, was the psychic world through which she wandered, searching for passage to the nether regions of Joakal's mind. Somewhere, she knew, waited the key to unlocking the full potential of the young King's powers.

Never had Troi found a task more difficult. Twice she believed she had found the passage she sought, only to have her efforts blocked by shields behind shields behind shields, in configurations she had never before encountered and for which all her Betazoid training offered no key.

The amount of psychic energy this effort was consuming was staggering. Alone, Troi knew she would have been forced to sever contact long ago. It was because of Mother Veronica that this effort could be made at all, and whether they should succeed or fail, Troi's gratitude to the nun remained the same.

To Troi, this was exhausting work, but for Mother Veronica it was like being caught in a nightmare from which there was no way to break free. Each thought, each image and memory that flowed from Joakal's mind through hers, was the personal horror, the years of striving and failing to be free of other people's minds, being condensed, intensified, and twisted. Joakal's thoughts were invading her as she was invading him. It did not matter that he had opened willingly to them or that their lives could well depend upon this action. Mother Veronica found each second of contact a soul-wrenching ordeal. She had to fight herself not to break away, not to retreat to the far corner of the room and beg to be left in peace.

And Troi experienced each second of the battle with her.

Troi would have spared Mother Veronica if it had been possible. It was not; it was only through her link with Mother Veronica that Troi could direct their efforts. She could use her knowledge and training as would any surgeon, but the nun's mind was the scalpel. Her telepathic abilities were the instrument that must be wielded if they were to find the pathway behind Joakal's shields.

Troi felt the nun's abhorrence as once again they attempted to delve deeply into the young King's mind. Images, voices, snatches of conversations, and half-remembered written phrases flashed from Joakal's thoughts, through Mother Veronica's, and into Troi's mind, instantly accepted and ignored. These were surface memories, the type that could be picked up on any finely tuned neuro-scanner, in presence if not in content. Troi rejected them at once, as she had been doing for the hours she and the others had been in contact.

Once more, Troi tried to encounter the neuro-synaptic network that would lead to the telepathic centers of Joakal's brain. Again her passage was blocked and her probing was turned aside like water hitting a wall. Her mind, and Mother Veronica's, crashed back in on themselves.

She broke contact. As physical sensation returned, she felt first the icy coldness of her own body, then the trembling fatigue coming from Mother Veronica. Troi saw how the effort of the last hours had drained the nun. Joakal's face, too, was possessed of a sickly pallor that had little to do with the pale green light cast by the surrounding stone. Only the captain, as he waited for her report, had any energy to give. Troi felt it emanating from him in strong and steady waves, and she held to his strength like a lifeline.

Before she could meet his eyes or answer the unspoken questions she knew would be waiting there, Troi closed her eyes again. She forced herself to breathe deeply a few times as she tried to banish the depression of her failure.

Another failure to report; too many failures.

She did not have to report it. The captain read it in her face and in her silence. He stood to ease the muscles in his back and legs that had cramped from sitting still for so long while he watched and waited, not wanting his movements to disturb their concentration. He strode briskly around the cell.

"I'm sorry, sir," Troi began, but Picard cut her off.

"You tried, Counselor," he said. "You all tried, and that's the most anyone can do. Now we'll have to try something else. But not until you've rested, and each of you has eaten," he added, gesturing toward the forgotten platter of bread and cheese and the pitcher of water Beahoram had brought with his last visit.

Troi managed a wan smile and a nod, relieved by the lack of recriminations in the captain's words and in his thoughts.

"That's better," he said as he squatted down to pick up the platter and pitcher and bring them closer to the others.

As he neared, Troi again felt the wash of his strength. Even here, he was *The Captain,* in command of himself and the situation, despite their captivity. This was the very strength and indomitable will that had allowed him to overcome the assimilation of the

176

Borg and had led not only to his own freedom but to the salvation of the Federation.

Never more than at this moment had Troi been aware of her admiration of the captain, and of her gratitude to Starfleet for assigning her to serve under Jean-Luc Picard.

Chapter Nineteen

WHEN ELANA HAD first fled from the palace and the man she now knew as Beahoram, she had been given a secluded room on the third floor of the Servants' quarters at the back of the temple. She was told it was a room where she would have solitude in which to meditate and recover. Now it had become as much a cell as the one in which she had found Joakal.

The Servants to whom Faellon had entrusted her after he discovered her in his office had not been harsh with her as they marched her through the corridors. But neither had they been lax enough for her to escape. They stood as her guards on the other side of the locked door.

In the hours she had endured this enforced retreat, Elana had pleaded and shouted, raged in anger against the Chief Servant and against the God, beat out her frustration on the door until her hands ached and her throat was sore. Then she had wept with bitter, angry tears.

Now she sat on the edge of the bed and stared at her feet. Her emotions were spent. From time to time a tear still rolled down her cheek and dropped unnoticed onto the hands that lay limp in her lap. Elana could not say from where the tears came; her reservoirs of both anger and sorrow were long empty. The tears merely *were*.

From within the temple, a fanfare blasted, announcing the entry of the royal procession. It sounded once and then again, and still it did not penetrate the fog that wrapped Elana's mind. But the third and final blast reached her. Like a strong wind and the bright, burning sun, it melted the mists that had enshrouded her will and Elana knew she could not give up.

She did not waste time berating herself for her depression. Time was too precious now; if need be, her self-accusations could come later. Elana lifted her head. Her eyes opened wide, and from some hidden reserve energy surged back renewed.

Her eyes searched for anything to which familiarity might have blinded her before. The door she knew was blocked to her, and she tossed that thought away as quickly as it appeared. The only other exit was the window. She had looked through it before and found no avenue of escape, but she now ran to it again.

The cobbled ground of the temple's enclosed outer courtyard lay thirty feet below, taunting her with the promise of unobtainable freedom. Too far to jump, there was no tree near enough to climb down, no tresses or latticework—nothing but cold, hard stone.

Elana could hear the melodic chanting of the Servants gently filtering up from the temple as they sang the opening responses to the coronation rite. She bent her head farther out the window, looking for some way, any way, to get free.

Four feet below her window, a small ledge, no more than six inches wide, stuck out from the stone. Another one was ten feet below that, marking the junction of the stories. They both ran the full length of the wall.

Could she do it? Elana wondered. By jamming her fingers into the cracks between the large stones of which the temple was constructed and keeping her toes on the ledge, could she slowly inch around the building and escape?

Elana drew back from the window. She leaned against the wall of her room and closed her eyes. What she was contemplating was crazy, but there was no other way. Did she have the strength? she wondered. Did she have the courage? Even as she asked herself these questions, she knew she had to try. She would never be able to live with herself if she did not.

Giving herself no more time to think, she bent and took off her shoes. She pulled the hem of her Servant's robe from back to front between her legs and secured it with the sash around her waist. Then she climbed out the window.

She sat for a moment on the sill, listening to the sounds around her. The chanting from the temple, the voices of children in the distance laughing and calling in their play, birds singing, the sounds of the city. The sounds of life.

Elana knew that if she fell, she would not survive. Yet there would be no life left for her if Beahoram was not stopped. Trying to ignore the sudden twisting of her guts, Elana turned and lowered herself over the edge.

Her stomach grated against the stone of the windowsill as she descended. Long heartbeats of panic swelled while her bare feet sought the relative safety of the ledge. Was it farther away than it looked? What if she could not reach it at all? Would she have the strength to pull herself back inside, or would she hang here until her fingers grew numb and she slipped, plummeting down to the courtyard and her death?

These thoughts flashed in an instant through Elana's brain. They were there in the sounds of her own breathing and the feel of the stone beneath her body. She did not want to think them. She tried to concentrate only on her actions, on each precious inch she covered. Finally, her toes touched the small stone outcropping. Her shoulders were still well above the sill, her arms could still reach inside her room. She rested her cheek against the stone surface where she had sat a long moment before and waited until her heart ceased its frantic pounding.

She did not look down as she moved on to the next phase of her escape. She would not look down again until she must. Instead her eyes scanned the large square stones of the temple, tracing the path her hands must follow.

Once, the giant blocks had fit together smoothly. But the passing centuries of sun and wind and storms had worn down the hard edges of the stones, creating cracks and crevasses. Hope replaced desperation. Confidence returned and Elana knew she could do it.

She began to inch away from the window. With her left arm still hooked through the window opening, she reached out with her right hand. Her fingers quested for the first of many holds until she found a place where her fingers slipped easily between the stones. She let go of the window and moved her left hand into position.

Inch by inch, she slid her toes along the ledge. She moved first one hand, then the other, cautiously, trying to find the rhythm of movement that would carry her to her destination. She did not dare make a mistake. Her senses heightened until she could feel each particle of dust beneath her fingertips, each hidden, undried drop of dew. Still she continued on, looking nowhere, thinking of nothing but the next place to put her hands, the next slide of her feet.

Her shoulders began to ache from the position of her outstretched arms. Her palms grew sweaty and her fingertips were raw. The muscles of her calves burned from the unnatural balance she fought to maintain. Perspiration soaked the back of her neck and pooled between her shoulder blades.

Finally, just when she thought she could go no farther, Elana reached the corner of the building. Here the stonemasons of that long forgotten era in which the temple was built had carved images of their faith deep into the cornerstones. These images were so familiar, Elana had forgotten their existence. Now she clung to the carving as a refuge and resting place. The cutwork was deep enough for her to stand and relieve the pressure on her strained, protesting muscles.

For the first time since starting out, Elana dared to look around. She faced another twenty yards of the same precarious travel she had just endured. Then the building turned again. From there, Elana knew it was only a short distance to the roof of the covered walkway between the temple itself and the Servants' quarters. If she could make it to that roof—and she would—then she would be safe. From there, she could find a way to the ground.

The throbbing in her hands and legs subsided and Elana began again.

While Elana traced her spiderlike crawl across the face of the building, Faellon stood at the high altar.

The opening anthems and chanted prayers that accompanied the King's entry into the temple had all been sung. The ancient regalia was in the hands of the coronation officers and they stood in their appointed places ready to bring each article to the altar, to be blessed, anointed, and applied in its prescribed function. The King himself lay prostrate on the crimson silken cloth, waiting to be raised up by consecrated hands and invested to his new status. All was as it should be.

Yet, as Faellon held his hands out over the great golden bowl ready to invoke the God's blessing and power on these proceedings, he felt something stir within his mind that had lain dormant for many years. The sensitivity that had first caused Faellon to enter the life of Service and had raised him to the Office of Chief Servant returned. For so long it had left him, faded through the years of disuse and hidden beneath the routine of daily duties.

Now it whispered a warning to him; something was wrong. There was a darkness here, an undercurrent of tension and fear that was swelling and had nothing to do with the solemnity of holy rite.

In the twenty-two years Faellon had been Chief Servant, he had officiated at many royal ceremonies, including the burial of Joakal's father and mother, and Joakal's own installment as King nine years ago. He remembered well the feelings, the emotions that had come from the young King then.

Now he sensed something entirely different, and his receptivity was frightening him. He no longer wanted to hear or to be the Voice of the God. He wanted only to perform this final duty to his King, then retire to quiet anonymity.

The sensitivity would not leave him. He tried to will

183

it away, but it was like water overflowing a dam—a trickle at first, slowly growing toward a roaring torrent.

The four Servants who stood near the altar to assist Faellon today were waiting for him to continue. Faellon could feel their impatient thoughts. Did they think he hesitated because he had forgotten the words of the rite? Faellon wondered. Could they, too, feel the emanations in the room?

Or, Faellon wondered—hoped—was he being foolish? Was this only the imaginings of a tired old man?

The congregations, spectators, and participants were also waiting for Faellon to proceed. The stillness was broken by the rustle of cloth as here and there people fidgeted in the pews. Faellon gazed down at his hands, then at the golden bowl beneath them. He raised his hands and his eyes toward the heavens, beyond which the God was said to dwell. His voice soared, filled the temple to the furthest corner.

"O most high and exalted God, who are above all things and above all men, we come before thee today to raise to the holy role of *Absolute,* Joakal I'lium, in accordance with the words and laws which thou did impart to our fathers. King he now is, and only by thy power, here given and received, will he be raised up to rule with Wisdom over thy people."

Faellon's hands lowered until they were outstretched to either side. Two of the waiting Servants stepped forward, each carrying a small crystal bowl and ewer of scented water. They poured a few drops of the water over each of Faellon's hands and caught the runoff in the crystal bowls. As the cool water touched his skin, Faellon continued his prayers.

"In the time that was before time," he recited, "clean was the world thou created. Clean was the air; clean was the water; clean were the hearts and the minds of thy people. Return us to that perfect state, that we may not sully thy laws."

Symbolic purification completed, the other Servants turned away. Faellon was now properly prepared to touch the vessels used in the elevation of the King. He picked up the golden bowl and held it high so that the people might gaze upon it. Then he turned to face his assistants. They stepped toward him, each carrying a crystal cruet. The first cruet contained water, the second red wine, the third held oil, and the fourth contained a pungent liquid incense. A small amount of each liquid was poured into the golden bowl and with this mixture, the swords, scepters, crowns, rings, chains of office, and finally the King himself would be anointed.

After the anointing, the two Robes of Service, to the God and to the people, would be draped about the King's shoulders, their weight a reminder of the burden of responsibility he was assuming. His boots would be removed and soft slippers of golden thread would be placed on his feet to symbolize the hallowed path he now must walk. Finally, the Circlet of Kingship would be removed from his head. The Servants of the altar, led by Faellon, would then gather around the King and lay hands upon him, becoming the channel through which the Power of the God would pour to enlighten the King's mind and create him *Absolute,* God-embodied. Once the King had been empowered, the final crown would be placed on his head, the scepter and sword given into his hands, and the coronation itself would be completed. Then remained only the closing prayers and the recession from the temple.

As Faellon received each of the offerings from the cruets into the golden bowl, he looked into the faces of his assistants. He tried again to judge whether they, like him, felt that something was amiss. But they concentrated on their functions and did not meet his eyes.

Faellon turned back around, ready to again elevate the bowl and utter the prayers to hallow its contents. The bowl nearly slipped from his fingers as a wave of adversarial emotions clashed within him. Impatience, arrogance, and impiety warred against regret and sorrow and fear.

Faellon looked out over the congregation. Where were these thoughts coming from? he wondered. They could not be from the King. Faellon had known Joakal all of the young man's life. There was no impiety in him, neither arrogance nor fear. The source must be elsewhere, whether from one or several, out among the crowd.

Why? Faellon wondered. And why should he be plagued today by the return of powers he no longer desired? He would *not* heed them. He set the golden bowl again on the altar and signaled for the four swords of virtue to be brought to him for anointing. His fingers dipped into the dark, viscous liquid.

Before he could again raise his voice in prayer, Elana's words as she was dragged from his office replaced the questions that plagued him and the voices that whispered through his mind. Was her voice the Voice of the God? Was it warning him that he had become too intent upon the outward forms of his faith and that he could no longer recognize the presence of Truth?

But what was the Truth, and whose Truth could be believed?

Faellon looked at the four swords in the hands of the Elders who stood waiting at the base of the altar. The points of the swords were lowered and pointed at him, ready to be anointed and consecrated before being touched to the neck of the prostrate King. The Elders were looking at Faellon with unrelenting trust.

Here was a Truth that had been proved over the generations. Here also was Faith made tangible. Faellon's uncertainties would wait until this day, and his duties, were done. In that instant his mind was made up. Tomorrow was the day he would retire. He had dreamed of this decision, toyed with it almost, but now he knew for certain. He would go home to the hills of the North-march and contemplate the esoterica of belief. Here, finally, was his one last duty and Service.

Faellon motioned for the first sword to be brought forward.

Chapter Twenty

TROI WAS NOT AWARE that she had dozed until the captain's voice pierced the silent blackness in which she was floating. When she opened her eyes, he was squatting next to her and speaking softly. She had to blink a few times to bring him into focus, for her eyes did not want to work, nor did her brain.

"I'm sorry, Counselor," Picard was saying. "I wish I could let you rest, but I need your help."

The captain's words cleared the last vestiges of sleep from Troi's mind. Apart from the hours that the drug had controlled her slumber, she had had very little rest. That coupled with the long, arduous hours she had spent working with Joakal and Mother Veronica made Troi feel as if she was calling on reserves of energy that no longer existed. She sat upright and ran a hand across her eyes to finish clearing them and tried to put her encroaching fatigue on hold one more time.

"What is it?" she asked. "What's happened?"

"Nothing," the captain answered. "That's the problem. I think we have to accept the fact that Elana failed in her attempt to contact the ship."

Troi nodded. "What do you think we should do?"

"I'm not sure, Counselor. I only know that Beahoram will return, just as he said he would, and I for one refuse to just sit here and wait."

Troi could not remain unaffected by the force of the captain's determination. She felt his confidence and a small, weary smile flitted across her lips.

"You have a plan," she said.

Picard snorted. "Well, I don't think it's good enough to qualify as a plan," he said. "But given the circumstances, any action is better than none."

Troi nodded. In a sudden flash of understanding, she realized the action the captain was about to suggest was going to include physical force. The realization brought a wave of anxiety, for although Troi was an officer and Starfleet trained, the physical arts of defense had never been subjects at which she had excelled. Still, she would do what she must.

The captain began outlining his plan. "What I am about to propose," he said, "will take exact timing. If it does not succeed on the first attempt, it will not succeed at all."

"Understood," Troi said. Her apprehension notched a bit higher.

"Beahoram will return," Picard said again, "but I don't believe he will want any witnesses for what he proposes to do. That's our one chance. When he arrives, you and the others must be sitting in plain sight—just talking, but quietly, as if I'm sleeping nearby. We'll take the blanket and roll it to look as much like a sleeping body as possible. It won't be exact, so you'll have to shield it somewhat with your bodies. In the meantime, I'll wait beside the door. When Beahoram enters, Joakal will stand and face Beahoram, which will draw his attention. I'll grab him from behind. The door opens inward and that will afford us some cover. Without that, we would have no chance of success. Even so we'll have to hope that Beahoram will be too intent on Joakal to notice much else."

Troi listened to the captain, seeing his plan in her mind's eye. He was right; if the timing was exact, it could work. She knew that Mother Veronica would be no help with this. Neither would Joakal. After his long captivity, his physical strength could not be counted upon. If it looked as if Beahoram was going to get away, Troi knew she would have to be ready to jump in and aid the captain.

"Any suggestions, Counselor?" the captain asked, pulling her thoughts away from their unpleasant path.

"About your plan? No, sir. But—" Troi looked over at Mother Veronica. The nun was sleeping, curled into a fetal position. Would she be willing to link with Troi one more time?

"There is one thing I'd like to try first, Captain," Troi said.

"Yes, Counselor?"

"Are you aware of the—relationship—Will Riker and I once shared?" she asked.

Picard cleared his throat. "I believe most of us realize that you and Commander Riker were once . . . close."

"Among my people, the kind of relationship Will and I shared allows them to read one another, to share their thoughts and emotions, mind to mind, regardless of race or telepathic abilities. In many ways, Will and I still share that bond. I'd like to use it to try and reach him now."

"Do you think it's possible?"

"I don't know, sir, but if Mother Veronica is willing to help me once more, we can try."

"Very well, Counselor. Make it so."

Troi nodded and crawled over to the nun's side. Mother Veronica was sleeping soundly. The evidence of the strain she had been under was plainly shown by the dark smudges beneath her eyes and the tight lines that ran from her nose to her mouth. As Troi watched, a frown marred the nun's features, creating deep furrows between her brows as if she struggled with some personal demon. Troi hated to wake her, but she put her hand on Mother Veronica's shoulder and shook gently, speaking the nun's name.

Mother Veronica moaned softly. Again Troi spoke the nun's name. This time Mother Veronica opened her eyes. She turned her head slightly to look at the counselor, and Troi was grieved to see the look of fear that flashed through Mother Veronica's eyes when she saw who was bending over her. Troi knew that the nun thought she was about to be asked again to delve into the young King's mind. Troi felt the hurt, the horror, then finally, her resolution.

"No," Troi quickly assured her. "We're not going to try that again."

Troi felt the nun's answering wave of relief. Mother Veronica uncurled and turned more fully toward Troi, wearily pushing herself to a sitting position. Too exhausted to be truly curious, she merely waited to hear what the counselor had to say.

"The captain has a plan for when Beahoram returns," Troi told her. "It's a good plan and it might be our only chance of escape. It includes overpowering Beahoram by force, and before then there is one thing I'd like to try. I need your help to do it."

Mother Veronica bowed her head. Troi felt her weariness like a stab wound in her own conscience. This was not the reason she had worked so hard with Mother Veronica, trying to teach her how to shield her mind.

"Do you remember the first day we began our lessons?" Troi asked. "I spoke to you then about some of the positive uses for telepathic communication, and I mentioned the possibility of thought crossing distances to bring help. That is what I would like to try now. There is someone on the ship, someone with whom I was once very close. I believe, I hope, he will hear us."

Mother Veronica looked away. Troi reached out and laid a hand gently on her arm.

"I know this is hard for you," Troi said. "I do understand. If I could think of a way to spare you, I would. But I don't believe I can do this alone."

Mother Veronica did not move. Troi could feel the internal war the nun was waging, the struggle between need and inclination, of faith and friendship over fear. Troi knew this was a personal battlefield and Mother Veronica's decision could only be reached alone.

"Often in my life," the nun said at last, "I have prayed for the strength to just make it through one more day—for one day of peace, one day without the voice of other people's thoughts in my mind. Throughout the years, God has chosen not to grant this prayer." She turned around to look at Troi. "And so it continues. What must I do?"

Troi released the breath she had been holding. She gave the nun a small smile that she hoped was reassuring and squeezed her arm in gratitude.

"Just open your mind to me," she said. "Our link will not be much different than the one we used on the

Enterprise for our lessons. Our minds together will send the message. Are you ready?"

Mother Veronica crossed herself, then she held out her hands. Troi took them in her own. She closed her eyes and reached for the bond that would pair her mind with the nun's. It formed easily.

Whether you realize it or not, she told Mother Veronica, *your abilities have grown. They're becoming stronger and more refined. You could accomplish a great deal with them, if you chose.*

The nun sent no answering thought and Troi did not press her. Instead she concentrated on Will Riker, calling up the image of him, the feel of his mind touching hers as it had in the sweet, golden time of their union.

Imzadi, Troi sent as the image, and the well-remembered sensation of their minds entwined, sharpened. *Imzadi, help me. Come to me. I need you. Imzadi. . . .*

At that moment, Elana was nearing the completion of her own escape, or so she hoped. She had made it around the outside of the Servants' quarters onto the covered walkway connecting the Servants' quarters with the temple itself, and finally onto the temple roof. From there, the going had become easier and she had quickly covered the distance to the front of the building. Now she had only to find a way to the ground without being seen and reported, and she would be free.

She crouched on the corner of the roof that covered the narthex. In front of her sloped the porch roof that covered and was held up by the Guardians, the four carved pillars at the top of the temple steps. If she could make it to one of them, she could slide-climb down.

There were people crossing in the city square in front of the temple. Soon a crowd would gather to watch the coronation recession and cheer the new *Absolute*. Elana knew it was now or never.

She started forward, staying as low to the roof as she could and trying not to attract attention. She kept her eyes on the passing people as much as she dared, but the roof tiles were slippery with accumulations of moss. Time and again she was forced to watch only her feet and hands and pray that no one would see her.

She reached the end of the roof. She lay down flat and prayed now that her luck would hold and her strength remain just a little while longer. Prayed that the God would not abandon her yet.

It seemed the God heard her, for the people crossing the city square went on their way. Suddenly the square was empty. Elana raised herself on her hands and knees. Taking a deep breath, she turned and swung her legs over the edge, scrambling through the air until they finally made contact with stone. She immediately wrapped her legs around the pillar. Using them to brace herself, she began to descend.

Here, as with the carvings at the corners of the Servants' quarters, the symbols on the stone had been deeply engraved. Her fingers found easy purchase, but these same carvings rubbed off the soft skin of her inner legs until the final feet of Elana's descent were agony. She knew she was leaving traces of her blood on the stone, but she dared not let it stop her.

The pain grew. It seared and burned until, finally, she could stand no more. Her legs fell from the pillar and she dropped the final few feet to the temple steps. A new pain jarred through her left ankle. Elana could not move. Her breath caught in her throat.

No, her mind screamed. If she was caught now, then it was all for nothing. She forced herself to her feet and started to hobble down the stairs. With each step, new fire shot up her leg, combined with the other aches the long travail had created in her body, and caused her to cry out. Tears sprang to her eyes and fell down her face. She bit her lip, forcing herself to breathe through her torment and to keep going. She had to reach the palace. Somehow, somewhere, she had to find someone to help her.

Will Riker sat at the desk in the captain's ready room, staring at the display screen of the computer. Trying to fill the time and keep his mind occupied, he had called up the reports of all contacts and treaties with the planet below them, all Capulon IV's recent history. But the pages were passing by unread, and had been for several minutes.

Finally Riker reached out and switched off the screen. He could not concentrate. He had waited hours for the captain to report in. He had reminded himself of everything from Picard's personal training and abilities to Starfleet's Prime Directive. But he could not shake the feeling that something was wrong, and his patience, never his strongest attribute, was at an end.

Riker pushed the chair back from the desk and stood, looking out the long, narrow viewport. From here only the edge of the planet could be seen. Surrounded by the infinity of space, it was a sight to stir the heart of any poet and the soul of any Starfleet officer. Will Riker was usually no exception. From the day of his first training cruise as a new cadet, he had known his home, his greatest joy, was among the stars.

Today even their beauty failed to enrapture him. With a sigh, he turned away and headed for the door that would take him again onto the bridge.

The bridge—the command chair—more waiting

and worrying. Cluck-cluck, his mind said; shut up, he told it.

The doors opened with their near-silent hiss. Will Riker stepped through and as he did, his eyes met those of his Chief of Security. The Klingon said no words, but Riker saw his own doubts about the safety of the Away Team mirrored on the warrior's face. Riker's intentions crystallized.

"Lieutenant Worf," he said as he strode across the open floor of the bridge. "Open a channel to the palace. It's time we got some answers."

"Aye, sir," the Klingon said eagerly, his approval spoken by the posture of his body and the glint in his eyes.

Riker sat down, preparing himself for a possible confrontation with whichever palace official answered the ship's hail. He would not sign off this time until he got what he wanted.

The hairs on the back of his neck prickled. Riker ran a hand across them, but the sensation did not go away. It intensified. It was as if someone had just poured itching powder between his shoulder blades.

He twitched and shifted in his chair. Nothing eased it. He stood and began to pace, aware that the other officers on the bridge had turned to look at him. He did not care; the discomfort continued to grow. He was about to call Doctor Crusher when he realized what he was feeling was not physical.

Deanna? he wondered. He tried to remember what she had taught him about opening his mind to her touch. It had once been so easy.

Imzadi? he thought, standing still and silent on the bridge. He closed his eyes and searched for her, not caring what the other officers on the bridge saw or thought. If Deanna needed him, all that mattered was that he hear her. Imzadi? he thought again, calling this time, and he picked up the faint but unmistakable essence of her mind reaching for his.

I'm coming, Deanna, he thought to her, not knowing if she could hear him. *Hold on, I'm coming.*

He turned to Lieutenant Worf. "Discontinue hail," he said, "and come with me. Have a security team meet us, with phasers, in Transporter Room Three. Whether they like it or not, we're beaming down to that planet. Something's going on and I intend to find out exactly what it is. Mr. Data," Riker said over his shoulder as he began to stride up the ramp toward the turbolift, "you have the conn."

Will Riker did not bother to watch the android leave his seat at Ops and take the command chair. Everything on the *Enterprise* would run efficiently. What Riker did see was the gleam of combat readiness in Worf's eyes as the Klingon met him at the top of the ramp. Riker knew the same light could be seen in his own.

Hold on, Deanna. We're coming.

Chapter Twenty-one

USING THE COORDINATES given to the first Away Team, Riker, Worf, and the six-man security team from the *Enterprise* beamed down into one of the reception halls of the palace. This time there was no delegation of Elders awaiting them. The room was empty, and the late afternoon sun that slanted through the windows created long pools of light and shadow.

Will Riker took this all in at a glance, then he looked over his shoulder to check the rest of his personnel. The security team stood at ready, phasers in their hands, and Lieutenant Worf held both his phaser and a tricorder. Riker waited while Worf moved the tricorder from side to side, adjusting its sensitivity while he tried to pick up the captain's communicator signal through the layers of thick stone that surrounded them. All the while, the subliminal call that had driven Riker here was growing more insistent.

Hold on, Deanna, he thought, hoping that he remembered enough of what she had taught him, hoping she would know he was on his way.

"Got it, Commander," Worf finally announced. With a quick nod, Riker led the way to the great double doors across the room and cautiously, not knowing what waited on the other side, he eased one of them open. Riker could hear voices in the distance, and the sound of running feet, but this corridor was empty. He slipped through the open door. Quickly and quietly, the others followed. Once all eight of them stood in the hall, Riker gestured for the Klingon and his tricorder to lead the way.

Worf was ready. He led them down the labyrinth of corridors, turning right or left or right again with unwavering certainty. The noises of the palace inhabitants grew louder: voices shouting orders, pans clanging, dishes rattling. Once a door opened and as Riker ran past, he saw a liveried servant, eyes wide with surprise, framed in the doorway. There was no time to stop or explain and Riker only hoped they could find the captain before the servant called the guards.

They turned another corner and found a staircase. The sounds of the kitchen crew preparing for the coronation banquet were louder here. *That explains the empty hallways,* Riker thought as he and the others began to climb the stairs.

He took the steps two at a time, wishing there was some way to go faster. Second floor; another corridor. Riker's heartbeat quickened. The servant they had passed could have called the guards by now. This was taking too long.

Worf stopped. "In here," he growled, motioning to two doors. The security team split up, four to a room, one team led by Worf and the other by Riker. Riker met the Klingon's eyes. No words were needed. Simultaneously, they opened the doors.

And found the rooms empty. Quickly they fanned out and searched, opening doors to closets, bedrooms, and baths. The furniture was neat and in place, no sign of a struggle—or of the room's inhabitants. Riker saw Deanna's uniform lying on the floor near a chair, and he picked it up. Her communicator was still attached.

"There's nothing here," he said, heading back to the corridor. The security team fell in behind him.

Worf met him out in the hallway. The Klingon held the captain's uniform just as Riker held Deanna's. Riker tapped his insignia, activating the comm link with the ship.

"Riker to *Enterprise*," he said.

"Enterprise, Data here," came the answer.

"We've found the captain's uniform, but there's no sign of the captain or the others. Have another security team standing by for my signal. I don't care if we have to take this place apart stone by stone, I'm going to find our people."

"Very well, Commander. A security team will be ready."

"Riker out." He turned to Worf. "Recommendations, Lieutenant?"

"The captain and Counselor Troi would *not* leave their rooms without their uniforms. They must have been carried off during the night. We should return to the lower floors and find a palace servant to act as guide. Wherever the captain and Counselor Troi are being held, it will not be in a place as easily accessible as this."

"Agreed," Riker said with a nod. "Let's go."

Again the *Enterprise* personnel sped down the corridor, retracing their steps. A part of Riker listened for the sound of pursuing footsteps or a call for them to stop, but all remained calm and silent. He knew from his recent reading about this planet that the palace had guards—why hadn't the alarm been raised?

They reached the stairway and began to descend, passing the floor on which they had entered and continuing toward the sounds of the kitchen below. The stairwell turned; there was someone crouching in the shadows. Riker held up his hand and the others behind him stopped, all phasers trained on the half-hidden figure.

The head slowly turned. Before Riker could make out any other details, he saw the fear in—her—eyes. Disheveled hair framed a pale and dirt-streaked face. She stood and at a glance, Riker took in the torn green robe, the scrapes and bruises, the look of exhaustion and the signs of a long and arduous ordeal.

"Who are you?" she whispered.

"Commander William T. Riker, First Officer of the *Enterprise*," he answered. The woman leaned back against the wall, her hand on her chest, and looked for a moment as if she might faint.

"The God has heard me," she said. Then she looked Riker in the face again, all trace of fear gone from her eyes. "I know where your people are. Help me."

With that, she started to crumble. Riker rushed to her side and caught her before she could hit the ground. As he lifted her, he noticed her torn and bloody hands, the swollen left ankle, and how very tiny she was—smaller even than Deanna.

Deanna, he thought/sent with all his might. *I'm almost there.*

"Where?" he asked.

"Down the stairs," the woman said. "But don't turn into the kitchen. We have to go through the wine cellar and the pantries. There is a hidden door in the room where the tapestries are stored for repair. That leads to a subbasement and the cell where your people are."

"Why are you doing this?" Riker asked.

"Because Joakal is with them," the woman whispered fiercely. Her eyes blazed with a spirit Riker knew he would not care to have turned against him.

"I'll explain more as we go," she assured him, "but we must hurry. And be careful—there are traitors in the palace and not everyone wishes to see the true King freed."

Riker turned and looked over his shoulder at Worf, grinning at the tone of command in the woman's voice. "You heard her, Lieutenant," he said. "Let's go."

They moved cautiously, one by one slipping past the kitchen door. Riker thought they were going to make it by unseen until, just as the last man was sliding past the opening, dishes crashed to the floor. Conversation in the kitchen stopped. A moment later a shout went up. That's it, Riker thought.

"We'll hold them here while you find the captain," Worf told him. "It is a defensible position."

Riker nodded. "Call the *Enterprise* if you need help," he ordered. Trusting the Klingon to guard his back, Riker looked down at the woman in his arms.

"Which way?" he asked. She pointed and he began to run. The sound of occasional phaser blasts provided the music of retreat.

True to her word, as Riker carried her through the palace cellars along a route as complicated and maze-like as the corridors upstairs, the woman filled him in on her identity and her knowledge of the Away Team's capture. She also told him of her own escape from the temple. That explained her condition. Riker was amazed at her strength and courage. Her words also explained why no guards had been called; the servant Riker had passed must have been one of the accomplices.

They finally reached the tapestry room and found the hidden door. It was locked.

"I'll have to put you down for a moment," Riker told Elana. "Can you stand?"

She nodded and gritted her teeth against the pain Riker knew the movement would cause her. He set her down gently where she could lean against the wall, and pulled out his phaser. It took only a short blast to release the lock. Then he picked Elana up again.

They went down yet another set of stairs, down to the cold subbasement of the palace. There was no mistaking the purpose of this area. Riker shivered, sick at the thought of Deanna, of anyone, being held prisoner in such a place.

"Down there," Elana told him. "The sixth cell on the right."

"Captain," Riker called out as he walked forward. "Deanna." For a heart-stopping moment, there was no answer. Then Riker heard the captain's voice.

"Over here, Number One."

Riker reached the cell door. Again he put Elana down. With her back against the wall, she slid to the floor on the far side of the corridor.

"Stand back," Riker told the prisoners as he again drew his phaser and fired. This lock held out longer than the one upstairs, and tiny sparks flew from it as the metal melted under the heat of the phaser beam. Finally, the door snapped open. Riker put his hand through the bars of the window and pushed until the door swung wide. Captivity was at an end.

Before Riker could step into the cell, a young man pushed past him and ran to Elana. He pulled her into his arms. Riker could hear their happy murmurings behind him as he stepped into the cell where Picard, Troi, and Mother Veronica waited.

They stood in a group looking cold and tired. Riker was relieved to see there was nothing more wrong with them, no signs of injuries or abuse. He glanced at Mother Veronica and nodded to the captain, but his eyes, and his heart, were fastened on Troi. Her smile, as she met his eyes with her own, assured Riker that she was all right.

Riker held out her uniform. "Imzadi," he said softly, for her ears alone, as she lifted the uniform from his hand. Then he turned to the captain.

"I'm afraid I don't have your uniform, sir," he said. "It's with Lieutenant Worf."

"Where is the lieutenant?"

"Guarding our avenue of escape."

"Very good," Picard said. "Let's step out while the counselor changes and you meet the King. Our work here is far from finished."

The captain put his hand on Riker's upper arm in an affectionate gesture, but there was no circumventing the friendly pressure that turned Riker toward the door. Still, he could not resist one glance over his shoulder, one more look at Deanna's smile. Then he was out of the cell and the captain pulled the door partway closed to afford the counselor the extra privacy.

"Your Majesty," Picard said to the young man now sitting beside Elana with his arm around her shoulders. "May I present my First Officer, Commander William Riker. Will—this is His Royal Majesty, Joakal I'lium, King of Capulon IV."

"Your Majesty," Riker acknowledged with a bow. "Elana has told me everything. I have a security team, headed by Lieutenant Worf," he added to the captain, "stationed up by the kitchens and another standing by on the *Enterprise*."

"Then as soon as the counselor is ready," Picard began.

"I'm ready now," Troi said, stepping out of the cell. She was dressed in her familiar one-piece uniform, with her nightgown draped across her shoulders. Although her feet were bare, she looked much more comfortable. Mother Veronica came out of the cell with her and stayed close by the counselor's side. Riker found himself wondering who was lending whom support.

Picard gave a curt nod, once more in command. "Counselor," he said, "I want you and Mother Veronica, as well as the King and Elana, to stay well back until we are out of danger. Is that understood?"

"Yes, sir."

"Then, Commander," Picard said, turning back to Riker. "If you're ready—"

Riker was prepared to carry Elana for the first part of their return to the upper levels. But when he stepped toward her, Joakal held up a hand to forestall him.

"Thank you, Commander Riker," he said, "but I'll take care of Elana."

"As you wish, Your Majesty." He waited until Joakal had helped Elana to her feet and lifted her. Then with one more glance at the captain, Riker led the way back up the staircase and through the twists and turns of the cellar, until they approached the kitchens. All was quiet.

"Lieutenant Worf," Riker called.

"Here, sir," the Klingon's voice boomed through the stillness.

They turned the final corner. Up ahead they saw Worf and his men sitting casually by the door. There was no sight of servants or guards, though the body of one man lay sprawled, unconscious, on the floor beyond them. Worf was grinning a warrior's grin.

"Report, Lieutenant," the captain ordered.

"When the palace staff tried to follow Commander Riker, we fired a few warning shots. Realizing they were not armed, we fired well above their heads. That one," Worf indicated the body on the floor, "would not be warned away. He is only stunned. Once he went down, the others backed away and we have not seen them since."

"Very good, Lieutenant," Picard said.

Worf then seemed to notice that the captain was in his sleeping attire. Looking slightly embarrassed for the captain's sake, the Klingon picked up the captain's uniform and held it out to him. Picard quickly pulled it on over what he was wearing.

Behind him, Joakal eased Elana out of his arms. Once she was safely seated, he walked up to Picard's side. "Captain," he said, "let me talk to the people out there. They are my subjects and my responsibility. They'll listen to me."

Picard hesitated, weighing the possibilities of violence and their chances of success. "All right," he said at last. "But please, Your Majesty, do not put yourself in plain sight until we are certain of their support. If they choose not to believe you and one of them is armed—"

"They'll believe me, Captain," Joakal said before Picard had finished. "Trust me."

Joakal crept forward until he was beside the Klingon. Worf's body tensed, ready to pull the King to safety if needed.

"Yesta?" Joakal called out. "Are you there? Can you hear me?"

"I am *Captain* Yesta," a deep voice answered.

"Who is it that calls me? Why have you defied the authority of the palace guards?"

"Yesta," Joakal called. "I am glad it is you, my friend. Listen to my voice. You know who I am. You've known me since I was a child and you served my father. Who am I, Yesta?"

"You have a voice like that of the King's. But you are a liar, for the King is in the temple at his coronation."

"No, Yesta," Joakal said. He stood. Worf put a hand to his arm, to pull him to safety, but Joakal shook it off. He stood regal and proud, looking like a King despite his haggard, unkept appearance.

"The one who has usurped my place in the temple is a liar," Joakal continued as he began to walk slowly forward. "Come out and meet me, Yesta. Look at me. Talk to me. Then come with me to the temple where I will prove I am who I claim to be."

A burly man with dark, gray-streaked hair stepped out from the kitchen. He was dressed in a long vest of thick brown leather over loose-fitting pants and a tunic of plain black cloth. On the right of the vest was stitched an insignia, and around his neck was a heavy chain, a badge of office. The only weapon he carried was a long, metal-wrapped club.

He and Joakal spoke quietly, a few brief sentences, then the captain of the palace guards dropped on one knee, offering his club two-handed to the King. Joakal laid his hand on the weapon in token acceptance, then he turned and gestured for the *Enterprise* personnel to join him.

"Yesta and his guards will accompany us to the temple," the King told the others. "But we must hurry now, before the coronation is completed."

Joakal and Captain Picard, side by side, led the way out of the palace. The others followed in a close group behind them, Capulonii and Federation intermingling as they ran.

Elana was carried in the arms of one of the *Enterprise* security men. Troi tried to stay close to her and to Mother Veronica, concerned by the fatigue she sensed beginning to descend on both these women. She could hold her own exhaustion at bay for a while longer. But when this was over, she promised herself, she was going to bathe, she was going to eat, and then she was going to sleep long hours where she was warm and safe.

They ran from the palace, leaving behind a bewildered kitchen staff. They ran down city streets and across the city square, ignoring the startled looks on the faces of the people they passed. They reached the temple and dashed up the long flight of stone stairs.

From inside they could hear the swell of music and the sound of chanting. Joakal paused at the top of the stairs and touched one of the Guardian pillars. He looked back over his shoulders and met the eyes of Elana. Troi felt the wave of love he sent her. Then he stepped forward, put his hands on the temple doors, and pushed. They flew open. The others stayed a few paces behind to let Joakal alone, as was his right, lead their entrance into the temple.

The young King marched forcefully across the narthex. Head held high, he entered the nave and strode into the long center aisle.

"Stop," he cried out in a loud, commanding voice. "In the name of the God who is above all, the God whose name is Justice and Truth, stop this unlawful rite."

Throughout the temple, voices faltered, heads turned and cries of alarm went up. At the altar, Faellon, who had been reaching to lift the Circlet of Kingship from Beahoram's head, ready to begin the most solemn part of the ceremony, the laying on of hands, took a step backward. He would have stumbled, had not one of the other Servants reached out to steady him.

Joakal continued down the long aisle until he reached the base of the altar. Seated on the draped and cushioned chair that had been placed on the third step, Beahoram had not moved.

Behind him Faellon looked up and met Joakal's eyes. Joakal uttered no word. His presence alone accused and convicted Faellon.

The Chief Servant slowly shook his head. His face paled, and he tore his eyes away from the sight of the identical features on the two younger men. Faellon looked out at the group of palace guards and Federation people that had mingled and filled the center of the nave. He caught sight of Elana in the arms of the uniformed security officer. Faellon saw the dirt and blood on her hands, her scraped cheeks and disheveled hair, the tears in her robe. Shame washed through him and Faellon buried his face in his hands.

Beahoram stood. "Who are you?" he demanded, his eyes burning with rage. "What is the meaning of this?" he roared.

Joakal finally turned his gaze from Faellon's face to Beahoram's. "The meaning, Brother," he said, mimicking Beahoram's own form of address, "is that your days of deception are at an end."

Beahoram turned to the Elders, the officers of the coronation who held the great swords in their hands. "Seize them," he shouted.

They did not move. Their eyes, like those of Faellon before, shifted back and forth between the identical faces. A little smile lifted the corners of Joakal's mouth. Beahoram saw it. His rage swelled and his face twisted into a snarl.

"Seize them," he shouted again. "I, your King, command you."

Beahoram took a step toward Joakal. His hands were raised and ready to close around his brother's throat, eager to squeeze the life from him. Joakal did not move. His eyes did not waver from Beahoram's face. The small smile that was his only weapon did not slip as Beahoram came closer still.

The sight finally shocked Tygar, the Head of the Council of Elders, into action. He stepped from his place among the officers of the coronation. In his hand he held the great Sword of Wisdom, and he brought it down between the two brothers.

"In accordance with our laws," he declared, "I proclaim this coronation at an end. The Council will convene in one hour in the Great Chamber. There we will discover the truth of who is King."

Beahoram tensed, ready to spring across the sword and still attack his brother, but Tygar saw him. He brought the sword up again. The tip of it pointed toward Beahoram's throat.

Joakal looked across the length of deadly metal. He saw the hatred that still blazed in his brother's eyes. It had no power over him now.

Slowly, the small smile that had not faded from his features turned cold and hard and broadened into a grin.

Chapter Twenty-two

TYGAR LOOKED UP at Faellon, but the Chief Servant had not moved. He still stood with his face buried in his hands, too stunned and shaken to command even his fellow Servants. Tygar took charge.

"Gibreh, Kithia, Leboath," he called to the three other Elders who carried the swords. Immediately, they stepped to his side and, at a motion, brought their swords to ready while they surrounded Joakal and Beahoram.

Tygar then walked over to the other Elders and ordered the rest of the regalia placed upon the altar. There it would remain under the guard of Yesta and his men until the coronation was resumed. Surprise had kept the Elders motionless, but now they hurried to comply. Each knew the law as well as Tygar and each was aware of what now must be done.

Even Faellon had finally been spurred into action. While the Elders carried the ancient instruments of crowning to the altar, the Chief Servant spoke quickly and quietly to his assistants. Tygar turned around to face the curious congregation.

"By the laws of our fathers," he announced, "this coronation is at an end. It will not resume until the Truth is found in accordance with Ways of the God. You are free to leave this temple, or to remain, but you may not interfere with the completion of the Council's duty. No one is to try to speak with or otherwise contact any participant, Elder, Servant, or Supplicant, until the court of Justice is at an end. To do so is a violation of the statutes of our world and will be punished."

Tygar turned away, ignoring the murmurs that spread among the people. He saw that Faellon and the other Servants, as well as the Elders, had surrounded the two who claimed to be the King. He nodded to them, then motioned to Yesta. The captain of the Palace Guards led his men to that altar and they took their places protecting the regalia. Again, Tygar nodded.

"To the palace," he said. The officials surrounding the brothers closed ranks. Tygar turned on his heel and led the way out of the temple.

Once they had gone, the congregation found its voice. People stood; the gentle murmurs became questions and speculations spoken back and forth across the long room. As the general din increased, Picard took advantage of the noise and motioned his people to him.

"Number One," he said to Riker. "I want you, Lieutenant Worf, and the security team to return to the ship. But stand by, ready to return if I call."

"What about you and Deanna?"

"I believe Counselor Troi and I should stay here."

"And Mother Veronica?"

Picard turned toward the nun. She was standing near the counselor, her eyes downcast and again clutching the cross that hung about her neck. She slowly raised her head, looking first at the captain, then at Troi.

"Here or there," she said dully. "It makes no difference."

"Good," Picard replied. "We may need you." Then he walked over to Elana, still carried by one of the security men.

"Elana," he said. "I cannot begin to state my gratitude, or my admiration. If you are willing to go back to our ship with Commander Riker, our medical staff will be able to effect a cure to your injuries. I promise you'll be back in time for the hearing."

"Thank you, Captain," Elana said with a weary smile. "I accept."

Picard tapped the insignia on his uniform, delighted to hear its small chirp of activation. "Picard to transporter room," he said.

"Transporter room, Tuttle here."

"Chief Tuttle, Commander Riker and his Away Team are returning to the ship, and they are bringing an injured guest. Please have Doctor Crusher standing by."

"Aye, aye, Captain."

"Thank you, Chief. Picard out."

Riker and the security force stepped off a little way from the others. "I'll stay in better contact this time, Number One," Picard told him.

Riker grinned. "Please see that you do, Captain," he said and he touched his communicator. "We're ready, Chief. Nine to beam up."

There was the familiar hum, the rain of silvered light, and then they were gone. Picard turned to Counselor Troi.

213

"Well," he said. "I think we should go back to our rooms at the palace. I don't know about you, but I'm hungry and thirsty and my feet are cold."

Troi smiled. "Agreed, Captain."

An hour later, the Council convened in the same chamber where Picard, Troi, and Mother Veronica had had their audience with the King. They stood now at the same great doors, ready to enter, but Tygar blocked their way.

"You are not of this world," the Head of the Council was saying. "The outcome of this judgment is of no concern to you."

Picard heard the transporter hum behind him, but he did not turn to look. He knew it would be Elana returning. He kept his attention on Tygar.

"On the contrary," he told the Elder. "The outcome is of great concern to me and to the Federation. We came here, at the King's and the Council's invitation, to sign a treaty. We were drugged, kidnapped, imprisoned by an imposter—"

"That has not been proved, Captain."

"Do you refuse to believe the evidence of your own eyes?"

"What I *believe* is of no importance," Tygar said. "We have *laws,* Captain. The judgment of this Council goes far beyond the question of identity, or even actions taken against you and your companions. One of these twins should not be alive, but now that he is here we must learn who is best fit to rule. This question must be settled according to *Law.*"

"If you had been in that cell with us—"

"Is there a problem, Captain?" Elana asked as she walked up to Picard's side.

"Lady Elana," Tygar said with a slight inclination of his head, "I was just informing the captain that these

214

proceedings are closed to him. He is not of our world."

Elana's face took on a look of deceptive passivity. Picard was no telepath, but even he could feel her outrage. When she spoke, her voice was steely quiet.

"*I* am of this world, Tygar."

"Yes, Lady, but—"

"These people are with me. Would you deny *me* entry, too?"

"No, Lady. Of course not, but—"

Tygar's voice faltered at the unwavering stare Elana fixed upon him. Picard admired the aura of command that surrounded the small woman. She was a strong ally and would be a formidable foe. Beahoram, he thought, had better be careful.

Tygar lowered his eyes and stood to one side, defeated. Elana lifted her chin, turned to the captain, and smiled.

"Will you give me your arm, Captain," she said sweetly. "The medical facilities of your ship are barely short of miraculous and I am well healed, but I still feel a little weak."

Weak, indeed, Picard thought wryly as he held out his arm. "I am honored, Elana," he said aloud.

Followed by Troi and Mother Veronica, Picard and Elana stepped past Tygar and into the Great Chamber. Again, the size of the room was overwhelming. It dwarfed the large array of tables that had been arranged in a semicircle in the center of the floor, and at which the Elders and thirty Servants sat as tribunal. Behind the tables, the throne sat empty upon its raised dais, waiting for its rightful occupant to be proclaimed.

Tygar walked over and took his place next to Faellon at the head of the tables. It was obvious they were to be joint arbitrators, sentinels to see that the laws of the God and of the people were justly observed. Joakal and Beahoram had been seated on plain wooden chairs in the center of the semicircle's opening. They were dressed in identical clothing, and now that Joakal had bathed and his hair and beard had been trimmed, the likeness between them was even more arresting.

When everyone was in place, Faellon stood and raised his hands. "The God declared unto our fathers," he began, *"My Truth shall be found in the minds of My people and My Laws shall govern their hearts.* It is thy Truth, O God, we seek. Let no falsehood remain hidden from Your light. Reveal Your Wisdom to us so that we may guard your laws and your people."

Faellon sat back down and folded his hands. He focused his eyes on his interlaced fingers, as though he could not bring himself to look around the room or bear the sight of the identical twins before him.

Without standing, Tygar took charge of the tribunal. He spoke to the two seated claimants to the throne.

"You will answer any questions put to you, no matter who asks. You will answer truthfully and without hesitation. Is that understood?"

Almost in unison, the two heads nodded.

"We will begin with the obvious. What is your name, the names of your parents and when and where were your born?"

"I am Joakal of the Ruling House of I'lium—"

"—Twelfth of that name—"

"—My parents were King Klavia and—"

"—Queen Irian. I was born—"

"—on the seventeenth day of Adin—"

"—here in the Royal—"

"—city of She'heldon."

The answers bounced back and forth between the

two voices, like lines of a well-rehearsed play. If this continues, we'll get nowhere, Picard thought. It can't continue for long—they grew up apart from one another.

But continue it did, for one hour and into the next, through more and more complicated questions. Standing next to him, Picard could tell that the counselor was growing increasingly uncomfortable. What is she sensing? he wondered. Before he could ask her, he saw Mother Veronica lean over and whisper something to Troi. The two of them conferred in quiet tones he could not overhear. Then Troi turned to him.

"Beahoram is reading Joakal's mind to gain his answers, Captain," she told him.

"Are you certain, Counselor?"

"Mother Veronica is. She can hear it."

"But how? The two of you were unable to penetrate Joakal's shields, despite your best efforts."

"I don't know, Captain," Troi said. "Perhaps it is because Joakal and Beahoram are twins and having the two of them together changes the frequency of their thought patterns. Maybe it's . . ." she shook her head. "I don't know," she repeated. "But I have been feeling Beahoram's growing confidence for quite some time. Of all the emotions in this room, it is the most dominant. If something doesn't happen soon to stop him, Joakal may still lose everything."

Picard turned to Elana. "I heard," she said before he could explain. "And I agree—we have to intervene. Your Mother Veronica can hear thoughts, and Counselor Troi can read the emotions of other people?"

"Yes," Picard answered.

"How accurate are they?"

"I'd trust them with my life."

Elana nodded. Without a backward glance, she

strode to the center of the room and stood between the seated twins. Picard and the others followed a step behind. Elana held up her hands in imitation of the pose Faellon struck for prayer.

"Cease this travesty," she ordered. "There is neither Truth nor Justice being discovered here."

"Elana," Tygar stood, angered by her outburst. "You were admitted here because you are E'shala, First Daughter of one of the thirty Gentle Houses. You are being allowed to *observe,* but you have not been called to participate."

"As First Daughter of the House E'shala, and as the future wife of Joakal I'lium who is King and true *Absolute* of Capulon, I claim and call upon an ancient right. I claim *Rhii'cha.*"

There was a stunned silence around the table. Faellon, who had sat mute through all the time of questioning, raised his eyes to Elana's face. "The powers necessary for *Rhii'cha* no longer exist among us, Elana," he said. "The God took them away."

"Just as twins do not exist, Faellon?" she asked him. He flinched at her words and at the unforgiving hardness in her voice.

She saw his reaction but did not relent. "As twins exist," she said, "so do these powers."

Elana motioned for Troi and Mother Veronica. "This one," she said, indicating the nun, "is granted the gift of Mind-share such as our ancient fathers possessed. And this one," she motioned to Troi, "is able to read the soul of a being, and to know the truth or falsehood of their words."

"These people are not Capulonii, Elana," Tygar said. "How can you say they have the Voice of the God within them?"

"They have the gifts. Are we not taught that all such

218

gifts come only from the God?" she countered. "Do you deny our teachings?"

Faellon looked at the captain. "Do you and your people agree to this?"

Picard hesitated. What is this *Rhii'cha*, he wondered, and how will Starfleet interpret my agreement to participate?

"There is no other way," Elana whispered to him. "Do not abandon us now."

Picard met her eyes. He saw the conviction and the pleading there. He nodded to Faellon.

"We agree," he said.

"Very well," Faellon replied. He stood. "The ancient way of *Rhii'cha* has been claimed. According to the ancient laws, it must be performed in the temple, before the altar of the God. The *Rhii'cha* will take place at dawn tomorrow, and there, by the Voice of the God, we will learn who has the strength and the courage necessary to best govern our world. So let it be."

Chapter Twenty-three

JOAKAL AND BEAHORAM were led away to be kept under close watch until morning. The Servants, led by Faellon, returned to the temple. Picard, Troi, and Mother Veronica went once more to their rooms in the palace. Elana joined them.

The first thing Picard did was report to Commander Riker and appraise him of the situation. After the communication ended, the captain turned to Elana.

"Now," he said. "Tell me what we've agreed to. What, precisely, is *Rhii'cha?*"

"It is a very ancient ceremony, Captain," Elana replied. "There are not many people on our world who even know of its existence any more. Faellon, as Chief Servant, and perhaps a few other Servants who are interested in the ancient ways. Joakal and I learned of it almost by accident."

"What do you mean?" Picard asked.

"Joakal will make a great ruler," Elana said, lifting

her chin a little as though daring them to disagree with her. "He truly cares. He has spent most of his life studying the old ways and looking for the means to improve the future of this world. He found many old and forgotten texts, both here in the palace and at the temple, writings that had not been looked at in centuries. Among them was the Book of Valpet. It is a codex of laws and rituals dating from before the last wars. It is in this book Joakal discovered the rite of *Rhii'cha.*"

"What does this rite entail?" Picard again prompted.

"According to the old texts, those who are skilled in the art of *Truth-saying,* those whom you call empaths and telepaths, are brought before the altar and purified by 'the touch and prayers of the Servants of the God,'" she quoted. "A laying on of hands. Then the accused are brought in and made to prostrate themselves before the altar. It is then the duty of those who are performing the rite to probe the minds of those before them and proclaim what is there. Especially in this, when the outcome is of such importance to this world, it will be demanded that Counselor Troi and Mother Veronica reveal not only *who* they discover, but *what* and *why.*"

"Counselor . . ." Picard turned to Troi. "What problems do you foresee?"

"None with the ritual itself," she answered. "On Betazed, much of what we now understand scientifically is still practiced in the form of religious ritual. We have found that it both opens the mind and allows us to focus on our inner realities. I believe this *Rhii'cha* will be much the same. But I am worried. In the cell, despite our best efforts, Mother Veronica and I were unable to reach past Joakal's most surface thoughts. These were easily read—you saw Beahoram

221

do it. But I don't know about a deeper probing. What if we fail?"

"You must not fail," Elana said. "The laws in the Book of Valpet are very clear; those who will not proclaim what is revealed in *Rhii'cha* are guilty of an offense against the God. This offense is punished by death."

Mother Veronica, who had been sitting with her head bowed and her right hand clutching the cross about her throat, sprang to her feet. She looked from face to face.

"No," she said loudly, emphatically. "No more." Then she turned and ran from the room.

Picard turned to Troi. His eyes said it all. Troi stood.

"I'll go to her," she said. "But I don't know how much good it will do."

Mother Veronica was staring out the window when Troi entered the room they shared. The nun held her back straight, her body calm and still, but Troi could feel the emotions that churned and heaved within her.

Troi came further into the room and sat on the edge of the bed, facing her companion. Mother Veronica did not turn away from the window. She gave no indication she was aware of Troi's presence until she spoke.

"I want to go back to the *Enterprise*," she said.

"Mother Veronica—"

The nun spun around quickly. Her eyes were filled with hurt and anger, and Troi could feel her rising panic.

"No more," she said again. "I can't do it. I can't go through it again. How can you ask it of me?"

"I need your help," Troi said.

Mother Veronica turned away again. She began pacing the room. "You need my help," she repeated,

222

her anger winning for a moment. "The planet needs my help. The children need my help. Everyone *needs*, whether I want to help or not. Well I don't—not this time."

Troi sat still, letting the nun vent her anger, knowing that Mother Veronica could not deal with her feelings until she faced them.

"It was bad enough," Mother Veronica continued, "before we came to the *Enterprise*. Since then, there have been so many minds all pressing in on me. I thought you wanted to help *me*. You did, it was better for a time. Then we came here. The cell . . . Joakal . . . forcing my mind to touch . . . to invade . . ."

The anger was spent. All the pain and despair of her many years of suffering was beginning to boil to the surface. Her steps faltered.

"Beahoram . . . so much hate . . . I can't touch . . . I can't . . ."

Mother Veronica began to cry. She dropped to her knees and buried her face in her hands. Troi went to her and, kneeling beside her, put her arms around the nun's shoulders.

After a moment, Mother Veronica's sobs subsided. "Please," she said without raising her head. "I want to go home."

Troi took a deep breath. She could not force the nun to stay, and in her present state Mother Veronica would be more of a hindrance than a help. If Troi was to have any chance of succeeding at the *Rhii'cha,* she knew she could not afford any distractions. Unless Mother Veronica could help her willingly, with a calm and steady mind, Troi knew she was better off on her own. She stood and stepped to one side. Then she tapped her communicator.

"Troi to *Enterprise,*" she said.

"Enterprise, Riker here."

"Will, Mother Veronica wants to return to the ship. She's here with me now."

"All right, Deanna. I'll see to it."

"Thanks, Will. Troi out."

A moment later the transporter beam caught the nun. When she was gone, Troi returned to the captain's room where Picard was still talking with Elana.

"Mother Veronica has gone back to the ship," she informed them.

"Will she return by morning?" Picard asked.

"I hope so," Elana said.

"So do I," Troi replied. Troi knew that Elana hoped for Mother Veronica's return for the sake of Joakal, and Picard hoped the same for, perhaps, the good of the planet. But Troi hoped Mother Veronica found the strength to return for Mother Veronica's own sake.

In the far west wing of the palace, Aklier had also returned to his rooms. It was over. Aklier knew that in a few hours the true Joakal would be proclaimed and Beahoram's plots revealed. With that revelation, Aklier's betrayal would also become known. For nine years Aklier had served on the Council. He knew the law. He knew he must die for his crime.

Aklier found he was trembling; a traitor's death was not an easy, painless one. He sat in his favorite chair by the window. Outside the darkness of evening was spreading across the city, and overhead the stars were beginning to twinkle in the velvet heavens. The city was beginning to twinkle, too. Lights shone out from the windows of homes and shops until the city looked like a mirror of the sky. It was too beautiful; Aklier could not bear to watch. He stood and pulled the heavy drapes shut, then touched a small switch on the wall to bring up the room's lighting.

The artificial brightness did not comfort him. He could still feel the darkness. It was waiting for him, waiting like the thick, rough braid of rope that would soon close about his throat in the traitor's noose. Aklier could already feel the abrasion on his skin as the rope grew tighter and tighter, cutting off his air, taking his life. . . .

Aklier choked some air into his lungs, forcing it past the terror that filled his throat. He lurched away from the window on unsteady feet. He kept moving; he could not bear to stay still.

He should not have come here. The room was suddenly too small; the walls felt as if they were pressing in on him. He should have gone to his other home, to the place where he had once been happy, and waited there for his death to arrive. He should have waited where he was surrounded by the memories of his wife, the things she had touched and loved.

Aklier stumbled about the room. On the sideboard by the door were a flagon of wine, a bowl of fruit, and a platter of cheese. In the cheese was a knife. Aklier rushed to it. He would not wait for the noose. He would end his life now, by his own hand.

A part of him welcomed the thought. A part of him had found life a burden for many, many years and was glad to be casting aside the lands and titles and responsibilities, and the bitter, aching loneliness.

He held the knife up to his heart. One quick jab and it would all be over. He would be reunited forever with Ilayne and with their daughter. He would go into the peace of the God.

No, he would not. The thought stayed his hand, stopped him just as the point of the knife began to press against his flesh. The guilt of his betrayal hammered at him, yet he knew that from it he still had some hope of the God's mercy. If he took his own life, he would be condemned to eternal darkness. It would be an eternity tortured by the shame and regret that filled him now. There would be no reunion, no peace after all.

Aklier dropped the knife. It fell to the floor and lay gleaming in the pile of the carpet. Aklier stared at it a moment, then turned away. He crossed the room and sat on the edge of the bed. It was too late now to wish things were different and that he had never met Beahoram. The most he could hope for now was to see Joakal before he died, to talk with him and, perhaps, hear his words of forgiveness.

It would be one less regret to carry with him when he faced the God.

226

Chapter Twenty-four

ALL NIGHT LONG, Mother Veronica struggled with her conscience. She was torn between the friendship she felt for Troi, Troi's need of her, and her own desire to be left alone.

She knew what her Order demanded of her. Saint Francis of Assisi, the patron of the Little Mothers, had once prayed, "Lord, make me an instrument of thy peace. . . ." and the words of his great prayer had become a credo for all those who followed his Rule. Yet right now, Mother Veronica could not find it within herself to seek to "sow pardon instead of injury, faith instead of doubt, hope instead of despair, or bring light into the darkness."

Other than a perfunctory greeting for Sister Julian, Mother Veronica said no word and her Sister, catching her mood, left her alone. Through the long hours, Mother Veronica sat in her quarters staring out the viewports. She did not eat or sleep or even pray. It was the longest night she had ever endured, and as dawn approached on the planet below, Mother Veronica knew she must go to the chapel. Maybe there, she thought, amid the familiar furnishings of her faith, she would regain the sense of who she was and who she was meant to be.

She left the stateroom and walked across the ship's corridor that had been dimmed to artificial night. The mental shields Counselor Troi had endeavored to teach her to use were in tatters, dissolved by her own inner tumult. Mother Veronica felt the weight of the many sleeping minds around her.

She entered the chapel and reached automatically for the holy water font. As she crossed herself, she saw a figure rise from one of the front pews and turn to face her. It startled her; she had not felt the presence of another in the room. Then, in the dim light of the altar candles, she saw the gleam of pale golden-white skin.

It's the android officer, she thought, trying to remember back to the dinner party when she had first come on board and the name she had heard. It was no use. She had been in too much misery to remember anything she heard that night.

"I did not mean to disturb you, Mr.—"

"Data," the android supplied. "You have not disturbed me."

"What are you doing here?" Mother Veronica asked. The question came out harsher than she had intended and she tried to soften it.

"I'm sorry," she said. "I didn't mean . . . You're welcome here, of course, but I didn't think an android . . ." Mother Veronica let her words falter.

"I am here trying to understand what draws humans to such places," Data said. "Can you explain it to me?"

228

Another need, Mother Veronica thought as she dropped to one knee in a genuflection toward the altar. More questions. How can I answer his when I can't answer my own?

"Why is it you want to know?" she asked as she rose again to her feet. She walked toward Data. As she approached, he stepped back into the pew and Mother Veronica followed him.

"I am an android," he reiterated once they were both seated. "I was built by a human. I serve in Starfleet among humans, and although it is true that I do not possess emotions such as desire, it is also true that if I were to be granted one wish, it would be to become human."

"And since you cannot become human, you study them," Mother Veronica added.

"Exactly," Data said. "I am currently endeavoring to understand the nature of religious belief. Before you and your companion came on board, I had given no thought to that aspect of human behavior. In the last three weeks, however, I have read everything in the ship's library on the subject. I have found that it has occupied a great deal of human thought over the centuries."

"I see," Mother Veronica replied. "If you have done all this reading, you have been in contact with far greater minds than mine. What can I possibly tell you?"

"Why did you become a nun?" Data answered.

Mother Veronica blinked. Data's question stabbed at the heart of what she had struggled with through the long hours past. She stared at the altar, at the candles and crucifix as if her answer might be resting there. But there was only silence.

"I don't know anymore," she said softly, honestly. "I thought I did once, but now I'm not so sure."

"Then you no longer believe there is a God?" Data's question, asked so innocently, was again like a knife thrust.

"Oh no, Mr. Data," she cried, turning to face him. "Never that. It's not God—it's me."

Mother Veronica turned again to the altar. It was more than her eyes that were fastened on the linen-draped altar and its golden crucifix this time. It was her soul.

"For so many years," she said at last, "I believed that my mind was an aberration and that by possessing such a mind, I was flawed, less than human in some way. I became a nun partly in reparation for this fault. I became a nun because of faith, because of a love for God, certainly, but also because at the convent there was safety. That safety is gone now."

Mother Veronica stopped. She finally tore her gaze away from the altar and closed her eyes. Her next words came out slowly as she fought through the pain it was costing her to say them.

"We came on board and Counselor Troi discovered I was a telepath. She offered me a way to keep all the voices out of my mind. I thought that was why God had brought me here. I thought that He had forgiven me at last. Finally, I was to be free of the stain of my sin."

Again, Mother Veronica stopped. The memory of that feeling brought a small smile to her lips, but it quickly faded. She opened her eyes once more, and once more she would look at nothing but the altar.

"Then we arrived here at Capulon IV," she continued. "Almost from the moment we set foot on this planet, rather than have those abilities locked away as I craved, I have been forced to use them. And I have heard the very abilities I grew up hating called God's hand, God's gift, God's voice. Now I don't know what to think, or what to do."

"Is it not then," Data said, "a question of faith?"

Surprised, stunned, Mother Veronica turned to look at him.

"Most of the religions I have encountered," he said, "contain the teaching of divine guidance and providence. Isn't yours the same?"

Mother Veronica nodded. "For we know that all things work together for good to those who love God."

"Romans 8:28," Data replied. "Perhaps I have misunderstood the quote."

Mother Veronica's eyes were once more drawn to the altar. The candles seemed to glow slowly brighter as the first light of personal epiphany dawned.

"No, Mr. Data," she said after a long moment. "You have not misunderstood. I have. I have misunderstood all my life. My sin has never been the abilities of my mind, but my fear of them. 'For the gifts and callings of the Lord are without repentance,'" she quoted.

The final words of Saint Francis's beloved peace prayer whispered through Mother Veronica's mind. She understood them then as she never had before. ". . . It is in giving that we now receive; it is in pardoning that we now are pardoned. . . ."

Her hand reached for and closed around the cross that hung at her breast. "I was brought here," she said, "not to close my mind, but to open it. To offer it. To learn to use it. That is the only way to gain the peace I have prayed for."

Mother Veronica stood and turned to Data. "Thank you," she told him. "I may not have answered your questions, but you have answered mine."

* * *

The soft light of dawn was just washing the sky when Troi, Picard, and Elana left the palace and walked across the city square toward the temple. Troi had no eyes for the beauty of the awakening day. Mother Veronica had not returned and Counselor Troi was worried, both about the nun and about the ritual ahead.

There was so much that could go wrong, she thought. I'm an empath not a telepath. Do the people here understand the difference? Will they accept it?

They reached the temple steps were they found a small delegation of five Servants and five Elders waiting to escort them into the building. Elana did not stop to greet them, but marched straight up the steps and into the temple. Troi and Picard hastened to keep up with her. The Elders and Servants fell into step behind.

Faellon waited at the altar with his back turned toward them. The royal regalia still rested on the sacred stone table, still watched over by the palace guards. Joakal and Beahoram were nowhere to be seen. The Servants who lived at the temple and the remaining Elders filled the front pews, but other than that, the temple was empty. There would be no large crowd of spectators to witness this ceremony as there had been for the interrupted coronation.

The procession reached the base of the altar steps. As the official delegation slipped silently into the pews they were to occupy, Faellon turned around. His eyes slowly slid over Elana, Picard, and then Counselor Troi.

"Where is the other one?" he asked.

"She has gone back to our ship," Picard answered.

Troi felt the anger mount in Faellon. "You agreed to

232

this rite," he said. "It is sacred. Would she go back on her word to the God?"

"No, she would not," a voice answered from the back of the temple. Troi turned to see Mother Veronica marching down the aisle. She and Captain Picard hurried to meet her.

"Mother Veronica," Picard said before Troi had a chance to greet her former student. "We're glad you are here. I know this is not the reason you came to Capulon IV, but we need you to use your telepathic abilities once more on our behalf."

"And I am ready, Captain," she replied with more equanimity than Troi would have thought possible a few weeks, or even a few hours ago. Something had changed for the nun. There was a new confidence in her voice and a peace in her thoughts. Troi hoped they would last through the ordeal ahead.

The three of them walked back to the base of the altar steps. Faellon stared at Mother Veronica for a moment, then he turned again to the altar. He placed his hands on either side of the golden bowl and looked down into the remains of the anointing melange. He did not speak for several seconds while the tension in the temple slowly built.

Finally, he raised his head. Without turning, he called to Liiyn, who had assisted him yesterday. She hurried to the Chief Servant's side. After a few whispered words, she turned and rushed from the temple, using the small door to the left side of the transept. She returned a few minutes later carrying a large book, bound in dark green leather and closed with a golden clasp.

"That is the Book of Valpet," Troi heard Elana whisper.

Faellon stood silently a moment longer, as if reluctant to proceed. Finally, he turned to face his assistant. She opened the book. Faellon read, renewing his memory of the ritual to come.

When Faellon finished reading, he turned toward the waiting assembly. "For the first time in more than thirty generations," he said, "there are two who claim the throne of Capulon IV. Each demands the right to the crown and power of *Absolute*. Because of our shame and our fathers' offense against the God, there are none among us who possess the ancient gifts that would show us the Truth and the Way of Wisdom. Yet, the God is not without mercy. He has sent from other worlds those who hear his Voice. They have vowed to accept our laws. Through them, the ancient way of *Rhii'cha* has been invoked. Through this rite, all things will be revealed."

Once more, Faellon stared at the group gathered at the base of the altar steps. His eyes lingered on each one, finally stopping at Elana.

"Elana," he said. "I give you one final chance to withdraw your call for *Rhii'cha*. Are you determined on this course?"

"I am," she said. "We all are."

Faellon stared at her a moment longer, as if trying to read her heart and measure the depths of her determination. Satisfied, he gave a curt nod. He lifted his gaze and let it flow again over Troi and Mother Veronica.

"Are you willing to dedicate yourselves in *Rhii'cha?*" he asked them.

Troi hesitated only a moment. Once begun, she knew there would be no turning back until this ceremony was completed. She wished she had time to talk with Mother Veronica, to find out what had happened to bring about the change she sensed in the nun. Troi wanted to know, needed to know, whether this new strength would falter just when she needed it most.

But Mother Veronica did not hesitate. She spoke loudly and clearly for all to hear. "We are willing," she said.

"So let it be. The *Rhii'cha* will begin."

Chapter Twenty-five

ALTHOUGH SHE WAS PREPARED, Faellon's last words still sent a chill up Troi's spine. Once again she thought of all that could go wrong, even with Mother Veronica's help. How deeply would they be expected to probe the minds of Joakal and his brother? Were they to be allowed to blend their abilities and perform the *Rhii'cha* together? What if they could not find a path through Beahoram and Joakal's shields? Troi caught the echo of Mother Veronica's thoughts whispering across the link the two of them had forged long ago.

. . . *For thou has delivered my soul from death, my eyes from tears and my feet from falling.* . . .

The words comforted the nun, but they did little to calm Troi's own fears.

Faellon spoke again. "Elana," he said, "you and the captain must leave your companions now. You may not speak or otherwise interfere until the *Rhii'cha* is completed. What must be done, you cannot do."

236

Elana laid her hand on the captain's arm. "You must have faith, Captain," Troi heard Elana say as she drew Picard outside the circle of Servants.

Faith again, Troi thought. That word and all the feelings, positive or otherwise, that it evoked had filled Troi's world since the Little Mothers had first come on board the *Enterprise.*

Once Elana and Captain Picard had moved away, Faellon turned his attention to Troi and Mother Veronica. "You are unfamiliar with the demands of the God," he said. "Therefore I will grant you a greater leniency in your behavior than I would to one of our own, and I will direct you. You will now come and kneel here." He indicated the third step to the altar. "Then you will bow low, touching your forehead to the step before you, in humble submission to the God. In your hearts, you will make your dedication to the God, offering your minds for use."

Together, Troi and Mother Veronica climbed the altar steps. But as they knelt, Troi found herself wondering to what she could make her dedication. To the God whom the people of this world embraced? No, nor to the God and the religion Mother Veronica followed. Truth and Life, these were the things in which Troi believed. They were the only articles of her faith, and she had pledged herself to them long ago. She would do so again. She made her bow.

Faellon extended his hands over them and began the ritual prayers. "O, Great and most Holy God," he intoned. "Infinite Source. We bow before you, offering to you all liberty, memory, understanding, and will. Purify us by your Divine Light. Let darkness and deception be banished forever. Let your Voice be heard."

Faellon lowered his hands. Troi and Mother Veronica again straightened their backs and looked up at the Chief Servant.

"You have bowed before the God and heard the words of our prayer," he said. "Are you now prepared to be consecrated unto the act you have undertaken?"

Troi glanced at Mother Veronica and saw her slight nod. "We are ready," they said in unison.

"Very well," Faellon replied. "But be warned, in the God's hallowing there is no mercy."

Troi felt a touch upon her head, her shoulders, her arms. All around, those of the thirty Servants who could not make contact with her or Mother Veronica, linked hands with one another until an unbroken circuit of energy was formed. Faellon again raised his hands in prayer.

"Circle of Light," he chanted. "Circle of Truth. Holy. Eternal. Unbroken. We enter the center where the God abides. We receive; we give; we receive again, bound and sanctified unto the God, forever consecrated unto the Holy."

The Chief Servant dropped his hands to Troi's and Mother Veronica's foreheads. His touch completed the circle. Troi felt a surge of energy fire through her brain, like a blinding flash of pure white light. It did not ebb. It kept growing, reaching toward the farthest corners of thought and the deepest centers of emotion. Troi struggled to hold her own identity against the combined presence of thirty other minds, all united for a single, unwavering purpose. She had once told Will Riker that her own emotions did not matter, but suddenly they mattered very, very much.

Automatically she tried to raise her shields and protect her mind. They would not respond. The energy pouring into her continued to build. It coursed through her mind and through her body. Troi felt as if she were standing in the middle of a pillar of fire. Her heart started to pound; she could not draw air into her lungs and still the flow of power did not relent. Troi wanted to scream for them to let her alone.

Then, suddenly, the light turned golden and receded. Troi's mind was her own again.

I was right, Troi thought. The Servants may no longer function as telepaths, but they are psychic triggers. This whole ceremony, the *laying on of hands*, is to unlock the psychic potential of the recipient. That's why the King is empowered at his coronation. His shields are released through the touch of the Servants. If this is the energy level it takes to break through, no wonder Mother Veronica and I could not do it alone. Can we do it now? she wondered.

Contact was broken. Hands were removed and Troi felt herself being helped to her feet. She opened her eyes and saw that the same had been done for Mother Veronica. Troi tried to reach out and touch the nun's mind. She wanted to know that Mother Veronica was all right and still able to proceed. To her surprise, Troi found the nun's mind shielded with strong, disciplined shields.

Mother Veronica looked at her and gave a small shake of her head. "Not yet," she whispered. Before Troi could respond, they were closely surrounded and led off to the side while Joakal and Beahoram were ushered forward for their preparation.

When Troi and Mother Veronica were escorted back toward the altar, the scene had changed. Joakal and Beahoram were lying face down, prostrate before the altar with their arms outstretched above their heads. In this position and in their identical clothing, there was no way to tell them apart.

Between them stood Faellon. He held the Sword of Justice in his hands. It was not as long as the great Sword of Wisdom Tygar had wielded, but it was thick and double-edged, and from the way the light reflected off the blade, Troi had no doubt that it could sever a man's head or cut deeply into a body with a single thrust. The look on Faellon's face proclaimed as loudly as any words that he would not hesitate to do his duty.

"Kneel there between them," Faellon ordered, and he pointed with the sword.

Troi and Mother Veronica knelt. Again, the Servants gathered in a circle around them. There was no touching this time, but Troi could feel the psychic force of their presence. She looked up at Faellon for direction.

"Singly or together, it makes no difference," he said. "Read them now, and proclaim the Truth."

Troi reached for and found the familiar link between herself and Mother Veronica. The rapport established quickly, as if this time the nun had been reaching for it.

I don't know what to do, Mother Veronica's thoughts immediately spoke in Troi's mind. The counselor was once again surprised, this time by the order and clarity with which the nun communicated.

Don't worry, Troi told her. *You've been hearing other people's thoughts most of your life. This will only be more focused, like a fine-tuned scanner.*

But how? There are so many people here. How do I tell one mind from another?

I'll guide you, as we did in the cell. Release control to me. This time I need it all. I can't do this if you fight against me. Are you ready?

I understand, Mother Veronica's thoughts assured her. *I promise I'll try. I'm ready now.*

Troi strengthened the link between them. As the nun completely lowered the shields Troi had taught her to use, Troi's own mind became bombarded by the cacophony Mother Veronica had daily endured. Once more the counselor marveled that Mother Veronica had survived; that she was sane and that now she was offering to help. Troi was not certain that in the same situation, she would have been this strong.

Quickly, Troi brought her own training into play. With cool efficiency, she blocked the external stimuli until the only ones she and Mother Veronica could sense were Joakal and Beahoram.

The emotions that flowed from the men battled against each other. They clashed and clattered in Troi's mind, like frenzied war drums. Images of people and places, half-remembered conversations whirled across the flow of mental energy. The separation of these thoughts was muddled, as if their proximity to one another was causing Joakal and Beahoram's minds to merge.

We must go deeper, Troi told Mother Veronica. *Down into their Self.*

Troi felt the nun falter. The link between them nearly severed. Troi could feel Mother Veronica fighting not to close her mind and back away. Troi hurried to reassure her, afraid that if Mother Veronica stopped now, a deeper reading would become impossible. What was more, Troi was certain that if Mother Veronica did not successfully complete this task, the nun would never consider furthering her training and becoming the skilled telepath she was meant to be.

Sometimes in order to heal, Troi shared, *a physician must cut into the flesh. And sometimes, in order to heal a mind, the barriers must be stripped away.*

"*If thy right hand offend thee, cut it off. . . .*" Mother Veronica quoted and Troi felt the nun's confidence return again. Once more the nun yielded to Troi's direction.

Troi focused on reading only the thoughts of the prostrate form on her left. She expected to encounter

Joakal, whose mind they had already touched and whose gentle inclinations would help ease this ordeal for Mother Veronica.

It was Beahoram. His confidence was in tatters, yet he had not totally given way to the fear that lurked and darted around the edges of his mind. He held it at bay by anger, the same dark and brooding anger that had driven him through most of his life. Both Troi and Mother Veronica recoiled from its touch.

Troi felt the cold point of the sword touch the base of her throat. It bit into her flesh, not deeply enough to draw blood—not yet. She opened her eyes and looked into the unyielding gaze of the Chief Servant towering over her.

"Proclaim what the Voice speaks to you," he ordered. "Fulfill *Rhii'cha*."

Troi hesitated. Mother Veronica's revulsion screamed inside her head, amplifying the feelings that were Troi's own. At that moment, Troi, too, would have liked to break away, to go back to the *Enterprise* and be cleansed from her contact with the blackness of Beahoram's mind.

Duty held her in place. Duty and the point of a sword. Both were sharp. Troi took a deep breath as she steeled herself to touch Beahoram's emotions again.

She reached; she touched; an answering wave of darkness boiled back at her. It slammed through her mind, battering at her defenses with the force of obsession. She was hardly aware that Faellon had removed the tip of the sword from her throat and again taken up his post between the prostrate bodies.

"Anger," she said aloud. Some part of her heard her own voice, but she could not spare the concentration to choose her words. "Pain and loss. Loneliness. I'll make them pay. Revenge. I'll hurt them for what they thought they did to me. I'll take back what is mine."

This was not enough. These thoughts were barely below the surface of Beahoram's mind. Troi knew she would have to go deeper. She withdrew a little, giving herself time to recover from the negative currents in which she had been immersed.

As she withdrew, she felt Beahoram's confidence return. He thought he had driven her off, but Troi knew otherwise. There was a technique for reaching past the imbalanced telepathic mind that she had learned in her training on Betazed. She had not needed it in the years she had worked among humans. She had almost forgotten it, but in the severity of her need, the memory of the training resurfaced.

Troi once again strengthened the link between herself and Mother Veronica. She wove their minds together, plaiting them into a single, bonded entity. Troi had not felt such complex psychic structures since she had bonded with her own teacher on Betazed.

Prepared now, Troi sent a Questing deep into Beahoram's mind. It stood out like a ray of light in the surrounding blackness, plunging and searching deeper and deeper. At any moment, Troi expected to encounter resistance, but unlike his brother, the layers of Beahoram's mind peeled easily away.

Troi knew then that she could shatter his mind with a single thought. She also knew that she would not. Her training, her sense of duty, and her devotion to the healing of the mind was too deeply engrained to let her do more than recognize the possibility and discard it. Instead she stripped away Beahoram's defenses. She laid bare to him the full darkness of his own mind. He tried to stop her, but he was powerless. Relentlessly, she delved into every memory, every action and plot, and revealed to him the true corruption of his motives.

Then she spoke. In the hush of the temple, her voice carried, revealing everything she learned to this inquisition of Servants and Elders that encircled her, and there was nothing Beahoram could do but lay groaning with frustration at her feet.

Troi opened her eyes. Faellon had left his place between the two brothers. He was straddling Beahoram's prostrate form, the Sword of Justice pressed into Beahoram's back. Gone was the bent old man who had hidden his face with shame when Joakal entered the temple and who had sat mute during the Council's interrogations. Gone was the Chief Servant of the temple, worn out with long Service. Faellon had become the avenging angel of his God. His eyes blazed with fury as they looked into Troi's, and she knew he would willingly wield the Sword.

"Complete the *Rhii'cha*," he ordered. "As you have read the heart and soul of one, now read the other."

Troi closed her eyes again. She focused her mind, still tightly interlaced with Mother Veronica's, on Joakal. Again she gathered their linked powers into a tight, penetrating beam of thought. But as before, Joakal's mind turned her away.

She tried again and again. Every time the way remained blocked. Surface memories—fears, beliefs, hopes, darted quickly over the external layers of his mind, but allowed no deeper entry.

Troi felt herself start to tremble with the effort. Finally she let out a gasp and sat back on her heels, her energy—and Mother Veronica's—spent.

"I cannot," she said. But that was enough.

"The God has protected His own," Faellon shouted triumphantly. He raised the sword. His muscles tensed as he prepared to plunge it down into the body of the imposter who had almost made a travesty of everything Faellon held sacred.

"No!" Troi screamed, lurching toward him.

Joakal sprang to his feet and caught the arm of the Chief Servant as it began to descend. Their eyes locked; Troi felt the pulse of their battle of wills.

Finally Faellon lowered his eyes. The sword in his hand dropped and clattered on the stone floor. He sank to one knee before Joakal.

"Your Majesty," he said. Faellon stood and turned to the waiting Elders. Aklier sat among them, his shoulders hunched, his head bowed. He made no effort to break from the hands that held him.

"Take him away," Faellon said. "And find his accomplices. They will await the judgment of the King."

"Wait," Joakal ordered. Movement in the temple stopped as he walked over to stand before the Elder.

Aklier did not look up. "Forgive me," he whispered. "I should have trusted you."

"Yes," Joakal said softly. "You should have. But I should also have trusted you. If I had not kept my plans to myself, if I had shared them with you, none of this would have happened. I was selfish, and though I did not know it, I was arrogant. You must also forgive me."

Aklier bowed deeply. Faellon came up behind Joakal. "Your Majesty," he said. "The coronation—"

"Will take place in two hours," Joakal replied. "With one alteration—me."

For the next two hours, the news of the *Rhii'cha*'s outcome was broadcast through the city. It was carried over communication systems, whispered from ear to ear, gossiped out doorways and windows until everyone knew the tale.

At the appointed time, the Elders once more gathered in the palace to escort the King to the temple.

Joakal requested that Captain Picard stand in Aklier's place in the procession and that Troi and Mother Veronica also walk with them.

It was the biggest crowd in living memory who turned out to see Joakal's coronation and elevation to *Absolute*. People lined the walkways and filled the city square, each hoping to catch not only a glimpse of their young King but to see the people from the Federation who had risked their lives to overthrow the usurper and protect the most hallowed right of sovereignty. Neither Troi nor Mother Veronica realized that to the people who whispered and pointed as the procession passed, they had already gained the status of living legends.

The procession reached the temple and once more ascended the long flight of stairs. A fanfare blew once, twice, three times. Joakal entered the hallowed structure and walked in triumph down the long nave to prostrate himself before the altar and be raised again as *Absolute*.

He had already been hallowed by his passage through *Rhii'cha* and therefore, when the coronation recommenced, Faellon chose to omit many of the prayers he had prayed over Beahoram. But the Chief Servant could not reduce the rite of anointing or the consecration.

At last, hands lifted Joakal from where he lay upon the crimson cloth. He knelt before the altar. Faellon stood in front of him and the four Servants, again assisting Faellon, came and laid their hands on Joakal's shoulders. Faellon recited the ancient prayer of consecration.

The prayer ended. Faellon dropped his hands to Joakal's head. At their touch, a warmth filled Joakal's mind. It expanded slowly at first, spreading outward and inward, warming and caressing him. It turned into a fire. It began to blaze. It scorched and seared. It burned its way through the layers of shields Troi had encountered, reaching deeper and deeper, down into the center of his brain and firing back outward again along all of the twisting pathways of thought, memory, reason, and belief.

Joakal rocked back and forth on his knees, he groaned as from deep within his mind, power flared, unleashed for the first time. It surged back up along the pathways that were now unblocked. It met with the energies that were flowing into his mind and blended with them, absorbed them.

It was as if a switch had been thrown in Joakal's mind. There was a flood of illumination and suddenly Joakal could hear the thoughts of those around him. He could read through the layers of their emotions and feel within himself the depths of their joys and triumphs, their sufferings and fears. He *Knew* them—all of them.

Then, just as he felt he could accept no more, he found he could shut them away with a single thought. The empowering was complete.

This is what Counselor Troi and Mother Veronica were trying to do for me down in the cell, Joakal realized. I did not understand.

He sent a single thought of affinity to them, brushing the minds of empath and telepath with his gratitude. Then he stood and met the eyes of the temple's Chief Servant. Faellon bowed low, acknowledging the new *Absolute* and in that instant, Joakal knew he had only to think a single thought to be able to read the mind, the heart and soul of the God's Servant. Such a temptation must be guarded against.

Joakal turned away from Faellon. He looked out at

the congregation. The faces that watched him held expectations and a little dread. He knew they wondered what kind of a man was now their ruler. They would know soon enough.

Joakal descended the altar steps. He crossed to where Elana stood with Picard, Troi, and Mother Veronica. He took Elana's hand into his own and raised it to his lips.

"My Queen," he said for her ears alone. "My friend," he said to Captain Picard. Then with two steps, he stood in front of Troi and Mother Veronica. He said nothing for a few quick seconds. Then slowly, he sank to one knee before them.

The people in the temple gasped; no *Absolute* had ever bowed to any but the God.

Joakal came to his feet again. He looked down into the tired faces of both women and he smiled a soft, warm smile.

"I owe you more than a life," he said. "What you have done will never be forgotten among my people."

He turned away and went back to stand at the foot of the altar. Once there he raised his hands. All eyes were fixed upon him. Joakal felt the surge of anticipation that flowed from the hearts and minds of his people as they waited to hear the first words of their newly consecrated sovereign.

"My people," he cried out in a loud and royal voice. "You have seen today the price of following an old law that has passed from the Way of Wisdom. The old laws will be reviewed and new laws proclaimed, and the first such law is this: No more children shall die for an accident of their birth. Life is the God's most precious gift. In revering it, we do homage to the God. Now is the quickening of a new era. We go forward together."

There was a moment of silence. Then, suddenly, a voice rang out. "The God's blessing upon the *Absolute*," it shouted. The cry was taken up by other voices until the temple rang with the accolade.

Joakal again crossed over to Elana and took her by the hand. She would walk by his side as he left the temple, as she would walk by his side through life. But he did not forget the people of the *Enterprise*.

"Captain," he said. "Will you, and the others if they are not too tired, be my guests at the coronation banquet? I believe we still have things to discuss."

"I, for one, would be honored, Your Majesty," Picard said. "Counselor—Mother Veronica?"

Troi smiled, but Mother Veronica shook her head. "If you don't mind," she said, "I'd like to go back to the *Enterprise*."

"Certainly," Joakal replied. "But I hope you will return to us soon."

Mother Veronica did not answer. She lowered her eyes and stood waiting. Picard tapped his communicator.

"Picard to *Enterprise*," he said.

"Enterprise, Riker here."

"All is well, Number One," Picard reported. "Counselor Troi and I will remain here for a while longer, but Mother Veronica wishes to return to the ship. Please see to it. I'll give you a full report later."

"Aye, aye, Captain."

"Thank you, Number One. Picard out."

He and the others stepped back a few feet to allow the transporter to work. As the effect took hold of Mother Veronica and before she had disappeared completely, she raised her eyes and looked at Troi. The counselor was uncertain what expression she saw there.

Then she was gone. Joakal, too, took his leave of them as he led Elana to their place in the coronation recession. Picard and Troi were left standing alone.

"Well, Counselor," the captain said, "I believe our young friend will make an excellent ruler for the people of Capulon IV, and they will be a welcome addition to the Federation."

"I agree, Captain," Troi said.

Picard held out his arm to her ready to escort her formally to the banquet. A wry smile touched the edges of his lips. "You'll have to admit that life in Starfleet is never boring."

Troi laughed. "It is certainly never that," she said.

Chapter Twenty-six

THE FEAST AND CELEBRATION were held in the main banquet hall of the palace. Larger even than the Great Chamber, it easily held all the people who had attended the coronation and the population of Servants from the temple, as well as the retainers and servers, the musicians and dancers and the other entertainers who would perform during the evening.

Joakal had ordered that Picard and Counselor Troi be seated near him at the high table. As the platters of food came and went, music played, toasts were given, and conversation crescendoed, Picard found he had little chance to speak with the King.

The first hour passed. The main dishes were cleared away and an array of desserts presented. More wine was served. The second hour was nearly spent when the evening's entertainment began with a chorus of children performing some old songs, written for past Kings but with the names changed to honor the new one. Next came tumblers and acrobats and a troop of dancers. Picard began to think about how he might make a graceful exit and return to the *Enterprise*. He turned and found Joakal watching him.

The new *Absolute* smiled and stood. Immediately the music stopped. Conversations halted in midword as throughout the hall, people sprang to their feet and waited.

Joakal motioned for them to sit. "You have feasted Us most wonderfully," he said, using the royal pronoun, "and you have shown Us your love and loyalty. We are appreciative of all you have done, but We must now take Our leave of you. Please, stay and enjoy yourselves in Our absence."

Joakal turned away from the table and as he did, he motioned for Captain Picard to follow him. Picard nodded to the King, then leaned closer to Counselor Troi.

"Stay here," he told her. "I'll try not to be gone too long."

Troi nodded. She and the rest of the room remainded standing until Picard had joined Joakal and the two of them left the banquet hall.

"They'll enjoy themselves more now that I'm not there," Joakal told Picard as they stepped out into one of the many palace corridors. "And I want—no, I need to ask your advice. Let's go to my private apartments where we can be comfortable while we talk."

"Certainly, Your Majesty," Picard said.

"Please, Captain, when we are alone, call me Joakal. My life will be filled with titles and formalities, with Elders and advisers and subjects, but there will be very few whom I can call friend."

"I shall be pleased to be among those few, Joakal. And my name is Jean-Luc."

"Jean-Luc—is that an Earth name?"

"Yes, from a country known as France."

"Now that we are to be a member of the Federation, I must learn more about your Earth."

The small talk continued while they walked down the corridors, but Picard knew that Joakal had other things on his mind. His chatter had a preoccupied quality to it.

Finally they reached Joakal's rooms. They entered and Joakal motioned for Picard to sit while he poured them each a glass of wine. When he had handed one to the captain, the younger man dropped into a chair and stretched his long legs out in front of him, crossing them at the ankles. He held his wine goblet up until the light touched the ruby-colored crystal at its heart and he sat contemplating it.

"Tomorrow," Joakal said at last. "Tomorrow is a great day for my people. I will sign the final treaty that brings us into full membership with the Federation. We will join that glorious brotherhood among the stars. It is a wondrous thing, Jean-Luc," he said, turning to look at the captain. "The treaty is a good document, one I'll be proud to sign."

"If it is not the treaty you wish to discuss," Picard said, "I don't see what else I have the knowledge, or the authority, to help you with. My experience with your people is quite—limited."

"The authority? No, now that I am *Absolute,* no one has that. It is a heavy burden to wear such a title and to wear it well. Perhaps that is why with the title comes this new power into my mind. Every action I take for the rest of my life must be for the good of my people—and how can I not act for their good when their hurts and fears are as clear to me as my own. In many ways, I *am* my people now."

"Then, what—"

"You do have a knowledge I need," Joakal continued. "And I would ask you for your advice."

"But you have advisers who are far more familiar with the ways of your world than I will ever be."

"That is why I cannot ask them." Joakal stopped and took a long drink of the wine in his goblet. Then he placed it on the small table between the chairs and folded his hands.

"Tomorrow," he began again, "I must pronounce judgment on my brother, and on Aklier, and the two who aided their actions. The laws of this world call for their deaths, as my advisers have already reminded me, several times. There must be laws. Society needs them or there would be chaos, and my people need them. They need laws they can believe in if they are to have any confidence in me as their ruler.

"But, Jean-Luc," Joakal continued, "I have said that I wish to enact new laws for my people. As an individual, I would offer Beahoram and Aklier mercy —but I am no longer an individual. I am *Absolute*. How, where, do I find the balance between mercy and law? What is justice?"

Picard took a deep breath and let it out slowly. It was a delicate question, and one that he had often asked himself over the years. But he was not burdened with the responsibilities Joakal faced. As captain of a starship, some aspects of his life could be compared to that of a ruler, but only on the surface. Picard always had other officers with whom he could share some of the burdens, and who had the authority to relieve him of command should he become unfit for his role. There were also other captains or admirals, and the whole great legal system of Starfleet and of the Federation at his back. He was never truly alone in his decisions. Joakal was.

Picard twirled the stem of his own wineglass between his fingers, staring down into the rich, golden liquid. His brow furrowed and his lips pursed as he tried to find a way to answer the young King's question.

Picard sat forward to put his goblet down next to Joakal's. "You told me a tale out of your people's history," he began, sitting back in his chair, crossing his legs. "It was the story of the first King Joakal and the two bakers. You said that this King knew the meaning of wisdom. On Earth, many centuries ago, there was a King by the name of Solomon. He was a very righteous man, a man of great faith who sought to serve both his people and his God to the best of his abilities. When he came to the throne, the one thing Solomon prayed was that God would grant him the wisdom to govern his people with both justice and understanding. It is said that God was so pleased by this request, that He granted it in full measure.

"Well, Solomon's new wisdom was soon put to the test. One day, two women appeared before him demanding the King's judgment. They had an infant with them. The women lived in the same household. They had each given birth, but one of the children had died within a few days. Now both women were claiming to be the mother of the remaining child.

"They argued back and forth as they stood before the King. 'It is my child who lives and yours who died,' they shouted. 'Give me back the child you have stolen from me.' Solomon let them argue while he watched their faces and tried to judge their hearts. Finally he stopped them. He took the child into his own arms. 'Bring me a sword,' he ordered. 'Since each of you claims this child,' he said as he held the child up, 'I will cut the living child in two and give half to each of you.'

"One woman nodded and said 'That is just.' But the

other woman cried out in horror. 'No,' she cried. 'Do not slay the child. Give it to this other woman here. I would rather my child be taken from me than that it should die.' By this King Solomon knew that it was the second woman who was the true mother. He put the child into her arms. And it is written that when the people of his land heard of Solomon's judgment, they said that the Wisdom of God was with him.'"

Picard finished his tale, and the two men sat in silence for a time, each in his own way contemplating the meaning of the tale. Finally, Joakal raised his head and smiled.

"Thank you, Jean-Luc," he said. He picked up both glasses and handed Picard's to him. Then Joakal lifted his own in toast.

"To our new era," he said. "And to Wisdom."

"To wisdom," Picard echoed.

Down in the banquet hall, Troi sat next to Elana at the high table. Troi did not notice when Faellon left his seat further along the high table, but suddenly he was there, kneeling on the floor between her seat and Elana's. Troi could feel the depths of his shame and sorrow.

"Elana E'shala," he said and he bowed low to her. "I have wronged you and I have come to ask your mercy."

Elana looked at him. There was a spark of anger that still burned within her, but at the sight of the old man, bent with the weight of his repentance, the spark flickered and died.

"Faellon," Elana said softly. "There is no need—"

"There is," Faellon countered, straightening. "Please hear me. I need to make you understand, at least in some small part, why I acted as I did, for truly I did not wish you harm."

Elana nodded and waited, allowing Faellon the dignity to say what he needed in order to make peace with himself.

"I am an old man," he began again. "And for most of my life, I have lived in Service at the temple. There are those who enter Service who yearn toward high office, but I was not one of them. I was content to Serve the God in quiet obscurity. Yet twenty-two years ago I was named Chief Servant. Since then my only thought has been to guard the ways of the God and to bring them to the people.

"But, Lady Elana," he said, and he paused for a breath. "I have grown old. More and more my thoughts have turned to resigning my office and retiring, to living the last of my days in peace. I had only one more act to perform—the coronation of the *Absolute*—before I could lay aside the title and responsibilities of Chief Servant. It became my greatest desire. More than hearing the Voice of the God, more than serving the God or the people or the King, I wanted obscurity and solitude. I wanted peace. And, though I told you that you must have faith, I had lost mine."

Here again Faellon paused. Elana reached out and touched his shoulder, offering her comfort and her forgiveness.

"Faellon," she said. "There is no need to go on."

"Yes, there is," he said. "You must know the fullness of my fault so that you can guard against it, both in yourself and in others. You are to be the queen of this land, and you will help the *Absolute* to rule."

"Go on then," Elana said kindly.

Faellon's breath, when he drew it this time, was ragged and shaky, but his voice was strong. "When you came to me," he said, "with your claim that something was wrong with the King, I did not want to

257

believe you. It would have meant a disruption to my life and the routine world with which I was familiar. I convinced myself that you were nothing more than an angry and disappointed lover. When later you told me of the *Absolute*'s capture by a twin brother, I still would not listen. Although I knew the particulars of Joakal's birth, I refused the memory. Again, I did not want to hear you. I did not want my peace disturbed. I wanted the actions of the God to conform to my needs and I refused to see beyond that. For my blindness, you and many others suffered. I am not fit to continue in Service. I ask your forgiveness, Gentleborn, and I shall spend the remainder of my days asking forgiveness from the God."

"Faellon," Elana said, "I do forgive you, and I know that Joakal does as well. You call yourself a tired old man. Yet, in *Rhii'cha* you held the Sword of Justice with strength. Without your help, Joakal would not now be upon the throne. You have paid your debt to us, Faellon. Your debt to the God, only your own heart can judge."

"Thank you, Elana E'shala," Faellon said, and again he bowed.

"I would add one more thing," Elana said. Faellon raised his head and looked at her. "You told me to have faith. Now I say the same to you. Have faith, Faellon. The ways of the God are sometimes hard to understand, yet I believe that all that has happened has been for a purpose. There will be less resistance to the changes Joakal wants to make, now that the people have seen for themselves the dangers of living only in the past. The *future* is our goal, Faellon, and it is full of bright hope for our people."

"You shall make a great queen, Elana E'shala," Faellon said. He stood and bowed again to her, then went back to his seat. But his back was a little straighter and his head was again held high. Troi could still feel his remorse, but could also feel the beginnings of his healing. She, too, thought that Elana would make a great queen.

Abruptly, the room hushed. Troi looked away from Elana and Faellon, and saw that the *Absolute* had again entered the hall. By his side walked Captain Picard. With a smile, Joakal waved his people back to their seats and motioned for the musicians to resume playing.

Troi watched Elana watching Joakal approach. Elana's eyes sparkled and she smiled a bright, delighted smile. Again Troi felt the love that ran between the two of them. It was a thread as strong as any alloy science had discovered, and far more indestructible. They were soul-bound together, and Troi was glad that she had had a part in reuniting them.

"Well, Counselor," Picard said when he and Joakal at last reached the table. "Are you ready to return to the *Enterprise?"*

"Yes, sir," she said, trying not to sound too eager or ungracious.

Joakal, however, was not fooled. He reached out and took Elana's hand, raising her from her chair and drawing her close to his side. Then he turned to Troi and smiled.

"Then, although both Elana and I will be sorry to see you go," he said, "we shall detain you no longer. We shall look forward to your return tomorrow, and to the arrival of the Little Mothers. Tell Mother Veronica for me."

Troi moved to stand next to Captain Picard, ready to beam up to the ship. As she passed by the new *Absolute,* Joakal laid a hand on her arm. She stopped and looked at him. He said no word, but she felt a brush of affection and respect within her mind.

I will never forget all you have done, his thoughts told her. *You offered your gifts unselfishly, which is the greatest gift of all. It will be an inspiration to me through all the long years ahead.*

Troi lowered her eyes, deeply touched. The sense of balance she had not realized she had lost returned and renewed as Joakal's words echoed a teaching from her own people's religion.

It is not the success or failure, she remembered, but the act itself.

"Thank you," she said aloud. Joakal lifted his hand from her arm and Troi continued on to stand by the captain's side.

Picard tapped his communicator. "Picard to *Enterprise,*" he said. "Two to beam up."

Chapter Twenty-seven

MIDMORNING THE NEXT DAY, Troi and Captain Picard stood on the transporter platform waiting for the Little Mothers to join them beaming down to the planet. Mother Veronica had spent the night in seclusion, refusing all of Troi's attempts to speak with her. Troi could not help wondering what decision, if any, Mother Veronica had reached about her future.

Troi thought back to the many hours they had spent together during their journey. Had she said enough? the counselor wondered. Too much? Did Mother Veronica realize the possibilities stretching before her if she would only choose to accept them?

The nuns finally arrived, but aside from a bare greeting, Mother Veronica was silent. What was more, her thoughts and emotions were tightly locked behind the shields Troi had taught her to use. Although a small part of Troi was pleased by her inability to read the nun, another part of her was still worried about the effect their time on Capulon IV, and especially the ritual of *Rhii'cha* in which Mother Veronica had participated yesterday, had had upon the nun's mental stability. Troi wished Mother Veronica would *talk* to her.

Beside the counselor, Captain Picard spoke. "Mr. Tuttle—if you please," he said.

The transporter chief gave them a half-smile as her hands moved across the controls, and Troi had no more time to worry over Mother Veronica's future.

They once again materialized in the reception hall of the palace and Tygar, as representative of the Council of Elders, was there to greet them.

"Welcome, Captain Picard," he said, stepping forward when they appeared. "Welcome, all of you. His Divine Majesty sent me to escort you to his presence. He is eager to see you."

"Thank you, Tygar," Picard replied. "We are looking forward to seeing His Majesty, as well."

"Then if you'll all follow me," Tygar said, "His Divine Majesty is waiting."

Tygar led them out once more into the palace corridors. As they walked, he began telling Captain Picard about the planned events of the day.

Today, on Joakal's first full day as the God-embodied to his people, oaths of allegiance would be taken, petitions presented, and judgments passed. The people of Capulon waited to see what kind of a ruler the God had given them. But it was already being whispered, Tygar told them confidentially, that this Joakal would prove to be as great a King as his ancient predecessor, Joakal I'lium the First.

"The last action today," Tygar concluded, "will be the formal dismissal of the Council of Elders. Now that His Majesty is *Absolute*, we are no longer required."

"So, King Joakal will have to rule alone, with no one to help or advise him?" the captain asked. "It is a terrible burden for one man to bear alone."

"His Majesty is free, of course, to retain his advisers, or to name new ones, or to have none at all. And you are right, Captain," Tygar said. "It is a heavy burden, but one His Majesty has spent thirty years in training to bear."

Picard cleared his throat and changed the subject. "Does the thought of dismissal bother you?" he asked.

Tygar shrugged. "I will continue to serve if His Divine Majesty asks me," he said. "But my wife and I have been away from our homeland for over nine years now and we would not be sorry to return to it."

They reached the Great Chamber. The massive doors stood open and inside several hundred people milled about, waiting for the business of the day to begin. At the sight of the newcomers, they parted, creating an aisle that led to the throne where Joakal sat, dressed majestically in crimson and gold. Jewels sparkled on his wrists, neck, and fingers. On his head sat the triple-tiered crown of the *Absolute,* and around his neck hung a thick golden chain. Suspended from the chain was a stylized bird of prey, the symbol of the House I'lium, made of gold and rubies. Troi could not help thinking what a different picture he presented from the filthy, haggard man they had awakened to find as their companion in captivity.

Joakal saw them. He stood and ran down the five steps that raised the throne off the chamber floor, a smile of welcome spread across his handsome features.

He stopped and approached them more sedately, as if suddenly remembering his rank. But Troi could feel his delight and his pride. He had something special, more than the signing of the treaty, he wanted to share with them today.

As Joakal neared, Captain Picard bowed. Troi and the others followed his example.

"Welcome, Captain Picard," Joakal said, giving a slight incline of his head in recognition of the captain's rank. "Welcome, all of you. We are pleased to have you here with Us and We are most overjoyed at the reason for your presence."

"Thank you—Your Majesty," Picard answered.

"Captain," Joakal said. "It is Our pleasure that you and the others sit near Us while We conduct the business of the day."

Joakal turned and walked back to the raised dais of the throne. He climbed the stairs and again took his place upon the royal seat of carved stone. Picard, Troi, and the Little Mothers followed him, but stopped at the base of the steps. With a sweep of his hand, Joakal indicated that it was on these steps they were to sit, Picard taking the place on the top stair.

Once they were seated, Joakal nodded to Tygar. The Elder walked out to the center of the floor, carrying a long staff of bleached wood that had been wound with gold. The top of the staff was adorned with a stylized bird of prey that matched the one hanging from the chain around Joakal's neck. Tygar struck the floor three times with the staff. The sound rang through the room and immediately all conversation died away.

"In the name of His Divine Majesty, the *Absolute* Joakal I'lium XII, Supreme and Most Holy Ruler, Voice of the God, King Nonpareil of Capulon IV, I call this court to order."

Again Tygar struck the floor. He walked down the length of the long room until he reached the open doors, then he turned and walked back again. Following him was Elana. Tygar escorted her to the base of

264

the steps where he bowed to the King. Without a word he turned away, leaving Elana standing alone before the throne.

She was dressed in pants and tunic of deep royal blue. Around her waist was wrapped a sash of silver cloth that sparkled with each breath she drew. A band of the same cloth pulled her hair back so that it cascaded like a golden waterfall down her back. Her eyes, as she looked up at Joakal, were almost as blue as her clothing.

Joakal bent toward the captain. "I wanted to take care of some of the happier business first," he whispered. Then he pulled himself up straight with his hands resting on the arms of his throne and looked down at Elana.

"Elana, First Daughter of the House E'shala, approach your King," he ordered. Elana climbed the stairs, walking between the seated figures but keeping her eyes on Joakal. When she reached the top step, he stood.

"Elana E'shala," he said. "We would have this world know the esteem with which you are held in Our heart. Without your faith and courage, We would not sit upon this throne. You have more than proved your love and your worth to Us, and to the people of this world. It is therefore Our pleasure to announce to Our people that our marriage will take place thirty days from today. But you shall be more than Our Queen and wife."

Joakal stopped. He lifted the chain from around his neck and placed it around Elana's. There was a ripple of voices through the room; no one but the *Absolute* was allowed to wear the golden bird.

"Elana E'shala," Joakal continued. "On the day to follow our marriage rite, you shall be crowned and consecrated to a new status. You shall, like Us, be invested and hallowed as *Absolute* unto this people, to live and rule by Our side through such years as the God shall grant us."

Again, quiet pandemonium swept across the floor as the people grasped the import of Joakal's announcement. Tygar gave them no time to talk, even among themselves. The Elder again walked to the center of the room and struck his staff upon the floor. The people quieted. Tygar then walked to the door, this time returning with Faellon and two fellow Servants.

Tygar led them to the throne and then again withdrew to the side. Joakal, once more seated on his throne with Elana standing by his side, looked down at the Chief Servant. Troi recognized the two Servants with Faellon as two who had assisted him during the *Rhii'cha* and during Joakal's coronation. One was an older man of about fifty and one was a woman of, perhaps, Joakal's age. Troi looked closely at the woman, feeling a connection of empathic powers with her.

"Faellon, Chief Servant of the temple here in Our royal city," Joakal began. "Our beloved Elana has spoken to Us of your wish to resign your office of Service. If this is truly your wish, We will not keep you from the years of rest you have earned. But We are sorry to see you go. You have served this people well and We bear you great respect and affection."

"Thank you, Divine Majesty," Faellon said, bowing. "But I am an old man and I am tired. The ways of our world are changing. Your Majesty will need a Chief Servant with the energy to help you."

"If this is truly your wish," Joakal repeated, inclining his head graciously. "Who would you name as your successor?"

Faellon motioned the two other Servants forward. "I present to Your Divine Majesty the two I believe are the most worthy. You must choose between them, for I cannot.

"This is Sambl, who has Served at the temple for thirty years." The older man bowed to the King. "And this is Liiyn. Although she is young," Faellon said as the woman bowed, "she is strong in the ways of the God. Either of these will serve Your Majesty and this world well."

Joakal stared at the two applicants. Troi felt the discharge of psychic power and knew that Joakal was using his new abilities to read the Servants.

"You present us with a most difficult choice," he said to Faellon after a moment. "And your words were full of Wisdom when you said that We will need the help of those at the temple during Our rule. In both We see the heart of dedication that would make a wise leader, but it is Our pleasure to name Liiyn to the Office of Chief Servant, to be so ordained at the date of your choosing. And may the God bestow to her the Wisdom and compassion that have so marked the years of your Service."

The three Servants bowed and backed away. Once more Tygar stepped out and pounded the floor with his staff. But this time no people were waiting at the great doors. Instead a small door in the back of the room opened and Yesta, captain of the palace guards, came through. Behind him, bound by ankle chains, marched Beahoram, Aklier, and their accomplices, Tymlan, the boy who worked in the palace kitchen, and Benget of the guards of Aklier's House.

Troi felt their emotions easily. Tymlan was frightened and a little bewildered by the rapid changes he had been through in the last two days. Aklier, alone among the prisoners, walked with his head bent. He was filled with contrition and yet resigned, accepting the fate he knew awaited him. Beahoram walked in

267

defiantly. Both he and Benget held their heads high and Troi could sense no remorse from either of them.

The prisoners were brought before the throne. The people in the room waited in a hushed anticipation that was almost palpable. Would the new *Absolute* act with vengeance? Would the ruler who spoke of new ways still demand the deaths of the offenders, as was the law?

Joakal did not look at the prisoners for a long moment. He stared at his feet as though still struggling with the judgment that was to come. Finally, he raised his eyes, but still he did not look at the prisoners. He looked at Captain Picard. Troi saw that the captain was watching Joakal intently, and she felt an unspoken message pass between them.

Joakal motioned to Tygar who stood at the base of the throne. The Elder banged his staff.

"Beahoram I'lium, Aklier Ti'Kara, Benget Marta, Tymlan Krai, you are here charged with the following crimes: Conspiracy against the King, now *Absolute*, Joakal I'lium; the abduction and imprisonment of the King; treason; blasphemy; the abduction and imprisonment of the representatives of the United Federation of Planets in the persons of Captain Jean-Luc Picard and Counselor Deanna Troi of the Starfleet Flagship, the USS *Enterprise*, and Mother Veronica of the Little Mothers.

"Further, Beahoram I'lium, you are charged with the impersonation of the King, now *Absolute*, Joakal I'lium, and the twice traitorous actions of attempting to usurp his crown, powers and titles, and making false our most sacred and holy rite of coronation.

"The law demands your deaths. The manner of execution as set forth in our laws comes from the time of our fathers. On the thirteenth day of—"

"Stop," Joakal commanded. Tygar swung around to

look at him, but Joakal would not meet his eyes. He looked at the prisoners.

"Our world knows no more foul or heinous crimes, save that of willful murder, than the crimes with which you are charged," he said. "The laws of this world call for your deaths. Yet, We believe there has been too much death upon this world. We would, therefore, be merciful." He looked now at Tygar. "For true Justice *must* have room for mercy."

Joakal turned back to the prisoners. "Yesterday it was Our great pleasure to abolish forever the old law that required the death of so many innocent children. This has been Our intention for many years and We have brought to this world the Little Mothers to help Our people learn to love those children the old ways would have destroyed. We understand that it was this law that sparked your actions. Because of this, We would offer you a choice. As punishment for your crimes, you may stay here on Capulon and devote your lives to Service with the Little Mothers, helping them in their care for our children, or you may leave this world and never again set foot upon Our planet. Choose now, but remember that this choice is a final one."

Aklier was the first to speak. Troi could feel his sorrow slowly transmuting to wonder.

"Please," he said slowly, as if hardly daring to believe what he had just heard. "I'll stay. I'll serve the Little Mothers and I'll gladly work with the children. Thank you, Your Divine Majesty. Thank you."

He bowed his head, tears running freely down his cheeks. But he smiled as well; he had been given a gift.

"I'll stay too, please," Tymlan said quickly. His voice cracked with nervousness and youth, but his fear was gone.

"And you, Benget?" Joakal asked.

"No, Your Majesty," he said. "I bear no ill to the Little Mothers and I wish them good fortune with the work that they will do, but I will not serve another House, even theirs. I would rather take my own chances and make my own way elsewhere."

Joakal nodded as if he knew, even understood, Benget's decision. Then, finally, Joakal looked at Beahoram. "And you, Brother?" he asked. "Will you stay?"

"Oh no—Brother," Beahoram said. His voice was hard and unrepentant and his eyes were still full of hate. "I made my decision long ago. Even without your 'mercy,' I would rather die than watch you rule."

Joakal stood. He walked slowly down the dais steps until he was face-to-face with his Brother. He stared for several seconds into his mirrored face.

"You still don't understand," Joakal said softly. "I would have shared everything with you. I would have opened my heart and welcomed you. I would even have loved you."

"What I understand," Beahoram said through clenched teeth, "is that I lost and you won. I have the stomach to accept that even if you do not. No, Brother, this world has never offered me comfort. I leave it gladly. Sit upon your throne, Brother. Be called Beloved by your people, but remember that there is one among the stars who does not revere the name of Joakal I'lium."

Joakal look sadly at Beahoram. "Very well," he said. "You have made your choice, and though We wish it could be otherwise between us, We will grant your exile. And We will pray that someday, somewhere, the God will grant you happiness."

Joakal turned and remounted the steps. He waved his hand and the prisoners were led away. He watched them go, and when the door had closed behind them, he closed his eyes and was silent for a moment more. Then he turned to the captain and smiled, and if the smile was a little ragged, no one but Picard could see it.

"Now, Captain Picard," he said. "It is time for the treaty."

Joakal stood. He held out his hand to Elana and together they descended the steps. Picard and the others followed. Tygar stepped behind the dais and brought forth a large silver tray that bore the copies of the treaty and two golden pens. He held the tray out to the King.

Joakal picked up one of the pens. "Captain Picard," he said, "it is Our great joy to put Our name to this paper as a symbol of this world's new union with the Federation." He bent and signed his name with a flourish to the bottom of the documents. Then he stepped back and waited for Picard to do the same.

Picard also signed the treaty and placed the pen back on the tray "On behalf of the worlds that make up the United Federation of Planets, I welcome the people of Capulon IV into our midst. We are all enriched by your presence."

Joakal picked up the golden pen Picard had laid down and handed it back to him. "Please keep this, Captain," he said, "as a small remembrance of your time among us. We hope that this day will begin a new era of exchange between Capulon IV and all other worlds of the Federation. Our home is open to all who would visit us in brotherhood and understanding."

Joakal now turned to the Little Mothers. "It is time for Our surprise," he said, smiling with delight. "Behind the palace is a stand of woods and in the middle of the woods is a lake. We believe this to be the most beautiful place in Our city. At dawn today, We sent a team of workers there to begin the construction of the home for the Little Mothers. This is Our gift to you." He looked directly at Mother Veronica. "If you will tell Us what you require, it will be provided."

Mother Veronica met Joakal's eyes for a moment, then she turned away. She walked over to Sister Julian. Mother Veronica reached up and removed the cross from around her own neck and lowered it over the head of the surprised nun. Then Mother Veronica returned to stand before the King.

Two feet away, Troi held her breath. She hoped she knew what was to come.

"On behalf of our Order, I thank you, Your Majesty," Mother Veronica said. "Your gift is a very noble and generous one. But I shall not be here to enjoy it. I will stay only until the other members of my Order arrive. Then Sister Julian—Mother Julian—will lead the Community."

Joakal frowned. "You're leaving?" he said. "But why?"

"I am leaving, Your Majesty, because God is leading me elsewhere. As soon as my Mother House can arrange it, I will be going to Vulcan to enter training in the mental disciplines they teach. I believe it is God's Will that I learn to use these gifts that He has given me."

Joakal reached out and took her hand. "We cannot argue with the Will of the God," he said. "But it will remain Our great hope that someday you will return to Us."

"The future, Your Majesty," Mother Veronica said, "is in God's hand. All we can do, is to have faith."

An hour later, Picard and Troi again stood on the bridge of the *Enterprise*. On the planet below, the royal court would continue throughout the rest of the day, but it stood in recess now while Joakal, Elana, and the Little Mothers said their good-byes. Their faces filled the main viewscreen of the bridge.

"We are sorry to see you go, Jean-Luc," Joakal was saying, "but we understand that duties are duties."

"And we hope that those duties will soon bring you back to our world," Elana added. "Capulon is an open planet to all members of the Federation, but we particularly hope that you and your crew will think of it as another home."

"Thank you, Your Majesties," Picard said. "And Joakal," he added, "King Solomon, and King Joakal, would have been proud."

Joakal smiled. He and Elana stepped back to let Mother Veronica say her farewells.

"Thank you, Captain Picard," she began, "for all you have done for us and for me. Our community will keep you and your people in our prayers."

"I hope the future will bring you the peace you desire, Mother Veronica," he said. "You have certainly earned it."

"The future, Captain, is in the hands of God—and it is full of promise."

Captain Picard nodded his farewell then returned to the command chair, leaving Troi standing alone before the big screen.

"Counselor Troi," Mother Veronica began, "you have taught me so much. How can I thank you?"

Troi looked at the image before her. She was no longer the haggard, desperate woman who had stumbled through Troi's door three weeks ago. Gone were the dark circles of exhaustion around her eyes; her skin was no longer stretched tightly across her cheekbones and her expression was not filled with fear.

"You already have," Troi said. Mother Veronica smiled at her. Troi started to turn away.

"Before you go," Mother Veronica added. "May I speak with Mr. Data?"

Data looked up from his station at Ops. He stood to address the nun. "Yes, Mother Veronica?"

Mother Veronica smiled at him, also. "Don't give up your search, Mr. Data," she said. "Don't stop asking your questions. Remember that the quest, like God, is eternal."

"Thank you," Data said. "I will remember everything."

The three figures on the viewscreen raised their hands in farewell and communication was severed. "Course, Captain?" Riker asked.

"Back to Starbase 212," Picard said as he took his place in the command chair. "We have a treaty to deliver."

Troi turned to leave the bridge. There were duties she had neglected too long, like the final log entry on Lieutenant Salah; she was ready to face that now. And she needed to write a letter to her mother. She also had patients waiting for her. Among them was Ensign Johann Marshall. Troi knew what to say to him now.

It's true, she thought as she walked up the ramp. The doctor is often healed by the patient, and the teacher learns from the student.

When she reached the turbolift, she stopped and turned around. "Data," she said, "was Mother Veronica able to give you the answers you were looking for?"

"Not entirely, Counselor," the android replied. "There are still many things for which I do not have an adequate definition. Although I have found some answers, I find those answers have only evoked more questions. I shall keep searching."

"That's all any of us can do, Data," Troi said.

Epilogue

COUNSELOR DEANNA TROI stepped into her quarters on her way to the transporter room. The ship was currently docking at Starbase 079 where it would receive Ensign Johann Marshall back on board. He was returning from a trip home to visit his family, his first in over two years, and Troi wanted to be there to greet him. She had only stopped by her quarters because the first grade class she had visited this morning had presented her with some artwork.

She carefully placed the small collection of youthful masterpieces on the table and turned back toward the door. Out of the corner of her eye, she saw the blinking light on her computer terminal that indicated a private message. Quickly, she crossed the room and switched it on.

It was a communiqué from Mother Veronica. Surprised and delighted, Troi sat down to read.

Dear Counselor Troi, it began. *I have been on Vulcan*

for six months now, and today my teachers announced that they were satisfied with my progress. I have learned that this is high praise from a Vulcan. I, too, am satisfied. I have learned far more than I ever imagined possible when I first left you, and I am learning more every day. The Vulcan dedication to nonemotional logic, which I feared would be an obstacle to our understanding one another, has proved to be quite the opposite. Their minds are so ordered that contact with them, even in deep telepathic rapport, is restful and makes learning a joy.

I have not written to you for all these months because I was not certain of my future plans. Until today. I have now realized that my place is back on Capulon IV. When I complete my studies, I shall return there and set up a school, as part of our Order's work, to help the people of Capulon IV rediscover their psychic heritage. I have written to King Joakal for his permission, and to my Mother House, but I am certain the permissions will be granted. It is indeed true that all things happen for a purpose.

You taught me so much and I shall always be grateful. Although I admire my Vulcan teachers, the lessons you taught me are the most precious of all. It was you, my dear Counselor Troi, who taught me by both your words and your example, that peace is only found through accepting myself. Because of you, I am free of the fears that held me captive for so long. For the first time and for all time, I am free to be alive.

Troi turned off the screen. She sat back in her chair and smiled. She was glad for Mother Veronica and for all the people the nun would help.

Her communicator chirped. "Tuttle to Counselor Troi."

"Troi here."

"Counselor," Tuttle said. "Docking is complete and

Ensign Marshalt has signaled that he's ready to beam aboard. Did you still want to be here to meet him?"

"I'm on my way. Thank you, Chief," Troi said and she stood. Her step was jaunty as she walked from her room. She smiled at people as she strolled along the corridors on the way to welcome back her recovered patient.

All in all, it had been a wonderful day for Deanna Troi.

Also available from Titan Books

STAR TREK®
THE NEXT GENERATION

HERE THERE BE DRAGONS

by John Peel

When Captain Jean-Luc Picard and the crew of the
U.S.S. Enterprise receive news of a human planet
hidden in the centre of an immense stellar cloud they
immediately investigate.

Penetrating the cloud, the Starship crew is shocked to
discover a world of knights and serfs lifted right out of
Earth's Middle Ages. Ruthlessly exploiting the planet
is a ring of interstellar trophy hunters preying on the
immense, native dragon-lizards, twenty feet tall and
armoured like tanks.

Beaming down, an away team soon becomes
embroiled in a web of intrigue and murder. Taken
prisoner, Picard, Data and Ro must somehow escape
and stop the hunters or face destruction from the
hunters ancient weapon, based on an advanced
technology capable of utterly annihilating the
Starship Enterprise...

STAR TREK®

WHO KILLED CAPTAIN KIRK?

by Peter David, Tom Sutton
and Ricardo Villagram

The *U.S.S. Enterprise* has encountered many strange beings and situations, but none has chilled them to the bone more than death. Someone aboard the Starship has killed Captain Kirk - or so it seems. While the Captain recovers, it falls to his loyal crew to uncover the facts behind the case and learn whether one of their own is a cold-blooded killer. The investigation is hampered by the unwanted arrival of the Klingons and an ill telepath who sends the entire crew on a journey through Dante's inferno. And then, just when everything is starting to calm down, Finnegan, Kirk's nemesis from his Academy days, arrives to take charge of the mystery. Murder, mayhem, a wedding and loads of action mark this graphic collection of stories featuring the acclaimed *Star Trek* author Peter David. Featuring a special introduction by George 'Sulu' Takei.

THE PRICE OF THE PHOENIX

STAR TREK®

ADVENTURES

by Sondra Marshak and Myrna Culbreath

"Captain Kirk is dead. Permission granted for *Enterprise* physician and party to attend."

Kirk and the crew of the *U.S.S. Enterprise* are investigating a strange conference of dissident factions at a freeport near the Romulan neutral zone. While on a delegates' tour of alien enclaves, Captain Kirk is pronounced dead after an attempt to rescue a woman and child being burned alive; a breach of the Prime Directive, or was it a set-up?

Spock must take over control of the *Enterprise* and join forces with an unlikely ally, as he becomes enmeshed in the subsequent dangerous battle of wits with the formidable Omne. At stake is the true fate of Captain Kirk, and the sovereignty of the Federation itself!

THE GALACTIC WHIRLPOOL

STAR TREK®

ADVENTURES
by David Gerrold

'Captain's Log, Stardate 4496. 1. We have broken off
our search to investigate the presence of . . .of a
sensory anomaly.'

On a routine mission in deep space, Captain Kirk and
the crew of the Enterprise discover a lost city, drifting
in space, more than twenty years from the nearest
human colony.

Its inhabitants are human, but so isolated that they are
unable to grasp the existance of other worlds beyond
their own. Outsiders must be 'demons'. Earth is a
place that exists only in legend, in the tales of their
ancestors. But time is running out for this forgotten
civilisation . . . their world is being pulled straight
towards the centre of a galactic whirlpool, two orbiting
black holes in space.

Can Kirk convince them to trust him, before their
world is destroyed forever?

For a complete list of Star Trek publications, please send a large stamped SAE to Titan Books Mail Order, 42–44 Dolben Street, London, SE1 0UP. Please quote reference NG27 on both envelopes.